In the Company of Shadows

The Night's Road: Book Two

The World's Pain

Andy Monk

Part One

Arriving

Chapter One

Madriel, The Electorate of Saxony, The Holy Roman Empire - 1630

"This is a mistake."

Most of the voices in the tavern, bar a drunk in the sooty back singing about a girl called Mathilda and her exceedingly fine cow, faded to hushed whispers or complete silence. Eyes - bloodshot, hooded, hungry, scheming and pretty much every other type he could think of - swivelled in their direction. Most lingered. Particularly the hungry ones.

"This is a *very* bad mistake," he repeated out of the side of his mouth.

Morlaine brushed past him, stared back across the shadowy tavern, challenging that sea of peering eyes, then pulled back her hood.

The remainder of the voices fell silent. Even the songful drunk, both Mathilda and her exceedingly fine cow, instantly forgotten.

"A really, really, very bad mistake..."

Crossing to the nearest empty table, Morlaine set the rushlights dancing in the swirling wake of her cloak.

Solace ignored his warning look. She didn't like to let the demon out of her sight as if fearful the creature might vanish in a puff of smoke if she strayed too far from her coattails.

Eyes followed Solace, too, though not as many as Morlaine. He had hoped her short hair and man's clothes, soiled by weeks of travelling, might make it easy, in the poor light, to mistake her for a boy. However, although her clothes were a man's, they weren't baggy enough to disguise the parts of her that were clearly not a man's.

He followed them, good hand resting on his sword.

By their appearance, most of the men were soldiers, and all were either drunk, well on the way to being drunk, or moving rapidly on to whatever state of inebriation existed beyond mere drunkenness. In hindsight, even passing as a boy wouldn't protect Solace from the attentions of some of these men.

"This is a-"

"Mistake?" When he continued to glare at Morlaine, she kicked back a chair from the table and jerked her head towards it, "Sit."

He glanced at Solace but found no help; she had already settled at the demon's side.

"Sit," Morlaine repeated, "people are staring at us."

"At *us?*"

Nobody showed any interest in him, other than perhaps a passing curiosity as to how a weakling with a withered arm got to be in the company of the two most beautiful women for a day's ride in any direction you might fancy heading off in.

Eventually, he slumped into the chair, too exhausted to argue further. They had walked for... he actually couldn't remember how long they trudged through the cold and the mud behind the swaying rump of Styx, the demon's stallion. Long enough for him to forget what sitting in a chair felt like anyway.

Morlaine had said something about getting a room. A room with beds. Perhaps she was right. Perhaps she knew what she was doing. Maybe if the locals decided to rape and murder them, they wouldn't bother troubling themselves with the weakling.

Conversation started to ripple through the shadows again, though plenty of eyes stayed on them. He kept his good hand on the hilt of his sword, thumb running up and down the worn leather strapping binding the grip.

A girl approached them, pale and thin, the hollows in her cheeks and bags under her eyes too deep and heavy for one so young.

"Can we have-"

The girl leaned in and hissed, "Most of these men are soldiers. 'tis not safe for you here, *fraulien*."

"Two plates of whatever you have that's hot, bread, a jug of wine and some water," Morlaine continued.

The serving girl frowned and leant in closer, "They are mercenaries, hired to protect the town..." her eyes darted about the figures hunched and sprawled around them, "...but there's no one here to protect us from *them*."

"And lodging, a large one if possible. Beds in separate rooms, ideally."

The serving girl flicked lank hair from her face, her eyes turning in his direction, "Please, sir, I don't think your lady quite understands..."

3

He offered her a shrug in return, "She's even less likely to listen to me than you..."

By the time the girl's attention returned to Morlaine, the demon's coins littered the table.

That was probably a bigger mistake. His grip on his father's sword tightened further.

"Hot food, bread, wine, water..." Morlaine's eyes didn't leave the girl, "...and a room."

"I can get you food and drink," the serving girl stepped back, the look on her face suggesting she'd decided she'd done all she could and wasn't going to let any subsequent rapes and murders trouble her conscience, "but no rooms... we are full. Everywhere in town is full, the churches are full, even the stables, outhouses and pig styes are filled with people fleeing the war," her face softened, a little, "don't matter how much silver you have, there's no rooms to be had in Madriel."

Morlaine nodded, "How much for the food?"

Ulrich's chin almost hit the scored and stained tabletop when the girl told her.

"How much?!"

She offered an apologetic smile, already scooping Morlaine's coins up, "'tis the war; we're short of everything. Everything save mouths to feed."

"But..."

"It doesn't matter," Morlaine nodded at the girl before asking, "who is the owner here?"

"Herr Kehlmann," she waved a hand at a ruddy-faced, balding man pouring ale. From the look of him, it was hard to imagine food was so scarce.

4

"Send him over."

"He-"

The demon silenced the girl by holding up another coin, which she span along her fingers before putting it in the opposite hand to the one holding the money for the meal.

"Yes, of course..."

"Do you think you have enough silver to get him to turf some soldiers out for us?" Ulrich asked once the girl hurried back to the bar, navigating the thicket of drunken grabbing hands with weary experience.

Morlaine gave him one of her expressionless looks; she rarely troubled her face with anything else.

When the demon said nothing, he added, "Given how much you just paid for food, you'd need a lot of coin."

"Is the meal expensive?" Solace asked, her face as blank as Morlaine's. He thought she was joking - it cost ten times what he used to pay in *The Bear Pit* back in Tassau - before it dawned on him she'd never bought a meal in her life.

He shook his head, letting his gaze drift to the fire. It was generous; fat flames greedily licking logs heaped in a stone hearth. Sadly, they were about as far away from it as they could get without sitting outside in the horse shit and mud of Madriel's market square.

Still, it was the warmest he'd been since leaving the ruins of The Wolf's Tower. They'd had little to scrape out a life with back there, but at least they'd been plenty to burn.

Exhaustion stayed his tongue. Why protest? Neither of them would listen. All he wanted was sleep. He was damp from the long unkempt tangles of his hair to the disintegrating, mud-splattered boots encasing his blistered feet. As best he could recall the only time it hadn't rained since they left The Wolf's Tower was when it sleeted.

How far had they walked? He didn't know. Hours and days bled into each other, an endless march through water-logged fields of rotting crops interspersed with thick clumps of dripping forest. Morlaine avoided roads wherever possible, crossing open country, following paths through woodland as likely made by animals as men. He could make no sense of their route, but Morlaine had seemed certain of it, and she'd brought them safely to Madriel in the end.

She'd avoided daylight too.

The walking started at dusk and continued through the long, cold nights, surrounded by shadows, surrounded by ghosts and phantoms, surrounded by the strange sounds of the night when all God-fearing folk stayed behind locked doors and beneath warm blankets.

They found shelter before the coming of each grey dawn. Old barns, burnt out cottages and any other abandoned structure they came across - the war had emptied much of the land and such places were not hard to find. They headed to where the trees were thickest when they couldn't, and Morlaine rigged a sheet of canvas between the trunks. Then she would squat in the shadow, huddled inside her cloak, hood drawn up, spectacles with smoke-blackened glass covering her eyes.

Solace and he slept in whatever dry patch they could find and if nothing was dry then the least damp spot. They

6

had brought what food they had, two blankets, a canteen and the few spare clothes they possessed. They filled a single sack he carried on his back in a makeshift sling.

It was not heavy, even for a weakling like him.

The first night he asked if Solace could ride on the back of Morlaine's huge, evil-looking black stallion.

"You chose to come," the demon had told him, not looking over her shoulder, "so, you chose to walk."

He didn't ask again. Instead, he stared at the swaying rump of the beast's arse and tried to avoid stumbling into its shit too often.

After the first night's walking, they made camp in a disintegrating woodsman's shack, abandoned long before the war swept through these lands and carried most of the people away.

Half the roof had collapsed, and, after tethering and feeding her stallion, Morlaine went to the far corner where the shadow lay deepest, threw down a blanket and sat on it, legs outstretched. She'd put on her smoke-blackened spectacles and then pulled up her hood.

"Sleep," she'd said.

They had two blankets of their own in his sack; he stamped down the fallen leaves and brown undergrowth before spreading out one for Solace. He handed the other to her once she crumpled onto it.

"Yours..." she'd mumbled, eyes already half-closed.

"No, my lady," he'd spread the blanket over her. She was asleep before he straightened up again. After retrieving his other shirt from the pack, he folded it into a thin pillow, and placed it under Solace's head. She'd stirred but did not wake.

Then he'd sat between Solace and Morlaine, back against the rotting timber wall, his father's sword across his lap.

"Sleep," Morlaine had said again, sometime later.

"Someone needs to keep watch," he'd jerked his head at the muted daylight creeping through trees dressed in the last of their autumn leaves.

"No one is close."

"How can you be sure?"

"Trust me."

"Still…"

"If anyone comes near us, I will know."

"How?"

"Vampires sleep very lightly…"

Her head turned a fraction; he sensed deep, dark eyes upon him within the hood's shadow and behind smoke-blackened glass.

He shivered despite himself.

He'd considered killing the demon as they'd trudged through the rain into that first night together, each step taking them inexorably towards the madness of Saul and his Red Company.

After the idea had crossed back and forth a few times, it came and sat in his mind to whisper and cajole while he waited for her to fall asleep.

Kill her. She is the same as Saul. The same as Alms and Cleever. The same as the others. A monster. Kill her before she kills you. Before she kills the Lady Solace. Kill her while you still can…

Could the demon hear those thoughts? Perhaps. Who knew what these things could do?

In the end, he closed his eyes. He would think more upon it. Rash deeds were seldom wise deeds. More of Old Man Ulrich's wisdom? Or was that one Sergeant Lutz's? He couldn't remember. He found it increasingly difficult to remember anything of his life before the Red Company came and ripped it to shreds.

Better the demon die. Better they not pursue Saul. Better they forget it all...

The next thing he knew, he was curled around his father's sword on the ground, near enough to Solace to hear her breath rattling the desiccated leaves she slept upon. A blanket covered him. At first, he thought Solace had given him hers, and a flush of annoyance that she believed he needed it more than her rattled him awake. When he'd forced his eyes open, however, he found Solace still sleeping between their own tatty blankets.

He sat up with a start, blinking. The world was still grey, still cold; it was raining again. Pattering through the trees to drum upon the remnants of the cabin's roof and the sodden forest beyond its rotting walls.

Morlaine was as before, legs outstretched, short sword at her side.

As he watched, she drew back her hood.

"The sun has set; we will leave as soon as you've eaten."

"The sun has set?"

"You've slept all day. You must be hungry."

He'd nodded, though he couldn't recall the last time he

hadn't been.

Dried leaves tangled his beard, and he'd swatted them away as he yawned.

The blanket covering him was much finer than the moth-eaten rags they'd salvaged from the Wolf's Tower.

"Yours?"

"Yes, you were shivering in your sleep."

"You should have given it to Lady Solace…"

"I did."

Glancing to his side, another blanket, as fine as his, covered his mistress.

He'd mumbled something within spitting distance of a thank you through both his broken teeth and his unease. The demon could have done anything while they'd slept. It would be as easy to slit their throats as to put blankets over them. The thought of her moving about them while they were helpless chilled him. He should have stayed awake; his weakness had risked their lives. Possibly their souls too.

"You cried out a lot while you slept."

He rubbed the balls of his palms into his eyes, trying not to wince at the effort it took to make his withered arm perform so simple a task.

"I suffer nightmares," for a second or two, he'd tried to stare at the smoke-blackened lenses of the demon's spectacles but found them even more unsettling than her eyes, "thanks to your friends…"

"They are not my friends. I am trying to kill them."

He'd shrugged. Maybe she spoke the truth; maybe she lied. The Devil was infamous for his deceits; his foul creatures were no different.

Morlaine took off the spectacles, her eyes narrowed as if bright sunshine raked the innards of the collapsing hovel rather than the feeble grey light of a late autumn dusk.

"I will be leaving in an hour. If you still wish to come with me. Eat and be ready."

"It won't take us an hour to eat."

All his pack contained was dried fish, the last of the carrots and turnips they'd managed to grow and a few sour apples.

"Make a small fire and eat as much as you can spare," Morlaine crossed the ruined cabin to the fallen wall, "The nights are long, and there's a lot of ground ahead of us."

Before he could snap out a reply, his eye fell upon two fat wood pigeons laid out next to his meagre pack. Their necks were broken.

"Where did they come from?" he asked, hating how his mouth was already filling with saliva.

"They came too close to me..." Morlaine paused at the edge of the cabin, one booted foot on the pile of green-mossed timber that had once been its north wall as she'd looked back at him, "...a thing that is always ill-advised."

With that, she'd clambered over the debris and disappeared into the coming night.

*

"There's only one bed..."

"'tis one more bed than many will have in Madriel tonight, fraulien," the serving girl, who'd told them her name was Anna-Lena said, moving to pass the flame from

11

her chamber light to the candles.

She followed Anna-Lena into the room. Renard hovered in the doorway, good hand on the hilt of his sword, peering about the room as if expecting assailants to come pouring out of every corner.

An unmade bed, its sheets and blankets tangled into snakes, dominated the room. Tobacco smoke and old sweat flavoured the air. No doubt, there would be plenty of people in town grateful to sleep in a bed with old, sweaty sheets too. So, she said nothing.

"Goodnight, fraulien," Anna-Lena nodded, first at her, then Renard. When he continued to stand in the door, the serving girl tilted her head and raised her eyebrows. He grunted and moved aside. He seemed to do everything more slowly these days. Even thinking.

Anna-Lena gave them a final look followed by a smile that didn't thaw her eyes, then the door closed, leaving them alone.

She supposed they made for a curious sight; a pair of filthy, bedraggled beggars, clothes falling apart, damp to the bone, covered in mud and still sporting a fair portion of the forests they'd tramped through in their hair. Yet they had the money for food and a room.

What they made of Morlaine, on the other hand...

"With your leave, I will take the chair, my lady," Renard said, hollow-voiced as he shuffled across the room. He carried their meagre possessions in a sack tied into a sling across his back with some old rope; he tugged it over his head like a handful of turnips and a few rags weighed

12

more than the Earth on Atlas' shoulders.

His boots scuffed the floorboards, trailing crumbs of dried mud in their wake.

"The bed is big enough for both of us."

He dropped their pack on the floor, eyes darting to the bed, then her, "'tis not seemly, my lady."

"These are strange days; what is seemly is no longer of much concern. We need to rest, to recover, to sleep. Sitting in a chair will not help you. And we have shared a bed before."

"That was different, my lady."

Yes, it was. He had been dying, shoulder and arm broken from his fall down The Wolf's Tower as they fled Saul and his minions; he had twice plunged into the icy water of the moat before they dragged themselves through the snow to her father's hunting lodge in the woods. With no fire, the only way to keep warm had been in bed, stripped of their freezing, sodden clothes under a pile of musty blankets.

He had been too weak and broken to take the kind of advantage low sorts of men might. But he wasn't broken now. Or not *as* broken. Still, they had spent nearly a year together in the ruins of The Wolf's Tower while he first recovered from his wounds and the fever that followed them, and then while they awaited the arrival of the demon the *sight* promised would help them find the Red Company and her brother.

If he harboured any desire for her, he hid it well.

"You are an honourable man; I trust you. I have no care about what the rest of the world thinks of the

13

arrangement."

"An honourable man..." Renard echoed, lips twisting behind his beard.

She held up her hand; she had heard it before. Many times. Honour was a subject best avoided around Ulrich Renard.

"'tis late. We are both exhausted. We need to sleep. There is much to do tomorrow, and I doubt Morlaine will want to tarry long here. We need to be prepared."

"Prepared, my lady?"

"We require horses, riding tackle, travelling gear, boots, food, weapons..." she ran hands down the stinking, rotten rags hanging from her "...we cannot find and face the Red Company dressed like a pair of wretched beggars with nothing but some mouldy turnips to throw at them."

She spoke light-heartedly, but no smile touched Renard's face. Instead, he dragged his feet to the door, "I will wait outside till you are... prepared."

Prepared?

That made her smile.

They had spent weeks sleeping in hedgerows, ruins, briars, barns, wherever they could find some respite from the weather and sanctuary from the daylight for Morlaine. Preparation had been no more than huddling beneath a blanket and praying for a few hours sleep.

Back in the *before*, things had been different; maids, ointments, soaps, powders, combing, bedpans to warm the sheets for her delicate skin, pillows to be plumped, scents to be dabbed. Fuss. Yes, the *freiher's* daughter had been the focus of an awful lot of fuss.

What preparations were required tonight?

Coals glowed in the hearth; they should spread their damp filthy rags in front of them. Dry clothes in the morning would be a novelty. Still, they would buy new clothing tomorrow, and these things could be burnt, along with the lice infesting them.

"I will not take long," she said as Renard paused at the door.

"My lady, everything here is in short supply. The provisions you seek will be expensive."

"What of it?"

"Your..." he lowered his voice and took a step back towards her, "...jewellery is all you have."

She raised her chin and repeated herself, "What of it?"

"'tis your future, my lady, with them you... can rebuild your life... anything you wish... but once they are gone..."

"What I wish is to find my brother, save him from the demons who took him, destroy the Red Company and see Saul the Bloodless' head on a stick. If that costs me every scrap of silver my family has left, I will consider it a fine bargain!"

She crossed the room as she spoke and spat the final words into his face. A full stomach, a fire and the prospect of a warm dry bed had lightened her mood considerably. She should thank Renard for focussing her mind on what was important. She glowered up at him till his eyes dropped.

"Yes, my lady."

"Wait outside."

He did as he was told, and she carried on staring at

15

the door long after he closed it behind him.

She let out a long breath. Sometimes she was too hard on him. She knew well enough he did not share her enthusiasm for pursuing Saul, but he followed her all the same. Honouring the oath he had made to her father. He could have fled the ruins of The Wolf Tower a long time ago, but he had stayed. Loyal to the last, despite what he saw as his own dishonour in helping the demons get into the castle.

Slowly she removed her clothes. How long had it been since she'd last taken them off? More than days, less than months. Weeks then.

The task was more akin to peeling than stripping. The rain had fallen incessantly, as if God had decided to wash away all the evil inflicting itself upon the Earth with another flood. The layers of linen and wool were ripe and rotten, crawling with lice and blackened with rot. The skin underneath bloomed with red blotches and scabs.

The room boasted a small looking-glass, but she lacked the courage to discover what had become of the pretty face she had once so admired. The pretty face *Graf* Bulcher coveted enough to hire the Red Company to seize her, wipe out her family and destroy her home. Yes. She often forgot Bulcher was as worthy a focus for her vengeance as Saul and his demons.

From Renard's pack she took a clean shirt. They had worn most of the clothes they possessed on the journey in a mostly futile attempt to keep warm in the biting wind, but she'd insisted he carry a few pieces for when they reached Madriel.

The shirt was a man's, like everything they had. They'd recovered no women's clothing from The Wolf's Tower, just some humble garments from one of the male servants' rooms untouched by fire. It covered her slight frame modestly enough.

A basin and pitcher sat in a corner of the room. A sliver of soap too. They would go to the bathhouse tomorrow. Clean the filth of the road from their bodies and restore themselves. By the time she finished washing her face and arms, the water was black. She poured it into the night bucket and sat on the bed.

Carefully she uncurled the crude belt from around her waist. Within the folds of linen resided all the jewellery she had managed to keep from Saul and his men. It rarely left her person. They were all she had. All her family had. And she would sell every piece to raise the money to save Torben and destroy the Red Company.

She slid the belt under one of the pillows. After a moment's hesitation, she fetched her knife and put it under the pillow too. Then she climbed into bed and pulled the blankets over her.

It felt strange.

"Ulrich!"

It was going to feel even stranger soon.

She rolled onto her side, one hand sliding beneath the pillow to rest on the jewellery belt.

The door opened and shut, followed by the sound of scuffing footsteps over creaking boards. Then silence.

"Take off your clothes, wash, douse the light and get into bed," just to ensure there was no misunderstanding,

17

she added, "then sleep."

"Yes, my lady," Renard sounded old and impossibly weary. She supposed she did too.

Perhaps she could persuade Morlaine to stay for a few days, let them recover their strength...

No! That was weak thinking. Saul already enjoyed the best part of a year's start on them. No more tarrying!

Despite her weariness, which sank deep roots into her bones, she felt vividly awake. A full stomach perhaps. It'd only been a gruel of barley and bacon rinds accompanied by heavy, gritty bread but they had devoured their meals like wolves.

Morlaine had watched them in silence, taking only water while they washed down the food with wine. It tasted more akin to vinegar but became palatable when heavily watered.

After Kehlmann the innkeeper came over, Morlaine stood and spoke to him, too quietly for her to make out what they were saying over the ructions of the busy inn. Frankly, whatever it was, the food was more interesting to her right then.

The innkeeper pulled faces, shook his head, wobbled his chins and looked apologetic. Whatever strange powers the vampire possessed, charming someone into conjuring a room out of thin air did not appear to be one of them.

Eventually, Kehlmann nodded across the room in response to a question. Morlaine thanked him, turned away and crossed to two men sat at the closest table to the fire.

She'd exchanged a glance with Renard, then Kehlmann. Renard shrugged before shoving his face back

18

into his bowl. Kehlmann stared at her like a man with questions to ask, so she returned her face to the bowl too.

When she next checked, Kehlmann was gone and Morlaine sat with the two men by the fire. They hid hard faces behind short beards. They looked much like the men who'd served Saul in the Red Company.

Part of her wanted to take Renard's sword and strike them down, part of her wanted to bolt for the door and the sanctuary of the night.

She did neither.

Instead, she sipped wine and studied Morlaine with the men. She sat close to the older of the pair, who boasted a long drooping moustache to accompany his beard, both shot with grey like his thinning hair. Solace didn't know if he was tired or suspicious, but he peered at Morlaine through half-closed eyes. Either way, she didn't like the look of him.

The younger man lounged back, drinking ale, an expression of faint amusement hovering on pinched features.

Several times Morlaine indicated them, and the older man's eyes followed.

Eventually a smile appeared, and he leaned across the table to speak to his companion. The amusement on the younger man's face melted into annoyance. The older man jabbed a finger at him. His friend stared back; ale pot poised in mid air. Then he nodded, drained the ale and left them.

The older man watched his friend cross the bar and talk to Kehlmann before leaning into Morlaine again.

"What's she doing?" Solace asked.

Renard was busy chasing grease around the bowl with the last sharp crust of his bread.

"Some devilry..." he muttered, not looking up.

She spooned another mouthful. A year ago, she would have probably spat such fayre out and demanded questions be asked of Herman, the cook. Now it tasted fit for gods.

"But what *is* she doing?" In the weeks they'd known the demon, she'd barely smiled, now she was beaming, laughing throatily and curling ringlets of hair around her finger, "'tis most strange."

She glanced at Renard and found him staring at her bowl, his eyes shot up to meet hers, "I have no idea..."

Anna-Lena appeared a few minutes later as she finished her food.

"Your room is on the second floor, last door on the left," she said, face blank but tone cold.

"Room? You said..."

The serving girl snatched up the plates, "Seems one of the rooms has been vacated unexpectedly, it must be your lucky night..." she looked at Morlaine, who was pouring more ale in to the moustached man's pot from a pitcher, whilst, to all intents and purposes, giggling, "...who would have thought, eh?"

"Oh, that is lucky," she found herself both grinning and frowning.

"Very," Renard agreed as Anna-Lena clattered his bowl atop hers, "is there any chance we could have some more?"

"Of course, I'm sure your friend can arrange for that too..." the serving girl replied before turning her back on them and stomping off across the room.

Chapter Two

"Not such a pretty thing now, but still..." the voice hissed "...pretty enough."

Ulrich's eyes snapped open.

They were here!

Alms was at the end of the bed, leaning forward, hands resting on the footboard, long curls hanging about his pale face. Cleever sat cross-legged atop a chest of drawers, Wendel stood by the door. He still wore Captain Kadelberg's face, but Ulrich knew who he was well enough. Jarl loomed next to him, back against the wall, bare-chested, ashen skin darkened by the tattoos swirling around his arms and torso. Callinicus too.

At least he thought it was Callinicus; he was just a shadowy mess of burnt and blackened flesh. Seared by burning oil and blown to pieces by gunpowder. Something plopped wetly on the floorboards between the demon's feet. White teeth flashed in the fleshy lump atop his shoulders.

Demons were even harder to kill than he'd imagined.

"You didn't think we'd forgotten about you, Ulrich, *did you?*"

The voice came from the window, the figure slouching against the frame, one booted foot crossed over the other. He was silver in the moonlight, save his liar's eyes, which glowed deepest blue.

"No... master..." he croaked, throat seemingly flooding with ash.

Saul the Bloodless chuckled and pushed back his hat. It had a wide brim and a feather, "I'm not much of a one for forgetting. Promises made. Oaths taken. Betrayals. Oh yes, I don't forget such things."

Alms drifted around the bed to stand over Solace, who still slept next to him.

"You should be running to the other side of the world, boy, not trying to find us..." the demon breathed, stroking Solace's hair.

He wanted to slap the creature's hand away from his mistress, but he could not move anything but his eyes. More wicked devilry!

"Tell me..." Alms looked up, his big, deceptively soft eyes glinting in the room's fey light, "...have you fucked it yet?"

"Leave her be, master, please!"

"If you don't want her, I'm happy to have a go before opening her throat," Jarl offered. Wendel forced a wet laugh through Kadelberg's nostrils. On the chest of drawers, Cleever's eyes moved from one to the other in turn.

Alms ran a finger down Solace's cheek, smiled and straightened up, "Frankly, this isn't my preferred meat, but you, pretty boy, should fuck this thing while you have the chance. We all know you're not going to live a long life..."

"Even more so if you try and find us," Saul said shaking his head.

"I don't want to find you!"

"Of course you don't. But you're too weak to stop her, aren't you?" Saul stepped away from the window, "One little girl. She says, you jump."

"Like she's got your cock on a string," Callinicus snorted. Another bit of him splattered on the floor.

Saul sauntered over the bed. Ulrich tried to push himself deeper into the thin mattress. One by one the other demons gathered around him, save for Cleever, who remained cross-legged, silently watching everything with intent dark eyes.

"To think this thing could have been like us?" Alms sighed.

"I'm usually such an excellent judge of character," Saul tipped back his hat further, "but even I can make mistakes."

"You could have been strong," Jarl sneered.

"Fast," Wendel added.

"Never grown old," Callinicus said, words bubbling from the ruins of his mouth.

"Had everything, done anything," Alms said, shaking his curls.

"Supped the sweetest, sweetest blood," Saul dropped to his haunches. The last thing Ulrich wanted to do was look into those blistering eyes, but his head turned regardless till Saul's face, handsome and strong, filled the room.

"You could have had everything, Ulrich, but you

24

betrayed us for one sweet piece of cunt you can't even bring yourself to try and fuck. It would be funny if it wasn't..."

Jarl laughed and slapped his thighs, "No, no it is funny!"

Saul twisted out one of those charming smiles that never touched his liar's eyes.

"And just think if you had stayed true to us. By now, you would adore the screams of women and children rather than have them haunting you," Saul reached out and placed a cold, cold hand on his check, "You did nothing; we tortured them, we raped them, we ate them, we killed them in such delightful, intoxicating ways. If only you'd been there, Ulrich, what a sight it was! What fun, what games, what beautiful darkness. You didn't want to be there, but you didn't want to save them either. You couldn't stand, so you run away with this little piece of cunt you'll never fuck instead. Not a man, not a hero, not a monster. You are nothing. Without honour, without hope, without a thing worth drawing the next breath for. We should come and slaughter you for betraying us. But... do you know what? We won't. We'll let you have your wretched, empty, honourless life following a piece of cunt you'll never get to fuck. And do you know why?"

When he said nothing, Saul flicked his chin.

"I said, do you know why?"

"No, master!"

"Because..." Saul leaned in so close he felt his breath, cold and foul as black snow, hiss across his skin, "...because your life is going to be so much worse than anything even I can think of..."

Around him, the demons laughed. And laughed. And laughed...

*

She awoke slowly.

The mattress was thin, the pillows flat, the sheets stank of whoever previously slept in the bed, the blankets coarse and scratchy.

She wasn't sure she'd ever felt more comfortable.

If I just keep my eyes closed...

She could pretend it was still *before*. Her maids would soon be making a fuss; she'd be fed, dressed, pampered and made pretty. Ready for another day of waiting for her prince to come, for Father to find the most advantageous match for the family. Her father had weighted rich and powerful far more heavily than handsome and kind. Still, perhaps not enough in the end.

If he had just agreed to *Graf* Bulcher's proposal, she would now be married to a loathsome old man, but her father would still be alive, as would Lutz and everyone else who'd died in The Wolf's Tower and Tassau.

But no, her father refused Bulcher. And insulted him grievously in the process. Her father, who she always feared never loved her enough, turned out to have loved her too much. At least too much to sanction a marriage to a disgusting old man. And in doing so, he had unleashed a company of monsters upon their home.

She opened her eyes. There was no purpose served in pretending she still lived in the *before*. She didn't. That world was gone. This was the only real one. The *after*.

Daylight snuck in through loosely fitted shutters. She had slept late. She glanced at the huddled form at her side. She had slept late with a man.

A strange little frisson ran through her.

How scandalous she was. What would everyone say...

Of course, nobody was going to say anything. They were all dead.

Her eyes lingered on Renard's turned back. He'd balanced himself on the very edge of the bed, as far as he could get from her without sleeping on the floor. He wore a coarse shirt, loose and much patched. She wondered what his skin would look like. She had seen it before, of course, felt it too. Like holding ice at first as they held each other beneath the blankets in the old hunting lodge, he shivering uncontrollably, she trying hard not to let her tears drip onto him. Slowly they had warmed one another, until his skin turned from blue to pink.

They had slept a long time then too. Later, the fever took him, and his skin burned. She knew his touch as ice or fire.

I wonder what it would feel like now?

She looked sharply away. Stupid thought.

Still, she did not jump from the bed. She could feel the warmth coming off him; it made her want to roll closer. Another stupid thought. Probably.

He was sleeping peacefully. Best to let him rest longer. He hadn't slept well during the night, several times crying out. Once, he'd shouted "No, master!" at the top of his voice. He'd sounded so scared she'd wanted to reach out and comfort him. But she hadn't.

She knew of his nightmares but had never been so close to them. Within The Wolf's Tower's shell, they had slept in different rooms, his night terrors muffled by thick stone walls. Later, as they'd travelled with Morlaine, she'd been too exhausted for all the hounds of Hell to wake her.

Here, in the same bed, his torments were closer, visceral beasts that woke her more than once.

There was much she wanted done but letting him sleep a little longer would not overly delay them.

She laid there, watching him breathe. Beyond, sounds drifted from the market square. Normal, everyday noises of voice and foot, hoof and wheel, as if the world were still a sane place not being ripped asunder by war. Nor tormented by demons.

This is soft. This is comfortable. This is stupid.

It wasn't going to save Torben, it wasn't going to avenge her father, nor The Wolf's Tower, nor Tassau. It wasn't going to avenge her.

With a strange reluctance, she pulled her eyes from Renard's back and pushed herself up till she was sitting.

Another day.

Another day to survive, another day to defeat. Another day closer to vengeance and retribution. She took in a deep breath. The room's smells were not wholesome, but she bore them well enough. If they turned out to be the worst thing she suffered before the midnight bell tolled, then it was going to be a better day than any she'd endured since... *before*.

Taking care not to wake Renard, she climbed from the bed and crossed to the window. Away from the blankets

28

and Renard's warmth, the room was wincing cold; the fire had burnt down to grey ashes from which but a few orange dots glowed like baleful eyes.

"I would rather you didn't do that," a voice said as she made to crack open the shutters.

Solace gave a start and jumped back from the window. Morlaine sat in the furthest and darkest corner of the room, legs stretched out, one foot over the other.

"Lord..." Solace swallowed and found a faltering smile, "...how long have you been there?"

"A while... but I saw nothing I shouldn't."

Solace padded across to her. She moved the room's other chair to sit beside Morlaine.

"There was nothing to see. We are not lovers! There was only one bed... and... and..."

Morlaine raised a hand, "I cast no aspersions on your honour, Solace; it would be hypocritical of me in the circumstances."

"Where have you been?" she asked in a low voice.

"Have you thought about becoming lovers? Perhaps you should."

"*What?*"

"Your lives are so very short," Morlaine sighed, "so... *ridiculously* short."

"I... well... that..."

The demon reached forward and took her hand, squeezing gently. Something similar to a smile ghosted her face.

Solace composed herself, "Where have you been?"

"I needed to eat too."

"Oh."

Morlaine released her hand and sat back, "Do not fret. No one died. Captain Lucien will have no complaints. We made a fair trade, I would say."

"Captain Lucien?"

"He commands the mercenaries billeted here. The man I spoke to last night. He graciously agreed to order one of his men to vacate this room for you two."

"Why would he do that?"

"So I might drink his blood away from prying eyes."

Solace's frown deepened as she asked again, "Why would he do that?"

Morlaine raised an eyebrow and the corner of her mouth in unison but gave no further answer.

"I don't understand?"

"She whored herself for a room," Renard said, patting down the tangles of his hair as he sat up in bed.

"Oh..." Solace's eyes widened.

"I would not quite express it so," the demon's dark regard turned on Renard.

"No? How would you describe it then?"

"I whored myself for a room and a man's blood. An equitable deal," Morlaine glanced back and forth between them, "I think everybody was happy with the arrangement. Though you'd need to ask Lucien to be certain."

"He was... happy to let you drink his blood in return for...?" somewhere under his wild beard, Renard looked either impressed or disgusted. Perhaps both. It could be hard to tell behind so much hair.

Morlaine shook her head, "He'd passed out by then.

30

He'd drunk a lot, and I have a sleeping draught a cunning woman taught me how to make many years ago. If suffices to reduce questions."

"But... there must be a wound?" Solace spluttered.

"A vampire's bite heals very quickly so long as the wound is not too savage; a couple of puncture wounds in the arm will have faded to blemishes long before he awoke. They will have vanished by tonight. He will feel weak and hungover. He will not see anything strange in that."

A silence descended. Renard remained in bed, the blankets around him, knees drawn up to his chest. Although the shirt she wore hung long on her, she found her knees were exposed. She made sure they were pressed together. She was shivering. Renard had the right idea. The temptation to crawl back into bed with him was great.

Just for warmth, of course.

Temptation, however, rarely got anything useful done.

She shot to her feet and clapped her hands, "Well, we have much to do. Soonest started, soonest finished!"

Renard and Morlaine both stared at her.

"We do?" the demon asked.

"We need provisions; I will sell some of my jewellery to buy horses, travelling gear, food, weapons... and such!"

"Where are you planning to go?"

She moved to the fire; the embers still offered some warmth, though the musty stinks of the clothes they'd laid out before it were stronger. They were far worse than the sweaty sheets she'd just spent the night wrapped in.

"With you, to find my brother..." she bent over and threw some more coal on the fire. The bucket was nearly empty. She supposed the room's previous occupant had paid for it, but that was for Morlaine's Captain to deal with.

"No. You're not."

Solace looked up from the fire.

"Yes, we are. You need us."

That earnt her one of those little twitches of the lips that were the closest the demon came to a smile.

"No, I don't, Solace."

She wiped coal dust from her hands as she straightened up, "We agreed,"

"I agreed to bring you to a place of safety," the demon waved a hand at the window, "Madriel is as close to safety as you're likely to find currently. Though, if I were you, I would use your jewellery to get out of the Empire. France, Spain, England... Naples, perhaps?"

"We are going to hunt the Red Company."

"This is a bad war. There is no other kind, of course, but this is a particularly nasty one, and I fear it is going to get worse," Morlaine continued, as if not hearing her, "I really can recommend Naples."

"We are not going to Naples or anywhere else. We are going with you."

"I am leaving tomorrow night or the night after. I shall leave alone."

She took a step towards Morlaine, then glanced at Renard; he still sat as before, though he'd dropped his eyes.

"We can help you; together-"

"I do not require your help. You are a child," her head moved a fraction in Renard's direction, "...and he is a child with only one good arm. I have no capacity to care for you both and find Saul."

"You don't have to care for us!"

"You'd have slept on the street last night if it wasn't for me."

"And we are grateful," she tried hard not to spit that gratitude out through her teeth, "but we discussed this before, back at The Wolf's Tower. I have the *sight*; you need me!"

Renard's eyes widened. She'd spoken too loudly. They no doubt burned witches as freely in Madriel as they did everywhere else these days.

"Has your *sight* said anything about the whereabouts of Saul since we left your home?" Morlaine asked evenly, voice lowered, eyebrow raised.

"No," she had to admit.

"The Red Company? Your brother?"

"No."

"Anything at all?"

There'd been nothing; she'd put it down to the exhaustion of the long walk from The Wolf's Tower. It was as good an explanation as any; she doubted it had left her permanently.

"It isn't a book I can pick up whenever I want. It comes and goes."

"But mostly goes."

"It will lead us to them eventually. It told me about you. It told me about the man you were looking for, the one who loves songbirds too much. So, why wouldn't it?"

"Is he here?"

"I don't know."

"I heard he might be; that is why I came to Madriel. If you could tell me such things, then you would be useful. If you can't..." Morlaine shrugged, "Something is useful only until the point it is not."

"We can help you."

"No!"

Solace resisted the urge to slap her hands against her sides in frustration. She was not a child, whatever Morlaine might think, but throwing a tantrum was not going to dissuade the demon of that foolish notion.

Taking a calming breath, she tried another approach.

"How long have you been looking for Saul?"

"A long time," Morlaine offered after a pause.

"Years?"

"Many, many years."

"And you've never found him?"

"Several times I have-"

"You've never found him?"

"No," Morlaine conceded.

"Have you met people who have?"

"A few. Most do not survive the experience."

"We met them," she took another step across the room, first jabbing a finger into her chest before pointing at Renard, "we met them all. The whole Red Company. We stood against them. We fought them. We killed some of them. And we lived. We paid a price, a terrible price, and we lost. But we're still here..."

She crossed the room, stood over the demon, then leaned down till her nose hovered but a finger's length from the dark-haired woman.

"I've looked in Saul the Bloodless' eye, and I've spat in it too. When was the last time you did that, eh, Morlaine? When? Tell me! When? When? When?!!!"

She wasn't aware of anything else until Renard pulled her away from the demon, wrapping his arms around her from behind as she sobbed.

Morlaine just sat motionlessly, no particular expression on her face, extraordinary eyes fixed on them.

As Solace's tears subsided, Morlaine unfolded herself from the chair and brushed by them.

"If you've both finished with the bed, I'm going to lie down. I've had quite a tiring night..."

Chapter Three

"Can you spare a coin or two, sir?"

Yesterday he dressed like a filthy, penniless beggar. Today the filthy. penniless beggars were asking him for money.

He'd scrubbed nigh on a year's grime from his body in the bathhouse, cut his hair to practical bristles and trimmed his wild beard into something that made him look like a man who still cared a shit about his appearance. His clothes were newly bought, if not new, his boots sound and keeping his feet unaccustomedly dry, while his stomach was pleasingly full. His left arm remained next to useless, but such things were more easily overlooked if you appeared to be a man of means.

The young woman smiled and looked hopeful; a child, barely old enough to stand, buried itself in skirts almost as soiled as the clothes he'd worn when they'd dragged themselves into Madriel the night before.

"I'm sorry..." he mumbled, wanting to hold her eye and return the smile but finding it quite beyond him.

The sun, which earlier managed to occasionally break free of the murky clouds, had set half an hour ago. Now a gloomy half-light pressed upon the market square. Most townsfolk had already retreated behind their doors, leaving the streets to the mangy stray dogs and refugees like the young woman, who dropped her outstretched hand to the child's tawny head.

"God be with you, sir," she said, still finding a smile as she turned to make her way back to the knot of people huddling beneath makeshift canvas awnings in the lee of the church wall.

"How did you come to be here?" Ulrich asked before he knew he was going to do anything other than scurry back to Solace and her demon.

"Running from the war," she said, looking back over her shoulder, "like everybody else, sir."

The skin below her eyes was slightly livid. Hair, the same tawny shade as the child in her skirts, hung in limp strands from under a linen cap. Her every movement seemed weighed down by black iron.

"Hopefully, it will be over soon."

"We all pray for it, sir."

His eyes dropped to the child, "Yours?"

"My daughter, Seraphina, sir."

His eyes moved to the people behind her. Most clustered around a small fire, sharing its meagre warmth. Some had blankets wrapped around them; most didn't. Few seemed to be paying him any attention, eyes remaining glassily fixed on the flames as if some promise of better hid within their dance.

"Your husband?"

Her shoulders moved up and down, "I do not know. He went to the war, thought soldiering would pay better than farming. That was two years ago now. Haven't seen nor heard from him since..." her hand stroked Seraphina's downy curls as her gaze fell to the dirty cobbles "...didn't really expect to. One way or another."

"He was a fool."

She found a rueful smile, "Yes, sir, that he was..."

Seraphina made a keening noise like a hungry kitten and tried to burrow deeper into her mother's thin skirts.

"Men with swords, they frighten her, sorry, sir."

"'She is wise to be wary."

"Brigands robbed us on the road. Had a mule and cart with our belongings..." the woman's voice both quickened and thickened, "...they didn't hurt Seraphina, but... but... they took everything else."

"I am sorry, truly."

"We walked after that. By the time we got to Madriel, we couldn't walk any further..."

A few coins nestled in his pocket, but there weren't his. Just a few bits of copper left from the earrings Solace sold to buy clothes and food. Would she really miss them? Or begrudge him giving them to this poor woman? Probably not. His eyes flicked to the equally bedraggled souls beneath the church wall. But what good would it do? He could not put the world to rights with a couple of copper coins.

"What is your name?"

"Madleen, sir."

38

"I will pray your fortunes improve soon."

Her face brightened, "I'm sure the Good Lord will hear the prayers of so noble a gentleman, sir!"

If God listened to anyone anymore, he doubted the prayer of a man who'd broken his oath and betrayed a whole castle to demons would catch his attention.

"Goodnight, Madleen. God go with you."

"Sir!" she put a hand over Seraphina's ear and pressed the girl's head against her leg before saying in a low voice, "there is an alley near by; we could go there, for a little silver you... you could do as you wish with me..."

"I..."

Her eyes dropped as her cheeks flushed, "Please, sir, we have no food, Seraphina is hungry, I am not... a fallen woman... but... we have *nothing*... and you have the look of a man who would not be unkind with me... please... do you not find me even a little pleasing?"

He held up his hands and stepped away.

"The men who robbed us found me pretty... but they were not kind... though they never touched Seraphina, and everyday I thank the Good Lord for that..."

The little girl began to wail. A screeching pained cry brought on by hunger and cold, but, to Ulrich's ears, it sounded the same as the ghostly cries that echoed around the broken shell of The Wolf's Tower at night, tormenting and reminding him of the fact he had done nothing to save the women and children of Tassau from the mercies of Saul the Bloodless.

"No, no, no..." he shook his head, as Madleen scooped Seraphina up into her arms.

He turned and walked away, new boots clicking on the cobbles as the little girl sobbed behind him.

He expected the sound to cut off sharply. The cries of the children's ghosts always did, but Seraphina continued to sob behind him as he hurried away.

A shopkeeper was locking up his store, an ironmonger, "They bothering you, sir?" he peered at Ulrich through fleshy slits as he drew close.

"'tis nothing," he said, wanting to be away from the child's sobbing but finding the man's bulk suddenly in his way.

"Vermin," the ironmonger spat, thumbs hitching under the straps of his apron, "Herr Aumann is right, beggars, whores and thieves, the lot of them! They've turned the town into a hovel. Should be moved on and put outside the walls with the other wild animals!"

"They're just running from the war," Ulrich tried to get around the man.

"Running? More like bringing it with them. Eating our food, clogging our streets, begging everywhere. This is a good town, always has been. Now 'tis barely fit for decent folk like us."

Ulrich stared at him. This time yesterday he'd looked as wretched as Madleen and the other poor souls in front of *St Lorenz's*. Today he qualified as *decent* folk.

"World's going to ruin, not a scrap of goodness left in it," he said, nodding at the ironmonger as he moved around him.

"Indeed, sir, indeed. Full of wickedness, weakness and vice. These are the End Days, most certainly!"

40

Ulrich walked on. Behind him, Seraphina continued to weep for the world.

*

"'tis all I have of my brother..." she stared across to the bed where the demon sat stretched out, then added, "...for now."

Morlaine said nothing. She had brief periods of garrulity, bookended by extended bouts of silence where she only expressed herself via curt looks and occasional twitches of her full lips.

Currently, her tongue was most becalmed.

"He never spoke. A mute. People thought him stupid, but I knew he was never that. Just different. Very different. He couldn't speak, but he was able to communicate through symbols and objects. He carried a bag, a satchel, which he wore wherever he went. He even kept it with him in bed..." the memory of Torben in his nightshirt, tousled hair and sleepy eyes, satchel strap wrapped and tangled about him brought a rare smile to her lips.

"Father always feared he'd strangle himself in the night. He tried to forbid him from taking it to bed. But Torben refused to sleep without it, and when Torben refused to do something, he refused *vehemently...*"

Looking up from her hands, she found the demon's eyes remained on her, dark, expressionless, fathomless. Did she blink less than people did? Perhaps.

"He collected all sorts of things in that bag, but he loved his wooden animals the best. They were made for him when he was little. They each took on a meaning, an

41

attribute and expression... they became his way of talking to a world that couldn't hear him."

She held up the little wooden animal for Morlaine to see. *The Lion.* Worn smooth by her brother's hands and scorched by the fires that destroyed The Wolf's Tower to cover the crimes of Saul and his Red Company.

"*The Lion.* It represents bravery. It was sitting on the stairs we always used to go up to the family rooms. Those rooms were gone, that whole side of the castle blown to rubble with gunpowder. I never found any of Torben's other figures, but this had been placed in the middle of one of the steps leading up to our rooms..."

She turned the wooden figure around in her hand. During the long slow days in the ruined Wolf's Tower, she tied a leather thong about it so she could wear it about her neck.

"It was a message. Left for me by Torben. Be brave... be strong... be a lion..." she thrust the figure at the demon, "...so, you see, when you tell me Torben is no longer my brother, that he is a monster now, that he will not love me anymore, that all I should do is grieve and let him go, that I cannot save him..." she closed her hand around *The Lion,* "...I know that you are wrong..."

Morlaine tilted her head a fraction.

Solace snorted and slipped the thong back over her head, "Of course, you probably can't understand such a thing as love."

"Or someone just dropped it there. You read much into little, Solace."

"It was a skill I learned well with Torben."

Before the demon could try to tarnish her hopes and dreams further, Renard opened the door and let himself in. He was much changed. Still gaunt, pinch-faced, withered arm held across his torso, but their visit to the bathhouse had at least restored some portion of the man he had once been.

He had shaved his long unkempt hair to stubble to get rid of the lice, while his beard was now short and as neatly trimmed as any gentleman's should be. The dirt and grime of their journey, along with the months in The Wolf's Tower where washing amounted to a few summer dips in the carp pond, was gone, leaving his skin flushed only with the cold.

He looked fine in his new outfit too. They would not be in Madriel long enough to have clothes made for them, but there were several pawnbrokers, all of which were doing a roaring trade from the refugees pouring into town desperate for money to buy food and lodgings.

They had found a stiffened leather jerkin and a heavy winter coat. some britches, a linen shirt and sturdy boots. She'd bought boy's clothes for herself, much to the curiosity of the pawnbroker who kept pointing her in the direction of more suitable clothing for a lady.

"We will be travelling soon. Dresses are not practical for the road."

The man stared over his spectacles at her, "Travelling? Fraulien? At such a desperate time? You have many soldiers to escort you, yes?"

"Just him?" she'd nodded at Renard, who'd been struggling to try on a coat without her aid.

"Oh," the pawnbroker said.

43

"The Good Lord will protect us."

"I will pray for you... may I ask where you are heading? Not far, I hope. 'tis likely there will be snow before Christmas."

"Naples," Renard shot before she could tell him anything.

"Well, you won't have to worry about snow there," the pawnbroker chuckled.

She'd asked Renard later why he'd told the man Naples.

"You sold him the finest piece of jewellery he'd seen in months. Hopefully, he is an honest man, but if the wrong ear were to hear that a young woman who owns fine jewellery will be leaving town accompanied by only a man with a withered arm..." he shrugged "...besides, if you'd told him we were heading north, he would be even more curious about us than he already is."

"Why?"

He'd stared at her as they walked along the street, ignoring the outstretched hands of the beggars who seemed to occupy every other doorway, "Because *nobody* is going north..." he'd added with a sigh "...nobody sane, at least."

Renard nodded at her as he closed the door behind him, "My lady." Morlaine he ignored.

"Do you bring good news?" she asked, tucking *The Lion* back under her new shirt as he moved to warm himself by the fire.

"No horses. The same story as everywhere else. Soldiers have bought every spare horse they could find for the war. Those left are not for sale at any price," rubbing his hands over the flames, he looked up, "I think some are being kept for food, just in case."

"Just in case?"

"The town apparently has enough grain to see them through the winter, but after that... There was no harvest this year; the peasants fled when a rumour came an Imperial army was heading this way to drive the Lutherans out. Soldiers and brigands have taken most of the livestock," Renard shook his head, "next year will be bad."

"But there will be supplies from the south, surely?"

"The war spreads chaos further every year and shows no sign of easing. Even if supplies came, they'd likely be seized or stolen before they reached the people in the towns. Things deteriorated much while we were in The Wolf's Tower. Everybody thinks it will get worse still."

"There must be horses somewhere!"

"The stable owner said he heard of a fellow who might have a horse or two for sale, but they will be *very* expensive..."

"You should stay here until the spring," Morlaine rose from the bed, "there will be people heading south then. Go with them and keep going till you are out of the Empire."

"We are going with you," Solace raised her chin and set her face hard. She hoped she didn't look like a stubborn and spoilt child.

"Solace-"

"You cannot stop us."

"We have enjoyed this conversation before. It will not end differently."

"But-"

"No."

"Where are you going?" Solace demanded as the demon opened the door.

"It is night. I will spend it with Lucien. I trust he is sufficiently recovered for my needs. Then I will look for Suleiman again; if he is not here, I will leave for Potsdam."

"Suleiman?"

"The man who loves songbirds too much. I was told he might know where Saul is, and someone else told me he was seen in Madriel, though, more recently I was told he was in Potsdam. I looked for him last night without success. It is probably a false lead; they usually are," the demon stared hard at Solace, "The Night's Road has many dead ends."

"I can-"

"This room is paid up for the week," Morlaine stifled any more debate by closing the door after her.

"Bloody woman," Solace said, shaking her head.

"She is not a woman, she is-"

"I know very well what she is!" Solace snapped at him, "She is our best hope of saving Torben."

"Yes, my lady..." Renard's attention went back to the fire "...have you checked your jewels?"

"Morlaine is many things. Most of them diabolical, but she is not a thief," when he said nothing further, she added, "Yes, Everything is still there."

She had left her jewellery belt with the demon, deciding it safer with her than in the public bathhouse. Renard, not a trusting soul by nature, had questioned the decision, but she doubted the creature would run off with it even if it wasn't daylight.

"Perhaps-"

"We are going north, with or without Morlaine," she snapped.

"Yes, my lady."

Renard straightened up and moved to the window. As soon as the sun went down, Morlaine had opened the shutters to stare out across the market square. He did the same. Stock still, eyes fixed on something distant, making no move to take off his coat despite the hearty fire that had long since dispelled the chill from the room.

"Go to this man first thing," she told him, "So long as the horses don't look like they'll die under us, agree to whatever he wants for them, and I will sell what I need to raise sufficient coin."

"You know the pawnbroker didn't give you a fraction of what those earrings were worth?"

"You are a jewellery expert?"

"No, my lady. I could tell from his face when you put them on his counter."

"They were my mother's. However much he gave me for them, it would not come close to their value to me."

He pulled out a couple of copper coins from his pocket, "This is all that is left."

"No matter. I have plenty more to sell. There may be a shortage of horses, food and lodgings here, but there appears to be a plethora of pawnbrokers and moneylenders."

"But it is all you have, my lady."

"No, all I have is my brother. Which is why we are

heading north."

Renard put the coins atop a chest of drawers, beside which sat the provisions her mother's earrings had bought. Everything they needed, save for horses and tackle.

He stood staring at the pile for a long time, "My lady, I met a woman in the square. A refugee. She has a small daughter. No money, no food, no shelter. Nothing. I wish to give her a blanket and some food. With your leave."

"Ulrich, your charity does you credit, but we need these things."

"We can buy more."

"I can buy more."

He returned his eyes to the provisions, clothes, weapons, dried food, travelling gear and blankets they'd bought for the challenges ahead.

"By my reckoning," he said in a quiet voice, "I am owed best part of a year's pay. I will accept a blanket and some food in lieu of some of what is due."

She stiffened, "Is that why you stayed with me? Awaiting your back pay?"

"No, my lady. 'tis more complicated than that."

"Is she young and fair, this woman you met?"

"She's alone, hungry, scared and has suffered a great deal. She has a young daughter, Seraphina. When the child started crying, it put me in mind of..." the words trailed to nothing.

She sucked in a breath, then waved a hand at their provisions, "Take what you want. Maybe God will repay the deed."

"Perhaps, my lady, thank you."

Renard crouched, took a blanket and put some food in a bag. When done, she said, "And what of all the other hungry, scared people in Madriel; what can you do for them?"

"Nothing," he admitted, "but I did nothing for the women and children in The Wolf's Tower either. I left them to die at the hands of monsters. I know I could not have saved them all, whatever I had done. But I could have tried to save someone. To suffer just one less life on my conscience would lessen my burden."

She didn't reply till he'd left the room.

"But you did save someone, Ulrich..." she whispered to the door, "...you saved *me*..."

Chapter Four

He found Madleen and Seraphina huddled together away from the main knot of refugees sheltering against the church wall. The night was sharp enough to frost his breath, but it was dry. The weeks of incessant autumn rain had finally ceased.

Around the fire, someone was singing; further along, a wizened man ranted about the end of the world. Most people, however, sat in silence, saving their energy to keep warm.

Madleen didn't notice him until he stood over them.

"Sir?" she peered up, one arm wrapped around her daughter's shoulders. Seraphina appeared to be sleeping, head resting against her mother's chest.

"My name is Ulrich... I... brought you... some things..." he handed her the blanket, which was thick and woven with good wool, followed by the canvas sack of food.

"The Lord be praised. Thank you!"

He crouched down and spread the blanket over them while Madleen clutched the food.

"I am sorry 'tis not more."

She shook her head and peered inside the bag.

"tis just some dried meat and dried fruit, a few apples too. Road provisions."

"'tis more than we have eaten in days! The church gives us bread and soup, but 'tis little more than hot water..."

"You will be here all night?"

"The church opens its doors for us once its business is done for the day. 'tis cold on the stone floor, but dry at least."

"I hope the blanket will keep you a little warmer."

"Oh, it will, sir! It will!"

He wanted to say more, do more. But had no idea what, so, instead, he smiled, nodded and made to bid her a good night.

"Sir!" she said, clutching the small sack with a fierce hand, "I see you are a man of means, a Christian man, a kind man. Would you have need of a maid? Sorry to ask, but I'm a hard worker. Dawn to dusk without a quibble, and Seraphina, well, she's no trouble. Barely makes a peep!"

"No, I'm sorry, Madleen, I do not."

"Oh... no need to be sorry, sir, but if you change your mind... or know of anyone..."

He shook his head, "I am leaving soon; I do not live here, I am just passing through."

"But when you get home, would you need help there? We're happy to travel. We can walk, sir, till our feet bleed we can!"

"I'm not going home, Madleen. I have no home. I'm sorry, truly."

"Where are you going?"

He was going to say Naples, but couldn't bring himself to lie, "North."

Madleen's eyes widened, "Don't go north! The war is worst there. Terrible it is. The things being done, the things I've seen, the things I've heard."

"I know. But I must."

"But why?"

Madleen and Seraphina sat apart from the other refugees, but not so far his words would not carry, and not so far curious eyes weren't already being turned in their direction.

Ulrich eased himself down next to Madleen, back against the cold, pitted brickwork of the church wall. They were sitting on old sacking spread across the cobbles.

"Because my lady wishes it."

"Why would she wish it? Does she not know?"

She looked at him with large, unblinking eyes. Beneath the dirt and tiredness, she was pretty; small nose, full lips, rounded cheeks, expressive eyes. He hadn't been with a woman since before The Wolf's Tower fell. He seldom felt the urge now; Lady Solace was beautiful, but she scared him, and she was his mistress, whom he had given his oath to protect, to whom he owed his life.

He had thought the horrors of the last year had burnt such desires from his body, heart and soul. But perhaps he had simply buried them to make a life lived alone with Solace possible.

Now he found he suffered a great urge to take Madleen's hand.

If he had any silver in his pocket, he wondered whether it would tempt him to press it into her palm for a favour or two.

He turned his eyes away.

"She knows. We know," he finally said, watching a skinny dog sniff around the deserted square in the hope of finding something edible the refugees had overlooked.

"Then why?"

"To find someone who wronged her. Wronged both of us..."

"You do not sound like you wish to go?"

He bit his bottom lip. Someone threw a stone at the dog, it missed, skittling over the cobbles, but it was near enough to send the animal scampering away.

"I am in her debt. I am honour-bound."

"Debts don't always have to be paid, sir. And honour ain't worth going to your grave for."

"Honour is the only thing a man has that cannot be bought or sold; he can only give it away..." he said, as much to himself as Madleen, "...something my father used to tell me."

"Did your father enjoy a happy life?"

That brought a smile to his lips.

"Eat, please. You are hungry," he said, troubled by the weight of her gaze. By taking an interest, he was giving Madleen hope; he wondered if that amounted to kindness or cruelty.

"I'll eat when Seraphina wakes; she doesn't sleep well.

None of us do."

Beyond Madleen, people watched them, noticing he had given the young woman and her child food.

"Best you eat it sooner rather than later... hungry people do desperate things."

She nodded, dropping her eyes, "I know... but I have to make it last. Don't know what tomorrow might bring, so always keep a little back. That was something my papa used to say."

"He sounds a wiser man than mine."

She shrugged, pushing a stray lick of hair back under her linen cap.

"Do what you think is best... but I will bring you more tomorrow."

Another smile flickered across her face; it was both happy and puzzled, "Why are you being so kind to me, sir? There are so many here going hungry. Why me?"

He eased his head back against the wall and stared heavenwards. Stars sprinkled the sky. It would be a dry night but a fiercely cold one, he reckoned.

"No one can save everybody, but everybody can save someone."

"Your father again?"

"No."

Save her, and you save yourself.

Lutz told him that before he'd given his life to the demons so they could try to escape. A vain sacrifice in the end, as a rock fall blocked the passage out of the castle, forcing the survivors to turn back.

It seemed, sitting here in the cold, Lutz's words fitted

Madleen as well as they did Solace.

This woman he could save. But Solace? She was taking them to their deaths as surely as Lutz walked to his after hiding the entrance to the tunnel in the family chapel.

But he had sworn no oath to protect Madleen. He owed her no debt.

"I ask only one thing in return?" he turned his head to look at her.

"Yes?" Madleen's hand tightened on the canvas bag.

"Don't offer yourself to a man for pieces of silver again. You are worth more than that."

Her hand moved towards him, brushed his leg and then pulled back, "My child is hungry. What else can I do? I am a woman; I have nothing else to sell."

It was a question he could not answer, "I am staying in the *Market Inn*, you know it?"

Madleen nodded.

"Once you leave the church tomorrow, come there. I will have hot food for you."

"Sir..."

"Ulrich, my name is Ulrich."

"You are too kind..."

"I am here for a few days. I will take care of you both till I leave. 'tis the least I can do."

"Mama...?" Seraphina stirred, two sapphire-blue eyes peeking out from behind her mother to peer at him.

"'tis our friend, Ulrich. Remember? From earlier? He has brought us a feast! A banquet!" Madleen rummaged in the sack and pulled out an apple. The little girl's eyes widened, and a small hand shot out to wrap around the fruit.

Seraphina took a chunk out of it, swallowed and then smiled about as widely as he'd ever seen a human face bear.

"Thank you," Madleen said again.

He nodded, eyes moving from the girl to her mother, "I will sit with you till the church opens its doors. Eat what you can before you go inside."

"I think I would have trouble stopping her," Madleen laughed as Seraphina devoured the apple.

"It might cost a finger or two," he agreed.

"'tis getting terrible cold tonight..." she lifted the blanket, "...come sit closer; it will help keep us both warm."

It was not a good idea for any number of reasons, but he shuffled up next to Madleen and let her throw the end of the blanket over his legs before he could let any of those reasons get a grip.

He took the other edge of the blanket and pulled it up to his chest.

Madleen was right; it was freezing, but, still, he soon found himself feeling warm for the first time since he'd been dragged from his bed to ride out to the burning village of Tassau the night The Wolf's Tower fell...

*

"You are wearing a dress, my lady."

Whatever else Renard had lost in the last year, his sense of observation remained as keen as ever.

Her hands smoothed down the gown, which was a plain and simple thing, "What do you think of it, Ulrich?"

56

He ran his eye up and down her, "'tis a dress, my lady."

Yes. Just as keen as ever.

In truth, it felt strange to wear such a garment again. It was more akin to what her maids might have worn than the silk and lace she dressed in *before* to look pretty in case a suitable prince or lord happened to drop in looking for a wife.

"I bought it while you were trying to find horses; it fits decently enough..." her eyes moved from looking down at the dress to Renard, his face still flushed red from the cold, "...I thought I might stand out less in this than dressed like a man."

"I believe you would stand out whatever you chose to wear, my lady."

That sounded very much like a compliment. She racked her brain to remember Renard complimenting her before. Perhaps she had misunderstood.

"Have you been drinking?"

"No, my lady."

"You were gone quite some time."

"I waited with Madleen till she went into the church for the night; I was worried some of the other refugees might take the food from her."

"I'm sure no one will be so base now they are in the house of the lord."

"No... but I made sure they ate everything while I was with them anyway."

She wanted to ask questions about this Madleen woman but forced them down. His charity was noble, and guilt about the women and children of Tassau they left to the demons when they'd fled The Wolf's Tower burdened him to the point of torment. His actions were commendable, even if giving away some of the provisions she'd sold her mother's jewellery for rankled.

She was certain he harboured no other motive. Entirely sure...

"Well, now I am hungry. That is the thing with food; once you start eating it again, you just want more..." she gave a feeble laugh. Renard forced a smile, and his eyes twitched to the window.

It looked out towards the church. She knew that well enough as she had stood and spied on Renard sitting with the woman and child many times whilst awaiting his return.

"Come, we will find a table downstairs and eat."

Renard nodded, but as he moved for the door, she put a hand on his arm.

"Morlaine..." she said, noticing the way his eyes narrowed and lips hardened at the mention of the demon's name, "...told her captain we are fleeing the war like everybody else. She said I am her cousin... and you are my husband."

His eyes stopped narrowing and widened instead.

"'tis... appropriate... I think. 'tis best not to be noticed. As man and wife, we will..." she shrugged, "...we should ensure we stay true to her story."

"Of course, my lady."

"So, please stop calling me "*my lady*," 'tis unnecessary anyway."

"Yes, my lady."

"Is this something requiring practice?"

"Yes... Solace..." he said the word as if it filled his mouth with some curious and exotic intimacy. They had faced so much together. Death, demons, illness, pain, loss, hardship and horror. They had held each other naked in bed, they had lived alone for the best part of a year without speaking to another soul. They had kept one another alive when death would have been so much easier. Yet he found it difficult to actually say her name.

She cleared her throat, "Do not call me that either. *Graf* Bulcher thinks me dead. I would imagine Saul thinks us dead too. 'tis best we do nothing to dissuade them of that fallacy."

She felt a cold smile upon her lips, "The next time *Graf* Bulcher hears the name Solace von Tassau it will be just before I slit his throat."

"You... intend to kill him too?"

"Am I being too ambitious? The Red Company was the means, but Bulcher provided the thought that sent them to us... Bulcher's was the lust... the madness..." she found she was clenching her fists; with an effort she stopped, forcing her hands to adopt a more suitably ladylike pose.

Renard eyed her in the manner someone might observe a dog to ascertain whether or not it was rabid.

She forced a softer smile onto her face, "There is no need to look concerned; we will probably die long before I get near enough to Bulcher to cut his throat. Or cut out his heart. Or..."

He stared at her for a long, drawn-out breath before

asking, "What should I call you, my lady?"

She coughed, then, "Celine."

"'tis a fine name."

"I think so! It was my grandmother's. I never knew her, and apparently she was a cantankerous, ill-tempered shrew, but, still, I like the name."

"Yes..." he frowned with the effort, "...Celine."

"Perfect!"

"Am I still Ulrich?"

"Does *Graf* Bulcher know you?"

He shook his head.

"Then I think you can remain Ulrich."

"And our family name?"

She doubted being known as Renard would present much danger; would Saul even know it? Still, something said no. A warning from her *sight* or just a silly pettiness? She didn't know. The *sight* had stayed quiet since Morlaine arrived at The Wolf's Tower, but if she had learned anything this past year, it was to always trust her instincts.

"Lutz."

"Very well," he nodded, "Frau Lutz."

She nodded back, "Now, come, husband, I am hungry."

Renard pursed his lips and opened the door for her, "Most wifely..."

Before they left the room, she placed a white linen cap upon her head. Being seen in public with your head uncovered signified a woman was either a virgin or a whore. As she was now Renard's wife...

Downstairs was much the same as the previous

evening, full of drunken soldiers. She wondered what state they would be in if an army ever did roll up before the town walls.

One difference was they no longer looked like vagrant beggars. She felt more eyes linger on her. Last night Morlaine drew most of the attention; now the demon sat at their captain's table and would later be in his bed. Perhaps the dress had been a mistake.

She had not planned to buy one; she was not some pretty little thing anymore. She was a warrior and a hunter of demons. She was vengeance, and vengeance didn't need to wear a dress.

She took Renard's arm as they crossed the room. It didn't turn any of the eyes away.

Anna-Lena served them. She didn't appear any cheerier. The food on offer was another thing that hadn't changed; she let Renard order it plus some ale and water. When Anna-Lena asked for money, Solace pointed across the room at Morlaine.

"Do you not recall? My cousin is paying for everything."

Anna-Lena made a faint snorting noise and negotiated her way around the tables, avoiding the groping hands, to interrupt Morlaine and Lucien. The demon put coins in the serving girl's palm without so much as a glance in their direction.

"One cannot fault her generosity, at least..." she muttered at Renard, who was playing his part well. Like most husbands, he didn't appear to be listening to her.

They ate in silence. Despite the food being the same, it

did not go down so finely. It was surprising the difference not being half-starved made to one's palate.

Once finished, Anna-Lena returned to slam a few plates around. When Renard asked for more ale, the serving girl shot him a venomous look.

"She's still paying..." Solace said.

A few minutes later more ale arrived, a fair portion of it sloshing straight on to the rough wooden tabletop.

"I don't think she approves of us..." Renard said, hand curling around the new tankard.

"Let us pray she doesn't get to know us any better," she diluted her own ale with water. It did little to improve the taste.

After eating in silence, they drunk in silence. Renard's hand never straying from the beer, his eyes distant.

Was he thinking about... what was her name? Madleen?

She let her gaze drift across the room, between the shadows and the drifting palls of smoke men with hard, sharp edges stared back. She tried not to catch anybody's eye. In truth, she hadn't wanted to come down here. Not being noticed was a lot easier when you were in a room on your own. But she'd passed every day since The Wolf's Tower fell in such a fashion. Alone, save for Renard and, latterly, Morlaine. Being around people again...

She hadn't expected to be unsettled by people, crowds, voices, by... the not being alone. But she was. And if she let that fear dig its talons into her any deeper, she'd just run away to some dark, empty corner of the world and not come back.

Which would make the business of vengeance so much harder.

A figure appearing over her jerked Solace's thoughts back.

"Your cousin has told me almost nothing about you, so I thought I should find out for myself..." Captain Lucien pulled out a chair and slumped into it.

"There isn't much to say," Solace managed to smile, glancing up at Morlaine, who stood, one hand resting on the soldier's shoulder, "we're very distant cousins..."

"War, it tears people apart. It brings people together. The world is a bubbling pot of stew, and war is the spoon that stirs it all up," Lucien smiled, seemingly pleased with himself.

"All we want," Morlaine said, slipping away from Lucien to sit between Solace and Renard, "is to escape the killing. Isn't it, cousin?"

Solace nodded. Renard managed the same.

Lucien's smile widened. She fancied he'd once been a handsome man, but now he was drawn, worn, greying hair and beard to match a grey pallor, bags weighed down eyes he seemed only able to half open. Several scars vividly slashed the square set of his face, his nose skewered to the right. When he smiled, he revealed mostly blackened teeth around the gaps.

How much of his appearance was due to the hardships of soldiering and how much to spending a night with Morlaine she could not say.

"Ah, now, that is the trick..." he snapped his fingers as Anna-Lena wandered by, pointing at the tankards once he'd earned himself a sour look, "I am Lucien, by the way. I have the honour of leading this rabble of drunken villains the upstanding burghers of Madriel's town council have seen fit to hire to defend their splendid community."

"An elite fighting force, I have no doubt," Renard muttered into his beer.

"Quite!" Lucien grinned, "You know a thing about soldiering, eh, Herr... you know, Morlaine has never actually told me your names...?"

"Ulrich Lutz," Renard said, "and my wife, Celine."

"Enchanted," Lucien's eyes swivelled between Morlaine and Solace, "what a beautiful family! Are the rest of you so blessed?"

"Everyone else is dead," Solace said before she could stop herself.

Lucien's head bobbed up and down, "Forgive me..."

She decided to reply with a smile accompanied by a deferential nod. Wives were not supposed to be much noticed, she reminded herself.

Husbands, on the other hand...

"Tell me, Captain," Renard asked, "do your men do anything other than get drunk?"

"Of course," Lucien beamed, "they also keep the town's whores well occupied. We provide a vital service!"

"So I see..." Renard sipped more beer.

"No, really. The town pay us with taxes from their coffers; almost all of that money is swiftly passed on to Madriel's many fine taverns and obliging whores, thereby returning the taxes raised to the people," he revealed more broken and blackened teeth, "'tis a most virtuous circle."

"I would have thought the burghers might expect a little more for their silver?" Renard kept pressing. She got the impression he was even less taken with Lucien than with Morlaine. Which was quite an achievement.

"Oh, that *stuff*..." Lucien flapped a hand, "...we patrol the streets, keep order, walk the walls, and ride out to clear brigands from the roads. But we can't spend *all* our time doing that kind of thing. Wouldn't be at all good for morale."

"I see."

"Trust me, I know about these things! The name of Lucien Kazmierczak is renown across the civilised world. A master of the noble art of soldiering known from Constantinople to Cadiz, from the Baltic to the Barbary Coast!" he thumped his tankard on the table, adding some foam to the puddles Anna-Lena deposited earlier, before grinning some more, "Known, though, I have to admit, rarely pronounced correctly..."

He did a lot of grinning. An ill-advised habit for a man with such dental wreckage decorating his mouth.

"I'm sure we can all sleep easier in our beds..." Renard said.

Despite herself, Solace glanced at Morlaine. Her face remained as implacable as ever.

"I see you carry a sabre, Herr Lutz. It has the look of a practical blade. You know a little of soldiering? Or is it for decoration?"

"It was my father's. He was a soldier. He taught me how to use it."

"I should hope so. A man should always be capable of

65

defending his woman," Lucien winked at Solace, "the world being so full of scoundrels and all..."

With that, Lucien emptied his tankard in one, save for a few more fat droplets that escaped to plop onto the table. Done, he slapped it down and jumped to his feet.

Quick as a flash, he pressed his lips against the back of her hand, "My great pleasure, Frau Lutz," once straightened, he shot another wink, this time in Renard's direction, "you are almost as lucky a man as I am..."

Morlaine rose unquestioningly to her feet too.

Lucien rested his knuckles on the tabletop and leaned on them, "My men are scum. And I say that kindly, but they won't give you any trouble. You have my word," his gaze bounced between them, "do let me know if that doesn't prove to be the case so I can have the skin lashed off the hide of the bastard. Men need a lashing now and then, not too many, just enough. That's good for morale too."

With that, he moved around the table and let Morlaine take his arm.

"Goodnight, cousins," she nodded at them before letting Lucien lead her towards the stairs.

Every pair of eyes in the room followed them.

Chapter Five

He awoke for the first time since the fall of The Wolf's Tower and found a worthwhile reason to open his eyes.

Curiously, that reason was not the beautiful young woman he was sharing a bed with. Next to him, Solace still slept, her breathing deep and slow.

He had thought of Madleen constantly, from the moment she shuffled inside the arched door of *St Lorenz's* till the second he opened his eyes. The only time he had not thought about her was during the fitful interrupted hours of sleep that split the night.

The only thought that came close to dislodging Madleen from his mind was the realisation he neither liked nor trusted Lucien whatever-his-name-was.

If he'd the misfortune to serve under such a louse, he would have made every effort to find himself another company at the first possible chance.

Still, he was not their problem. Let him rut the night away with a demon and suffer the consequences. A blood-sucking fiend and a louche fool. A fine couple!

His snort was loud enough for Solace to stir next to him. He held his breath till she settled. She needed to sleep, to recover from all she'd endured. At least in body, if not mind.

He remembered how her eyes flared when she'd talked of slitting *Graf* Bulcher's throat. It'd only been there for a second or two, but, for a few heartbeats, she'd looked more demonic than Morlaine ever had.

That such a slip of a girl could do anything to frighten him...

But she did. Like Morlaine did. Like Saul, Alms and the other demons of the Red Company did. And fear of them all had become his closest companion, chained to him with hard, unbreakable iron, a demented creature forever hissing in his ear about the pain, misery and despair awaiting him before his imminent death.

Yet when he'd sat with Madleen that choking dread, a weight he'd carried ever since riding into the burning village of Tassau to discover demons really did stalk the night, had shrunk, and shrivelled to nothing.

How was that possible?

His eyes moved to the window again; darkness still pressed against the shutters.

Twice already, he had climbed from bed to pad across the room, crack open the shutters and stare across the square. The first time due to a restlessness that kept him from sleep; the second was because a crying child woke him.

He didn't know if it was a real child, a ghost from The Wolf's Tower or just a dream. He'd hoped the one grace of following Morlaine would be to leave those spectral sobs and wails within the shattered walls of the broken castle. But they had come with him. While they'd slept in the open, he knew they could only be ghosts. Here, of course, there were real living children, like Seraphina, to cry.

By the time he reached the window to see if it *was* Seraphina, the crying stopped. There were no refugees huddled against the church wall; everyone was inside, and the square was deserted save for a solitary figure making its way across the already frosty cobbles. A three-quartered moon hung over the town, dressing the market square in silver-grey.

His breath caught in his throat. The figure was Morlaine. He recognised her long hooded cloak; he'd spent much of the last few weeks staring at her back after all.

Off to look for the man she sought. Suleiman. Who liked songbirds too much, whatever that meant? Perhaps he would point her towards Saul and The Red Company if she found him. He should pray that she didn't. If she got word of their whereabouts Solace would be even more determined that they follow the Night's Road the demon walked.

As he watched, the figure halted, twisting around to stare over its shoulder. The hood was up, obscuring the face in its deep shadow. But it was Morlaine; no breath steamed from the hood. He took a step back from the window. It was not possible she could see him halfway across the square, and he only peering through shutters that weren't a quarter open.

Maybe she couldn't see him, but she knew the window

of their room. Perhaps she was wary one or other of them might be watching, might see her out and about the dark work of demons in the smallest hours of a freezing moon-washed night.

Still, he'd silently closed the shutters and returned to bed. Letting Solace's warmth dispel the chill of the night that wrapped itself about him in the few minutes he had been at the window.

He lay awake till dawn's first suggestion teased the window hours later. At least no child screamed or cried through the remainder of the night, which was a mercy.

Solace didn't wake or stir. Her sleep deep and untroubled. Perhaps she dreamt sweet dreams of vengeance. After dressing quickly, he carried his boots, coat and sabre out into the hallway. Not pulling them on until far away from Solace's door.

Downstairs several of Lucien's men were about, some cradling steaming mugs to their red-flushed faces after a cold night walking the walls and streets. Others appeared to have slept where their beer left them the previous night.

A couple of glances came his way, but as he wasn't Morlaine nor Solace, none lingered.

Madleen and Seraphina had not yet arrived. The refugees had to leave the church at dawn to make way for morning worship. Beyond the inn's leaded windows, a greying dawn light pressed, so they would not be long.

Anna-Lena came and asked what he wanted after a few minutes. She always seemed to be working; perhaps that explained her permanently foul mood.

He ordered some watered wine, sweetened with

elderflower syrup.

"Your *cousin* paying, is she?"

"She has the money," he replied, rubbing sleep from his eyes.

"I suppose there's always plenty of coin to be had in her line of work..." Anna-Lena sniffed before spinning on her heels.

He ignored the barb. Whatever she or anyone else thought of Morlaine, the truth was far more terrible.

Eyes fixed on the door, he became unaccountably fidgety, squirming in the chair to find a comfortable perch. When he found one, restless fingers drummed on the table or ran through the unfamiliar bristles of his newly trimmed beard instead.

When the door finally did open, he half jumped to his feet, only sinking back down as two soldiers, slapping the cold from their arms, came through it.

When Anna-Lena slammed his drink on the table and asked if he would be eating, he simply growled, "Later," at the woman.

The sweetened and watered wine sat untouched before him. He didn't even want wine; it'd simply been the first and only thing to pop into his mind. Would Madleen think him a drunkard? Why did it matter what she thought? He'd done far worse things. How might Madleen react to those if she did not approve of breaking fast with wine?

Foolish thoughts chased their own tails, making his head spin far more than a barrelful of weak wine ever would.

The door opened again. He managed to stay on his

arse this time, which was just as well as it was only another of Lucien's men.

He sat, fidgeted, stared at the door, stared at the wine, stared at the gradually brightening window. Waited.

When full sunlight started making the frost coated windows sparkle, he got up, rubbed condensation from the glass with his sleeve and peered across the market square towards the church.

The morning was unseasonably bright. Harsh, startling light raked the square from the low winter sun, spearing through the streets, alleys and gaps to the east, to glisten upon the still ice-coated cobbles. The refugees already gathered against the wall separating the market from the church grounds. Huddling under their rough canvas awnings, clustering around fires they were trying to relight.

Madleen would be here soon.

Wouldn't she?

Why would a woman with a hungry child turn down a free meal?

Yes, of course she would come.

And then?

They would eat, and spend some time together. He would try to save them, because everybody could save someone, and then he would follow Solace to their deaths. Whether with Morlaine or not, whether at the hands of Saul's demons or the more mundane monsters blighting the war-ravaged land. They would die, Madleen and Seraphina would remain penniless and hungry. Nothing would change.

He returned to the wine and sat down.

Perhaps he should go back to Solace. He was doing no good here. Just foolishly pursuing a pretty face. Was he trying to save Madleen or bed her? Perhaps a bit of both.

More minutes passed.

A knot grew in his stomach. Worrying why Madleen had not yet come, worrying about what would happen if she did.

Eventually, he pushed himself to his feet.

The wine sat on the table. Untouched. Scooping it up, he downed it in one. It was sickly sweet and made his guts roil. No matter. He stood, staring at the empty mug, unsure what to do.

How had his father become a drunk?

A man is not born to it, after all. It was a vice that took him by degrees. Had there been a moment, a choice, a decision? Have another drink or leave. A fork in the road. Two paths leading to different places. If Old Man Ulrich had chosen that other path...?

Or had there never been a decision to make? Was choice nought but an illusion? Everything decided already by a greater power, and we just dance about the world in time to the pull of hands upon invisible strings, to some divine script.

God saved us for a purpose...

That was one of Solace's favourites. As if it explained everything that had befallen them, excused every death, every cruelty, every suffering. God had a plan, and they were His agents.

He snorted at the thought.

74

Solace. Madleen. Hard-drinking.

What plan was most likely God's? What plan the Devil's? What plan the dishonoured coward, Ulrich Renard's?

When you put it like that...

He pushed the mug away and headed for the door.

*

A man stood on the crest of a grey hill.

Smoke billowed around her, intermittently obscuring the figure. Sometimes she could see the cloak snapping around him, the wind teasing long, unkempt hair. Then another curtain of sharp, acrid smoke swished between them, and he became but an indistinct ghost her smarting eyes could not distinguish from the whorls and swirls engulfing the hill.

"Torben!"

The smoke caught in her throat, making her cough to the point of retching.

He didn't respond. He might have been looking at her; he might have been staring sightlessly into the middle distance, his eyes turned inwards, the world forgotten.

She pushed on. The hill was not steep, but her calves burned all the same. She wore a dark green gown trimmed with Flanders lace, not designed for charging up hills. She gathered the skirts and tried to run as best she could. It was a lovely dress. She'd worn it when *Graf* Bulcher came to visit and had refused to wear it ever again.

Father thought Bulcher had come to make a match for his son, Leopold, but the *sight* had whispered something different.

Father never listened to her, not about anything, but certainly not about her hunches and feelings. So, he'd bought her a beautiful new dress to show Bulcher how desirable she was, what a fine match she'd be for his son.

She'd have guessed Bulcher's motives even without the sight as soon as his greedy, piggy eyes fell on her. He'd heard she was a beauty and had come to see for himself. He was a rich and powerful man, and he'd taken time off from the murderous business of war and politics to travel to a tiny barony to cast his eye over a young woman.

She looked wildly around, suddenly certain Bulcher lurked in the smoke, but there was no one to see bar Torben. In truth, it would have taken a *lot* of smoke to conceal something as vast, hideous and unholy as *Graf* Bulcher.

After Bulcher left, the very sight of the dress made her flesh crawl, reminding her how the fat old *Graf's* eyes had roamed over it - exploring, imagining, devouring.

Father never talked of what passed between Bulcher and he after he'd excused her from dinner the night before the *Graf* left.

He'd asked for her hand, not for Leopold or his other sons, but for himself. He'd said no such thing that she'd heard, but she knew. And had known before he squeezed out of his carriage, like some bloated, malevolent spider, whose eyes sat on stalks and tongue lolled from its mouth whenever she was in the same room as him.

Father had said no. Bulcher was as hugely rich as he was huge. A man well used to the world giving him whatever he wanted. And he wanted her. Perhaps if Father had just said no. Politely and firmly, that would have been the end of it.

But perhaps not.

Father insulted Bulcher and sent him away with a flea in his ear. Had called him a pig. That was not like Father. Bulcher must have angered him greatly to react so vehemently, must have made demands, made insinuations, made threats when Father refused his proposal.

But Bulcher didn't take no for an answer.

He sent the Red Company to seize her and wipe their barony from the face of the Earth. To slaughter everyone she knew, to roast Father alive all because he had called Bulcher a pig.

So Saul the Bloodless told her anyway. In most things she would believe nothing that monster said, but she saw no reason for him to lie about Bulcher. Sometimes even demons spoke the truth.

And now, here she was, struggling up this grey hill towards the brother Saul took from her in the dress she'd worn for *Graf* Bulcher.

Did that mean anything?

"Torben!"

He didn't respond. She tried running faster, but walking was difficult enough between the heavy skirts in her hands and the whalebone corset. Haste was not required when one dressed to stoke the fires of your suitors.

She slipped and had to let go of her skirts to save her face - that pretty, coveted face some men would most definitely kill for - from smacking into the ground.

She found her hands grey with greasy ash when she pushed herself back up. The wind tugged at the blonde tresses her maids spent so long teasing into shape for the approval of *Graf* Bulcher's lecherous eye. She wiped the ash onto the embroidered bodice of her gown, then tried to rip the skirts off, but the material was too heavy to tear.

She gave up, gathered the skirts once more and started clambering up the slope again. She wanted to pant, but her corset disapproved of such unladylike pursuits.

What was this place?

Her feet, encased in their dainty silk slippers, dug into the grey hill as she climbed, sending small puffs to swirl around her skirts. Occasionally they crunched into something more substantial, but she kept her eyes on Torben. She didn't want to see what made those crunching noises. She really didn't.

Torben faded in and out of the smoke; each time it thinned, she expected him gone. Each time, she was wrong. He stayed motionless, as he often did. His pose, slightly hunched forward, hands clasped before him, was the one she knew so well. The wind played with the long fair locks she remembered - he hated having his hair cut and allowed only Solace to do it, and even then, only under great duress.

It looked the same Torben she knew and loved. Her big brother who didn't fit into the world everybody else inhabited. Kind, gentle, surprisingly funny when you learnt to grasp the ways he expressed himself, full of peculiarities that could equally charm and infuriate. The same Torben as ever was.

Save, he wore a soldier's garb.

A dented gun-metal cuirass over a leather jerkin, a baldric crossed his chest from which a sheathed sword hung, cavalry boots came to his knees, pistols were thrust into a wide weapons belt alongside a dagger.

They fitted him well; they fitted him awful.

He had always yearned to be like other men, but he was never a fighter, never a killer. He dreamed of being a soldier like a boy dreamed of it, of being a hero, a champion. Of being like your father.

And now he was.

Slowly she crested the hill; beyond the incessant eddies of smoke, clouds broke to reveal a bloated red sun teasing the horizon, its light igniting the smoke, turning it to bloody steam.

Her feet crunched, and she slipped the last few strides to her brother.

"Torben!" When his attention remained elsewhere, she said, more softly, "Torben?"

Slowly his eyes focussed as his mind returned to his body. She'd seen it countless times before as they transformed from glassy mirrors into something human, as life washed back into flesh.

This time, however, it was different.

Torben's back straightened, his shoulders raised, his hands unclasped and fell to the heavy buckle of his weapons belt.

"Sister..." he smiled.

She wanted to cry, she wanted to hug him, she wanted

to turn and flee back down the slope of ash.

She had often wondered what his voice might sound like if God were to miraculously restore it one day. But she had never expected it to be so deep and harsh.

Perhaps because it wasn't God who'd given Torben his voice.

"Is this but a dream?" she asked. The setting sun raked across the ash, turning everything to the colour of blood, even her brother's face.

"Everything is but a dream," Torben replied; he sounded like a man who'd only just survived having his throat crushed.

"Are you real, or is this just a conjuring?"

Torben tilted his head. He was smooth-shaven she noticed, the downy beard he'd grown to try and ape their father gone, "Do not follow me, Solace. I will not be able to save you twice."

She tried to step toward him, but something tugged her back. Looking down, she found a bony hand protruding from the ash, skeletal fingers catching the hem of her dress.

Swallowing she attempted to yank herself free, but she was caught fast. The hand and forearm were slight. A child's...

"They took everything from me," she hissed, "you are all I have left."

"They took me too. You have nothing left but your life..." his eyes moved past her, "...do not waste it on a folly."

"I will save you! I will avenge Father, Lutz and

everyone else who died in The Wolf's Tower and Tassau! I swear it!"

"Go, Solace. Get out of the Empire. Do as Morlaine says, take Mother's jewels and build a life with them. Be happy. 'tis all I want from you."

"No!"

When he continued to stare over her shoulder, she twisted around to follow his gaze. The sun was gone, leaving rubicund banners across the horizon to mark its passing. Through the smoke, figures approached the hill, boots crunching through bone, adding more dust to the air.

"What is this place?" Solace kicked at the bony hand till it cracked, and her foot sent its fragments skidding down the slope.

"The place where flesh becomes bone and ash," Torben said, "the place we all come to in the end."

"But why are we here?"

His eyes came back to hers, "Because 'tis the only place we will ever see each other again."

She moved to stand before him, chin raised, nostrils flaring as the wind whipped ash and smoke around them.

"I don't believe that."

"'tis the only way it can be."

"And you have seen this with your *sight?*"

"If you try to find me, you will die..." he swept a hand towards the horizon; through the smoke, she could see other hills, other mounds, scattered about a dusty plain stretching for as far as the eye could see, "...and then you will be here for good."

"Where are you, Torben? Tell me where you are, and I

81

will find you. I will save you!"

"You cannot save me."

"I love you! I am your sister! I can do anything!" she slapped her hands against the metal covering his chest. It was like hitting ice.

Torben seized her wrists and held them tight, "If you love me, leave me. Forget me. If you don't, you will die."

Distantly, she could hear the crunch of boots as the figures approached the hill they stood atop.

"Who are they?"

Gently, Torben lowered her hands to her sides and released them.

"The undead, coming to feast upon the World's Pain."

"The World's Pain?"

Torben shook his head, setting licks of hair whipping about a face she knew better than any but no longer recognised.

"You must leave. Please, Solace, find somewhere safe, beyond the war, beyond them... beyond me."

"You are not like them. You are not!"

The sound of boots on ash, boots on bone, boots on the dead grew louder all around her.

"Yes, sister, I am, and I will feast on the World's Pain as readily as them all..."

Then his face changed in a heartbeat, no longer the soft round features of the brother she had loved all her life, but something stretched, ashen and awful.

"This is what I am now..."

All around her, the sound of boots grew louder. Louder than the wind, louder than her heart, lounder than

Torben's voice, louder than her scream that pierced the thickening, ash-choked dusk.

The sound of the undead coming to feast upon the World's Pain.

Chapter Six

At first, Ulrich couldn't find either Madleen or Seraphina amongst the refugees huddled against the wall.

He walked along the debris-strewn length of their camp, scanning faces. Some stared back, a few pleaded for charity, a couple spat on the cobbles and glared at him like the Devil himself was out for a morning stroll. All struggled to keep warm.

Finally, he spotted Seraphina with a clutch of children of various ages at the far end of the line. He recognised the tawny hair sprouting beneath a moth-eaten woollen cap only after he realised the blanket wrapped around her was the one he'd given Madleen the previous night.

A middle-aged woman stood with the children, leaning against the wall. She looked like she might once, in better times, have been fat, but the fat, like the better times, was long gone, and now skin hung loosely from her bones, each line and wrinkle deepened by the gauntness of her flesh.

"Do you know Madleen?" he asked her.

The woman nodded, blowing a cloud of frosty breath

into her hands, and then rubbing them together.

"Is she around? I wish to speak to her."

"You tell me."

"Pardon?"

After extracting herself from the gaggle of silent children the woman moved out into the square. A few stalls were being set up, and the men working on them were shooting sour looks at the strangers. It was a market day, but there didn't appear many people were coming to sell.

"She went with you last night, so, you tell me where she is? I got enough mouths to care for as it is..." a jerk of the head towards the children accompanied the hiss. Seven, including Seraphina. Seven children would usually be a recipe for noise and boisterousness, but they all sat on the cobbles in sullen silence. Too cold and hungry for anything else.

"I was not with her last night."

"Saw you myself! Cosying with her beneath that fine blanket you gave her, bold as anything! Blanket to keep her daughter warm in return for her keeping you warm. That's how it works, isn't it?"

"I left her when she went into the church with Seraphina. I haven't seen her since. I was going to break fast with them, but they did not show. So, where is she?" He wasn't going to be shamed by the woman's barbs; he'd done nothing wrong. He held her eye and demanded an answer.

"She went out again once Seraphina were settled. Gave me her soup and bread as she'd eaten already, thanks to your... *kindness*... so, I was happy to oblige. These are the days we live in, after all, where you'll turn your eyes from sin for thin soup and stale bread."

"Sin?"

The woman snorted again and shook her head, "Some of the women, the younger ones, go out at night to find some coin for their families. I don't cast no stones at them; hard to think about sin and righteousness when you've nothing in your belly, and your baby's crying with the cold. But the men who use them, take advantage of their misfortunes; they're no better than..." she spat at his feet.

When he raised his eyes from the steaming gob of phlegm by his boot, he asked, as calmly as he could, "Where do these women go to find their coins?"

She pushed her lips so firmly together they went as white as the rest of her. She pointed to the east, "*Baumwollstraße* has any number of alleys coming off it, all dark, narrow and mean. The men who haven't got a bed to take them to, do their fornicating there. Out of the eyesight of decent folk," she lifted her head and held his gaze, "but not out of the eyes of the Lord. He sees all, knows all, and ensures there's always a reckoning."

"I-"

He found a grubby, quick-bitten finger under his nose, "You best be remembering that, sir. These are the End Days, and the reckoning is coming for us all. Mark my words, they are," with that, she spun away and stomped back to the children.

His boots started taking him back to the Inn, bitterness swishing with the acidic sweetness of the wine in his belly. He considered forgetting Madleen and going to find that man who might have horses to sell. Madleen made her choice, preferring to sell herself than accept whatever it was he was offering.

What *was* he offering, exactly?

As he didn't know, he supposed he could not blame Madleen for not figuring it out. He was a stranger who would be gone in a day or two, leaving her and Seraphina hungry in the street with only the prospect of a long bitter winter ahead of them.

Perhaps men who gave her silver rather than kindness were a more practical proposition.

He stopped halfway across the square; he clenched the fingers of his bad arm. The biting cold made them even more numb than usual.

It still did not explain why she'd failed to break fast with him. Or returned to the church for Seraphina. Perhaps she'd found a man with a warm bed for the night to go with his coins.

His boots started taking him east.

Perhaps not.

He wasn't entirely sure what he was doing or why. He liked Madleen, and that was a novel enough feeling in itself. Sitting with her had felt normal, well as normal as shivering under a blanket on the cobbles surrounded by hungry refugees ever could, but compared to everything else he'd experienced in the last year...

No one can save everybody...

If he closed his eyes long enough, he would suffer the cries and screams of children echoing around his mind, as he always did. So, he kept his eyes open and went looking for Madleen instead.

It was a short walk to *Baumwollstraße*. If this was where women came to sell themselves, there was no sign of it now. Though early morning, especially such a cold one, was not the most conducive time for sinning.

This seemed an older part of Madriel than the market square, where fine stone buildings rose on three sides and the church of *St Lorenz* on the other. Here the buildings were of wood, lathe and straw; the upper storeys hung over a street marked with mud rather than cobbles.

A red-faced woman hung washing from a line strung between the houses. The sunlight carried little warmth, and the wind cut bitter, but after weeks of rain, it at least allowed the possibility of getting something dry.

He touched his hat and smiled; she scowled back and slammed the window shut.

Perhaps she had seen too many men ambling back and forth outside her home in search of women lately.

He walked slowly, bad hand in his coat pocket, good hand never straying far from his sabre's hilt. Trouble seemed unlikely, but...

Always be prepared...

Old Man Ulrich's voice whispered in his ear. An older, more familiar demon than the ones who'd been plaguing him latterly.

As the spitting woman promised, *Baumwollstraße* boasted a surfeit of little alleys. The poorer parts of towns often did. They often boasted plenty of cutthroats and robbers too, though, as with the whores, this wasn't the best time of day to run into any.

Ulrich walked the length of the street, boots squelching in the morass of mud and shit cutting between the houses. He counted seven alleys. All as mean, shady and narrow as his spitting friend said.

Seven alleys. Seven children. Did that mean anything?

No, probably not. He didn't believe in signs and portents. Such things suggested someone was paying attention, and the sorry state of the world made that seem damn unlikely.

An old woman, her crooked back bending her almost double, was poking her way through the rubbish in one alley; an equally sorry-looking dog did the same in another. Both sniffing around for food. Judging by how thin the pair were, neither had enjoyed much luck.

Ulrich stopped at the far end of the street. An unappealing tavern sat on the corner; a man squat on the step begging. Seeing Ulrich, he scooped up his hat and thrust it in his direction.

When he shook his head, the man's shoulder's slumped, and he dropped the upturned hat back into the mud.

If you were a young, pretty woman, would I be more generous?

Ulrich turned around and made his way back up *Baumwollstraße*.

Am I truly trying to save anyone, or am I merely disguising my lust in a coat of noble colours?

Whatever he was doing, he was wasting his time. If Madleen came here to sell her favours last night, she was long gone now. He could scour Madriel for her, but to what end? She'd likely just found a man with something more to give her than a blanket and some road provisions, even if he wanted more in return than Ulrich did.

The thought rankled. But there it was. In truth, he'd never had much luck with women, whether he was trying to bed them or save them. He had tried to woo Erna, and she rejected him for dull Kapsner, but they were both long dead amongst the rubble of The Wolf's Tower, so he did his best not to be bitter about that. He saved Solace to save himself, as old Lutz had advised, and ended up broken and tormented, while her desire for vengeance was driving his mistress half insane.

No, perhaps it was for the best.

The old bent-backed woman emerged blinking from her alley into the sharp light raking the street. She gave a little start on seeing him, but when he made no move to rob or kill her, she pulled her tatty shawl tight against the biting breeze before shuffling off to search the next alley.

Ulrich hurried on. Best he see about those horses. If God was feeling merciful, the man wouldn't have any. With any luck Morlaine would soon be gone; Solace would realise pursuing the Red Company was madness, that her brother was gone and only death awaited them in the north.

He checked each alley again as he passed, not knowing what he was looking for. Each remained as they were before, save for that mangy dog had found something to nose and worry at the far end of the final one before he got back to the start of the street.

He walked on a few paces before coming to a halt.

It was probably nothing. An old bone or some such.

Except, no one threw old bones away in a town full of hungry people, they broke them open and got the marrow out, they boiled them down for soup, they...

Ulrich turned around and headed down the alley towards the dog. The place stank of cold piss. Shards of glass crunched under his boots along with the frost; everything was deep in shadow. It'd be a long time before the winter sun found its way down here.

The piles of shit were plentiful; a couple still steamed gently. The content of night buckets, either emptied out of the overhanging windows or carried down here. He almost stopped. That was likely all the dog was sniffing.

The mutt didn't notice his approach. It was nosing at something under a piece of old blackened canvas, so rotten even the homeless had no use for it.

"Scram!" he yelled, stamping his foot.

The dog cocked one ear, eyed him for a second, and then went back to licking at something. He was in no mood to give way and, like the rest of the world, saw little to fear in a weakling and coward like Ulrich Renard.

He found a piece of broken brick, hopefully it was one of the things no one had gotten around to pissing on down here, and threw it at the dog.

"I said scram!"

The brick thudded into the canvas, the dog yelped and bounded off down the alley.

"Next time, it'll be your head!"

In truth, he'd been aiming for its head this time, but he was prepared to be magnanimous about it.

He stood over the canvas, carpeted with needles of

discoloured frost. His stomach was bubbling, and it had nothing to do with wine and elderflower syrup.

Even with gloved hands, he did not relish touching the canvas, so he drew his sabre, slipped the tip under the rotting edge, and lifted it up to see what the mangy dog had been so interested in under there...

*

"Solace?"

A hand, cool and soft, touched her arm.

For an instant, she thought it was Renard, but Renard's hands, she knew from the very few times he'd had cause to touch her, were neither cool nor soft.

He also didn't have a woman's voice.

She peeled open her eyes.

"Morlaine," she was as surprised by the demon's presence as much as the fact daylight snuck around the edges of the shuttered window.

"What time is it? Where's Renard? Why are you here?"

Morlaine straightened her back, "It is morning. I don't know. It is morning."

"I see..." Solace shuffled herself up the bed till her back pressed against the headboard. The demon was both fascinating and terrifying, and she continually found herself see-sawing from one to the other.

"You had a nightmare?" the demon crossed her arms and stared at her, head tilted slightly.

"No. It was Torben."

"Your brother?"

Solace nodded, "He told me not to try and find him."

"Excellent advice."

"He was waiting for me atop a grey hill of ash and bone. Do you know of such a place?"

The demon shook her head, then retreated to the dimmest corner of the room, "It was just a dream, Solace."

"No, it *was* Torben. He found a way to speak to me, to warn me."

"Did he say where Saul was by any chance?" the scepticism dripping from Morlaine's voice reminded her of Father.

"My *sight* is real. I thought you of all people would be prepared to believe in such things."

"There are many people who believe in such things. And most of them would happily burn you at the stake for it."

In fact, she was reminding her of Father more and more.

"But you don't believe me?"

"I believe you had a dream. Nothing more. You claim to have the *sight*, Solace, but I have seen nothing of it in the weeks we have been together. Better to believe what my own eyes and ears tell me than accept the claims of others. Caution is a virtue that keeps you alive."

She wanted to slap her hands on the bed in frustration, but that had never worked with Father, so doubted it would with Morlaine either. Strange that the pair of them should be cut from the same sceptical cloth.

The thought of Father sent a snarling torrent of anger, grief, horror and disbelief rushing through her mind. In these moments, sudden and unexpected, she felt almost lost to herself, consumed by emotions and feelings she could not control. It would wash her away if she let it, the knowledge of how he had suffered, how he had died, how she had run away and left him to Saul and his fellow demons

She sucked in air, curled her hands into fists and drove the fingernails into her palms.

"Suleiman is not here, so I will be leaving for Potsdam tonight. Alone," the demon said, Solace suspected she might have said more before that, but for a handful of heartbeats she'd been able to hear nothing bar Father's screams serenaded by the crackle and snap of the flames that had roasted him alive.

"You need me," Solace managed to hiss.

"I need no one."

"I can lead you to Saul."

"Even though your brother neglected to tell you where he was. In your dream."

"It wasn't a bloody dream! He was there, he was different, but he's still my brother. He can talk now..." her voice dropped as her eyes slid away "...and he is like you..." When Morlaine continued to stare at her, she spat out the word the demons used to describe themselves, "...a vampire..."

"Let us hope it was a dream. Far better he is dead than that."

She turned Torben's words over in her head, searching for something to both find him and convince Morlaine she could be of some use to her.

Whether or not it was the *sight* or just common sense,

she knew that without the demon's help, she would have little chance of avenging Father and the others who'd died at the Red Company's hands.

"The World's Pain?" Solace said, furrowing her brow, "Does that mean anything to you?"

"Was that something Saul?" Morlaine asked, leaning forward.

"No. Torben. In my *dream.*"

Morlaine frowned, then shook her head, "More likely it was Saul, and you have forgotten..."

"Every word that creature said to me is burned into my soul. I hear them every night when I close my eyes," Solace hugged her knees, "he said nothing about the World's Pain. What is it?"

"What exactly did Torben say...?"

"He said..." she pursed her lips. The memory wasn't fuzzy like a dream would be; it wasn't fading in the morning light. She just wanted to be sure she got it right, "...the undead are coming to eat the World's Pain."

Morlaine shuffled on the chair, uncertainty flickering over her usually expressionless face.

"No..." Solace shook her head, "...that's not quite right... there were figures at the bottom of the hill, this huge mound of ash and bone; I couldn't see them clearly, there was smoke, and the wind was whipping up the ash too. The sun had just set; it was getting dark. I asked him who they were, and Torben said, "the undead, coming to feast on the World's Pain," what does that mean?"

Morlaine continued to watch her silently across the room.

"And do not tell me it is nothing. Your face doesn't often give much away, but..."

"It is... a vampire fantasy. Nothing more."

Solace held her eye. The demon was going to have to give her more than that.

Morlaine ran a hand over her mouth, "The World's Pain is humanity's suffering. War, famine, pestilence, disease. The gifts of the four horsemen. Where the World's Pain is at its greatest, so some vampires claim, the living is easier for us. Where the corpses pile high already, who will notice a few more? Where law has broken down, who will care about lives being taken? They argue the greater The World's Pain, the greater our pleasures. That one day, the World's Pain will engulf everything mankind has built, and amongst the corpses, the vampires will walk like kings and queens upon the dust to feed freely from the remaining mortal cattle."

"A cheery tale."

"Indeed. 'tis just something the undead amuse themselves with, a fireside yarn, a tall tale of better days to come. We do have a lot of time to kill."

Solace looked to the window; muffled voices babbled in the square beyond the shutters. It sounded normal enough, save there was precious little to buy in Madriel.

"The war..." she muttered "...I was a child when it started. A small child. People say this is the End Time. The apocalypse is coming, Satan will walk the Earth, and the dead shall rise from their graves. The war, this endless war, is just the start of it."

"The same tale told from a different side of the coin."

"Are they coming here because of the war? To feast on the World's Pain?"

"Vampires have always been attracted to war, the worst of us particularly so. And this is a war like few before it... when man wrecks such atrocities upon his brothers, what are a few bodies drained of blood?" Morlaine twisted out a rare smile, though it was a bitter one,

"And that is why you are here?"

"I am here to atone. Nothing more."

Morlaine pulled off her boots, then rose from the chair and crossed to the bed.

"What are you doing?"

"I'm going to sleep. It may be sometime before I have a bed again."

Solace eyed the demon as she stretched out next to her.

"You can go or stay. You have nothing to fear from me."

"Are we going to leave at dusk?"

Morlaine peeled open an eye, "Suleiman is not here; therefore, I will leave at dusk. Or soon after. You-"

"How are you going to find Saul?"

Morlaine sighed, "I keep following the Night's Road until I find him."

"Is that a poetic way of saying you don't know, but you're hoping to get lucky?"

"Saul will be where the war is worst. The war is worst in the north. I will keep going north."

"Because Saul is feasting on the World's Pain?"

Morlaine closed her eyes, "If you like."

"Just as Torben told me..."

"The answer is still no."

Solace rolled her bottom lip between her teeth, thinking.

"What if I know how to find the Red Company?"

"You don't. Unless you intend to have a conveniently revelatory dream before sunset, I-"

"No," she shook her head, "I know how to find him and 'tis nothing to do with the *sight*."

Morlaine opened her eyes again, "How?"

"First," Solace grinned, "You've got to promise to take us with you..."

Chapter Seven

"The man had horses."

"At last!" Solace's smile faded when he did not mirror it.

"But they are only worth buying if you're interested in meat or glue."

"Perhaps-"

"Are you interested in meat or glue, my la... Sol... err... Celine...?"

Several expressions flickered over her face before disappointment settled.

"No."

"The fellow did give me another name."

"Are you going to tell me his horses were even worse?"

Ulrich shook his head, "No, he has a farm, an hour's ride south of town. One of the few still working around here, so 'tis possible he does have horses."

"Why hasn't he fled like the others?"

"He has a fortified manor house and has hired men to protect his family and workers. Apparently, he is as stubborn as a mule."

Solace leant against the wall next to the shuttered window; she stared at him, "An hour's ride, is-"

"A long walk."

She peered at the shutters as if trying to ascertain the time from the amount of light sneaking through them.

"If I set out now, I might get back before dark..." when she stared at him some more, he shrugged, "...I am a fast walker."

"Take my horse."

His eyes darted to the bed where Morlaine stretched out, fully dressed save for her boots.

"That evil beast?"

"It will be faster than walking. Unless he throws you and tramples you to a pulp..."

They both eyed Morlaine uncertainly; she wasn't, in their experience, much of a one for jokes.

"You *can* ride?" the demon asked.

When he snorted, she opened her eyes, fished in the pocket of her jacket, and tossed something at him. Fortunately, she threw it to his right side, so he could make the catch. It was a wooden token with the number seven carved into it.

"Give that to the stable master in *Engelshof,* and he'll let you take the horse. Don't lose it, hurt it, or lame it. Be back by dark and..." she gave him a stare intense enough to make him squirm "...don't make me come looking for you."

"I can walk," he spat, making to throw the token back at the demon until Solace grabbed his wrist.

"Thank you, Morlaine."

"My-"

"Go to this farm, buy two horses, come back," she gave his wrist a firm squeeze before releasing it, "by sunset."

He wanted no more to do with the huge stallion than he did the demon herself, but the look Solace gave him brooked no argument.

"Very well, but we need to get some coin first."

"Will this be enough?" She put a purse in his palm.

It was heavy. When he opened it, silver talers and Imperial florins glinted back.

"My lady, you shouldn't have gone alone to sell jewellery, 'tis too dangerous!"

"Ulrich, if I can't make a deal and navigate a few streets without being robbed and murdered, I fear I will not get far with Saul and the Red Company..."

"But-"

"Is there enough?"

He bounced the purse in his hand; she'd sold a lot more than a pair of earrings this time. He nodded, "There's enough."

"Good, I'll buy the rest of the provisions we need while you're gone. We're leaving tonight."

The weight on his shoulders grew heavier, sinking his heart further under its burden. His eyes bounced between Solace and Morlaine.

"All of us, together," she had the air of a young woman who'd just talked her father into taking her to a ball rather than one who'd just persuaded a demon to take her to her death.

"Yes..." he whispered. His fingers turned around the bag, his good hand momentarily feeling as numb as the bad one. He put the silver in his coat pocket and turned for the door.

"The roads are thick with robbers," Morlaine said, "I believe Lucien's men are patrolling the south road today. I suggest you go with them."

"I can look after myself."

"I was more concerned about my horse."

"She's right," Solace said, taking the demon's side again, "go and see Lucien first."

Before he could protest, Morlaine said, "From what I understand, Lucien's men are as likely to rob you as any bandits you come across. It is better they know you are under their Captain's protection; they will ensure you have safe passage then."

"You think your Lucien is trustworthy?" he demanded.

"I have met many hired killers in my life; I can assure you, he is not the worst."

To his ears, that was far from a glowing recommendation.

"Do as she says," Solace said, "I do not wish to lose you, the silver or the horse."

After a breath, he nodded, wondering if she had the order right.

Lucien was downstairs eating bread and cheese. The bags had darkened under his eyes; he looked pale and drawn beneath his stubble and drooping moustache. His spirits, however, seemed high.

"Of course, my friend!" Lucien boomed after Ulrich

asked him if he could ride out with his men, ushering him to sit down, "I know that place. Old Janick's men regularly take pot shots at my lads."

Ulrich raised an eyebrow.

"Oh, nothing to worry about. They're just larking about. Never hit anyone yet..."

"Thank you, Captain," he nodded, making to rise.

"You know, 'tis such a fine-looking day..." hand wiping crumbs from his moustache, he glanced at the windows, "...well, 'tis not raining for once. A ride will blow away my cobwebs. I think I will come with you. What do you say to that?"

He'd rather take his chances with the brigands and highwaymen, but, as with most things, he found he had few choices to make these days.

"I'd be honoured."

"Excellent," Lucien slapped the table, "It will be good for morale. Nothing the boys like more than seeing their beloved leader roll up his sleeves and do some work. Always best to keep the boys' peckers up. First rule of soldiering. Keep the bloody peckers up!" Lucien laughed and whacked the table some more.

"Quite..." he managed to say.

*

Styx was as much of an evil, short-tempered creature as his mistress.

He'd saddled the beast without getting kicked or bitten, but, from the gleam in the monster's eye, he had a hunch the surly creature was simply bidding its time till it could do the most damage.

Still, despite its foul, diabolical nature, the horse was a beauty. Something else it had in common with its owner.

Lucien said he should be at the south gate for noon, which gave him time to visit the refugees in the square again. The spitting woman, who'd begrudgingly told him her name was Carola, still had Seraphina with her own sullen brood of shivering waifs. Madleen had not returned.

"Another bloody mouth to feed!" Carola grumbled, "Madleen's no doubt found some rich fool in need of his own personal whore."

She'd eyed him balefully enough to suggest she thought that rich fool was standing right in front of her.

He wasn't so sure.

The coppery stink of blood rising up from beneath that pile of rotting canvas teased his nose again. A dark, still sticky puddle soaking into the underside. The stench reminded him of the slaughter in Tassau, when the Red Company massacred his comrades before the burning church. Another memory he was unable to exorcise.

Of course, it was impossible to know whose blood it was. It might have been an animal's. But it was fresh, and there was so much no one could have survived such a wound if it was human.

That canvas sheet hadn't blown over it by accident either. The wind was sharp in the alley, funnelled by the buildings on both sides, but the canvas was far too heavy. Someone had put it there on purpose to cover the blood.

He had pressed one if Solace's silver talers into Carola's grubby hand, which at least shut the bloody woman up, "Ensure the children are fed. I will be back later to make sure you haven't drunk it."

"How dare-"

He'd swivelled away and headed for the stables before she had the chance to vomit up her outrage.

Perhaps Carola was right. Perhaps the blood had nothing to do with Madleen. Perhaps...

He pushed the thoughts aside. He had enough problems. If she was dead, what of it? Soon he and Solace would be joining her; better he concentrate on that.

After saddling Styx, he put on the reins despite the creature's baleful stare and even got the bit into its mouth without losing any fingers. The thought struck him that he now had a fine stallion and a purse of silver.

He didn't have to go with Lucien, he didn't have to buy horses, he didn't have to ever see Madriel again. Or Solace von Tassau and her new demon friend. He could ride south. Ride hard and keep going till the war and its monsters, human and otherwise, were all far behind him. He could find...

Sighing, he raised his eyes to the heavens.

He could do anything he wanted, but he owed Solace his life. She had his word, his sword, his honour. He had absolutely nothing else of worth in this world.

Honour is the only thing a man has that cannot be bought or sold...

"Stupid, drunken old fool," he spat.

Somewhere in the distance, a cackling laugh echoed. It almost certainly wasn't his father's shade, but a shiver ran through him anyway.

Numerous eyes followed him as he rode, outstretched hands and beseeching cries too. Surely, a man on such a fine horse must have a coin to spare?

Styx's ears pricked up, and he tossed his head. Ulrich swore the beast started prancing upon the cobbles; he seemed to like the attention. Given that his mistress spent her time skulking around at night, attention was no doubt a novelty. And when you were as fine-looking as Styx...

Lucien waited with half a dozen armed men in the lee of the stone arch leading through the town's south wall. Their conversations dried up as Styx's iron hooves clattered towards them.

The mercenary captain whistled, "Now *that* is a horse!"

He offered a thin smile in return as he reined Styx in; the beast's uncharacteristic good mood evaporated at the sight of the other horses. It started to whinny and paw the ground. He didn't seem particularly tolerant of lesser beings.

Lucien vaulted smoothly into the saddle of his own chestnut gelding. He nodded at the militiamen guarding the gate and led the group through the arch. The two old men leaning on their pikes glowered back and muttered darkly.

"We are so beloved in Madriel..." Lucien shouted back over his shoulder as they passed through the gate, weeping stonework momentarily replacing the sky, "...they shower us with affection, garland us with appreciation. We do so much for the local people! Of course, being a reticent, unemotional breed, they endeavour tirelessly to keep that joy from ever bubbling onto their faces!"

Once on the road, Styx immediately pushed himself to

the front alongside Lucian, nipping and snarling at the mercenary's gelding whenever it made the mistake of coming too close.

"A temperamental beast?" Lucien grinned. He seemed remarkably cheerful for a man who'd suffered a demon drinking his blood for two nights running.

"Like his owner."

Lucien cocked an eyebrow, "He is not yours?"

"No, he's... my wife's cousin."

"Really?" the eyebrow climbed higher.

"It would be a long walk without a horse."

"Not recommended either. Once you're out of sight of the walls..." he spat, "...bad times."

That, at least, he could agree on.

"Morlaine..." after a long pause filled with only the snorts and hooves of the horses, Lucien continued, "...a remarkable woman. But, perhaps, a little... peculiar?"

"Oh... I haven't really noticed."

"Not just because she rides a warhorse, carries a sword and dresses like a man. Yet she is - and I am fortunate enough to be able to attest to this - very much a woman."

"As you said. Bad times."

"She talks little. About anything, really. Another strangeness in a woman. How long have you known her?"

Lucien's eyes were on him far more than the muddy road and ice-skimmed puddles ahead.

"Not long, my... wife and her are not close."

"Yet here you are together. You and your wife arrive looking like the lowest kind of vagrant beggar, accompanied by one of the most beautiful women I have ever seen. Who rides a horse worth more than I lost at cards last year. A man cannot help but be curious."

"I suppose not."

"Then, please, sate my curiosity..." Lucien's attention remained on him, but now there was no grin beneath his drooping moustache.

"There is not much to tell. We were attacked. Our home destroyed, family, friends, servants all killed. Celine and I escaped with our lives. We found Morlaine; she brought us here. We are going to Naples."

The man was suspicious, and this was not a good time to attract suspicion. He kept his own eyes front and hoped remaining vague would ensure he did not contradict anything the demon had told Lucien. Neither being burnt as a witch or hung as a spy greatly appealed.

"A terrible tale... who attacked you?"

"Brigands, bandits, deserters, a foraging party. I do not know. They came in the middle of the night. We did not ask."

"No, I suppose you wouldn't..." Lucien's eyes still weren't budging from him, "...is that how you hurt your arm?"

The fingers of his bad arm spasmed and twitched, "An old injury. I fell. It has never healed."

"I am sorry. Did you get it soldiering? You have that look soldiers sometimes carry."

"Look?"

"Old before your time. The soldier sees too much of the worst of us. That comes with a price."

"There are things I do not wish to think about," Ulrich said carefully, "or talk about."

"Of course! I did not mean to pry. Now tell me more of Morlaine."

"I think you already know her a lot better than I do."

When Lucien finished chuckling, he said, "She is extraordinary. Her beauty takes my breath, but if I stare for long enough into the pools of her eyes, I see flashes of something that scares me."

"Scares you?"

"I have lived an interesting life, Herr Lutz; I have travelled far, I have loved, I have killed, I have broken and built, I have stolen, I have given. Many, many things... so many I thought there were no surprises left in this world for Lucien Kazmierczak to experience. Then the most beautiful woman I have ever seen appears out of the night and offers herself to me in return for a room for you and your wife..." the mercenary's shoulders twitched, "...I am not complaining. I just wish to understand my good fortune."

"You think her beautiful?"

"I find her... *bewitching*..."

Ulrich's eyes snapped to the captain. Bewitching was not a word used lightly these days, "If that is your way of asking..." he said quietly out of the side of his mouth, "...no, she is not a witch."

"A witch? No, no! I would never accuse her of such a thing!" Lucien exclaimed, throwing out his free hand, before adding, "the pyre would be a dreadful waste of such a beautiful woman. Dreadful!"

He didn't know quite what to make of Lucien, but he

didn't like him much from whichever direction he looked.

As the mercenary leaned across to say more, his horse followed the lead and moved closer too. Styx seemed to care even less for the gelding than Ulrich did its rider and immediately tossed its great black head and tried to bite the intruder.

The gelding shied away, whinnying and almost bucking Lucien from his saddle. To the barking laughter of the men behind, the horse left the road, and Lucien had to wheel it around in a circle to regain control.

Ulrich took advantage of the distraction to nudge Styx into a trot.

He patted the stallion's neck and muttered, "You know, you evil bastard, I think you're starting to grow on me..."

The horse's snicker sounded a lot like a chuckle.

*

He'd hoped Lucien and his men would leave him at Janick's farm to continue their patrol. He was disappointed.

"I know the leader of the men guarding the place. A dear old friend! We are almost brothers. He will be delighted to see me! I can't pass the opportunity to bid him good day and see how farm life suits him!" Lucien punctuated his words with a volley of grins as they turned off the sodden road onto an even smaller and muddier track.

Despite the dark tales of brigands and cutthroats infesting the roads, they'd seen no one bar a few hollow-eyed peasants trudging wearily towards Madriel.

"Do not fear good people!" Lucien cried as they approached the cowering group, "we are merely keeping the road safe for honest folk. Walk on, knowing none other than Lucien Kazmierczak is protecting you!"

The peasants cringed in silence as the passing horses splattered them with more mud.

A low ridge crested with ash and alder screened Janick's farm from the road. Once they cleared the trees, Lucien slowed the horses, pulled out a handkerchief that might once have been white and held it above his head.

"Nobody likes surprise visitors anymore," Lucien sighed, "terrible times."

A stone wall as tall as a man surrounded the manor house, the track took them to the stout gates set into it. Behind the wall, two musketeers stood atop a wooden tower. The wall and gate appeared seasoned and time-worn; the tower was much more recent.

The gate had several firing slits and as they came closer, muskets began poking through them.

Once in shouting range, they reined in their mounts.

"What do you want?" one of the men atop the tower shouted.

Lucien gave him a black-toothed smile and opened his palm towards the gate, "Off you go, Herr Lutz, state your business. We'll stay here for the moment. Some of the lads here can be a bit trigger-happy..."

Slowly he walked Styx forward; behind its frosted plume of breath, the beast's ears were pricked and alert.

"My name's Lutz; I'm looking to buy horses. I've heard you might have a few fit for something more than glue!"

"And them?" the man atop the tower jerked his musket at Lucien and his boys.

"They're from Madriel. Patrolling the road, they kindly offered to escort me here."

The two men closed heads and muttered to each other, then "Wait there!"

He twisted around to look back at Lucien, but the mercenary was too busy playing with his moustaches.

He patted Styx's neck and tried to soothe the beast. It was skittish, sensing the tension in the air.

There would have been a time when, if you turned up on someone's doorstep with a bag of silver, you would have been welcomed like a returning son. But those times were long gone. He'd been a boy who still idolised his drunken father when the war started in Bohemia before spreading across the rest of the Empire and beyond; he didn't expect to be alive to see its end. Perhaps no one would. Maybe these really were the End Days the doomsayers kept preaching about.

He couldn't say. He was just focusing on breathing from one day to the next. He didn't know whether or not finding the horses Solace wanted would hasten their end, but riding to your death was a lot less tiring than walking to it.

After a few minutes of shivering atop Styx, a wooden hatch snapped open and a face, the colour and texture of tired old leather, appeared.

"You want to buy horses?"

"Yes, sir!"

"You got coin?"

"Yes, sir!"

"Show me its colour, young man."

Ulrich dismounted. Not trusting Styx, he kept hold of the reins and led the horse to the gate. For a moment, he feared the beast would make him look a complete fool by refusing to budge. Instead, after the barest hesitation, Styx threw his head, snorted and disdainfully put up with the imposition of following him.

He fished out the purse of talers and florins. Bouncing it up and down, the distinctive jingle of money cut through the frosty air to compete with the bird song for a second or two.

"Show me," the man insisted, "could be anything in there."

Ulrich poured a few silver coins into his hand before holding out his palm to show the man the emperor's head, "Does this get me past your gate?"

"Guess so," the man said, somewhat begrudgingly, before his eyes rose to the midnight-black stallion looming over Ulrich's shoulder. He didn't check, but he thought there was a fair chance the beast was giving the man an exceedingly dirty look.

"I got horses to sell. None like that thing, though."

"I'm not looking for thoroughbreds or warhorses. Just a couple of mounts that won't die on me after a day or two."

The man nodded, his attention moving from Styx to Lucien and his men, "The horses for you or them?"

"Me..."

"Suppose that must be true. Those bastards wouldn't be offering silver for anything," the hatch snapped shut,

114

and after some grunting and squeaking, the gates swung open.

The leather-faced man turned out to be short, portly and sporting a shock of vividly white hair.

"Janick," he held out his hand, "don't be causing me no trouble, son."

"Ulrich," he said, taking a hand that felt like leather as much as it looked like it. He wondered if the old man ever went indoors, "I want horses, not trouble."

Janick glanced at Lucien and his men, "Pardon me for saying, but you're not keeping the right company if that's the case."

"They're just making sure I got here safe."

"How much you have to pay them for that pleasure?"

"Nothing."

Janick raised a snowy eyebrow.

"Lucien is friendly with... my wife's cousin."

That earnt a snort, "Tell your wife's cousin to keep a hand on his silver. You'd be well advised to do the same around that snake."

"I will. And my wife's cousin is a she."

"Ah... then she should keep a hand on her virtue as well."

He smiled thinly, it was too late for that, but there was no need to be ungallant, even about a demon.

"Keep those bastards out there," Janick growled at the men around the gate while jerking his thumb in Lucien's direction. "I don't want to lose any more fucking cows."

Lucien grinned and waved back.

Janick's men didn't appear any better than Lucien's to

Ulrich's eye. The only thing obviously in their favour being they weren't riding with Lucien Kazmierczak.

A squat, solid-looking manor house with thick walls and narrow windows stood, surrounded by a collection of stone and wooden outbuildings.

"Used to be able to leave the livestock in the fields and send a boy to check on them now and then," Janick said, leading him around the manor house, "not any more..."

"Why are you still out here?"

"My family's been here for three hundred years, lad. I am only leaving in a box."

"And you can afford to hire mercenaries?"

Janick shot him a gap-toothed grin, "My family's also been fleecing the locals for three hundred years. I don't stay here to make money anymore; I stay here to ensure there's still something to pass on to my sons. War ain't going to stop that, nor is money."

One of the stone buildings to the rear of the manor house was a stable; once they reached it, he could see several more wooden towers. Firing platforms had been erected along the perimeter walls at regular intervals.

"Ain't gone help me if a proper army comes through, but it keeps the brigands out," Janick said, noticing his interest.

Before following the old man inside, Ulrich hobbled Styx, who acquiesced with an insolent toss of the head.

There were four horses Janick was prepared to sell, plus a dozen others he wasn't. Ulrich looked them over; one was lame, one too old and saggy-backed, the remaining two - a dun gelding and a bay mare - were better than he expected. Not great, but better.

He inspected each horse in turn, patted them, ran hands over their flanks, checked their feet and teeth. Then he did a fair bit of face-pulling and head-scratching.

Finally, he made an offer for the better two.

When Janick finished laughing, he told him how much he wanted. Ulrich neither called him a thief nor questioned his mother's virtue, but the implication was there all the same.

They traded insults and exclamations until Ulrich haggled Janick down to a price that was merely extortionate. Out of the goodness of his generous heart, Janick threw in a couple of old saddles and tack - for an equally exorbitant price.

He was paying far more than any of it was worth, even in such dark times, but Ulrich consoled himself with the heartening fact it was Solace's coin, and they'd both be dead soon anyway.

As he counted out the silver, the smile on the old man's face said he'd been taken for more of a ride than any of the horses in the stable ever had. Still, at least he helped him saddle up the two nags and lead them out into the sharp sunlight.

Styx cast a disparaging eye over the two newcomers before snorting out a cloud of frosty breath.

"Better not let them get too close to that beast till he's used to them," Janick nodded, "looks like he's got a questionable attitude to me..."

They walked back to the gate, Janick chatting affably about how shit the world had become.

"Managed to get the wheat in, but I've had to leave half my fields to the weeds. Not enough labourers to tend them, not enough soldiers to guard them."

"And with half of Madriel starving," Ulrich said.

"Aye. Not just Madriel either, same everywhere. Worse in the north. If the war doesn't kill you, likely you'll starve to death."

"That's why we're going to Naples."

"Get out while you can. The Empire is finished; it'll be nothing but rubble and ash by the time they sort out which fucking way we should all be worshipping God properly."

Returning to the gate they found Janick and Lucien's men hurling insults and hand gestures at each other.

A round-faced man with a shock of auburn curls rolled his eyes as they approached.

"Anyone died yet?" Janick asked.

"Another five minutes," the man replied.

"My son, Jacob," Janick said.

"Ulrich. A fool with too much silver and a need for horses," Ulrich took the man's hand.

Jacob grinned, "Always welcome, unlike your friends."

"They don't like each other much?"

"History," Janick worked his tongue through one of the gaps in his teeth, "that and the fact Lucien is a cunt. No offence."

"I have much the same opinion."

"Glad to see you're a better judge of men than horses," Janick chuckled.

Ulrich conjured a tight grin before climbing up onto Styx, who was casting an eye around the surrounding

118

armed men as if he couldn't quite decide who to kick first.

He'd attached rope (graciously thrown in for free by Janick) to the bridles of the dun and bay and he tied the other end off on Styx's pommel. The rope was a generous length; he didn't trust the stallion not to bite chunks out of the pair if he got the chance.

Janick reached up and shook his hand, "If you ever need more horses, son..."

"Then you won't need to bother putting *any* wheat in your fields."

Janick laughed, then said in a low voice, "Be careful around Lucien. He's a snake. Only reason him and his men are protecting the roads rather than robbing them is the burghers of Madriel offered him more than they could steal for a lot less trouble. Don't matter how many times you pat a wolf on the head; it ain't ever going to be your dog."

Ulrich nodded.

"I know his type."

As he walked Styx and his new horses back to Lucien, he thought there wasn't much difference between the men with him and the ones who'd served Saul and the demons in the Red Company.

He shook that away. Didn't matter. There'd soon be leaving Lucien behind. And however much of a rogue the mercenary Captain was, he doubted he drunk human blood or strung up plump whores by their ankles.

Lucien gave him a black-toothed grin as he approached.

Probably.

Chapter Eight

It was nearly dark by the time they reached the walls of Madriel.

To be fair to Lucien and his men, they had not once tried to rob him of the remainder of Solace's silver or his horses. The captain, however, hadn't shut up all afternoon.

Robbery would undoubtedly be more costly, but...

"Nothing like a good hard ride to work up a thirst, eh, my friend?" Lucien yawned, looking far more ready for his bed than an evening's carousing.

Ulrich smiled but said nothing. He'd spent most of the journey back saying nothing, but it'd done little to deter Lucien's incessant prattling intermingled with questions about Morlaine and Solace.

"And our mission was a complete success. You found horses! Something to celebrate, eh?"

He got the distinct impression Lucien wanted to continue their rip-roaring camaraderie over a few flagons of ale. He probably assumed there was some money left over from the horses.

"Having to part with a small fortune for two unremarkable nags and some half worn out tack is not a reason to celebrate," he said.

"Alas, these are the times we live in. Everything is bad..." a grin, splitting his face from ear-to-ear interrupted Lucien's shake of the head, "...unless you're a soldier, of course. *Lots* of work for us."

"Lots of misery for everyone else."

"Good if you have things to sell, too. Like that old miser Janick. He must be making a fortune from that fortified farm of his..."

Ulrich shrugged.

"And whores, of course, they're doing very well."

That made him think of Madleen, which annoyed him. Both because he didn't want to think of her as a whore and trying not to worry about her. Or worry why he was worried about her.

"Do you know..." Lucien started leaning towards him, then remembered how much Styx liked the taste of horse flesh and thought better of it "...they say before the war there wasn't a single whore to be had in Madriel. Can you imagine? What a fucking boring town it must have been then. So, you see, war isn't all bad. Yes, all the killing, hardship, suffering, that's bad, but there's always another side to every coin? Don't you think?"

He managed a grunt, which was more than such bilge deserved.

"And we do our bit to make things better. The strangers, for instance. Hungry, cold, not two coins to rub together by the time they reach Madriel. Where would those poor souls be if my boys weren't prepared to fuck their women for money? An even worse place, that's where they'd be. Not everyone sees it, but I know how caring, selfless and altruistic these boys of mine are," Lucien said, hitching a thumb back at the grim-faced, hard-eyed killers trailing behind them.

"The first rule of soldiering, my friend, know your men!"

"Your men fuck a lot of the refugees, then?" he found himself asking, even the fingers of his bad hand tightening.

"Whores are important for morale. I've told you about the importance of keeping peckers up, haven't I?"

"Those women aren't whores."

"No?" Lucien frowned, "But they fuck for money. What would you call them?"

They were approaching the town gates. A night with Lucien and his boys appealed even less than tramping through the pitch-black woods behind Styx's swaying arse again.

"Desperate and taken advantage of?" he offered.

"I prefer my definition," Lucien pulled a long face, "fewer syllables…"

"Where do they go? These women?"

Lucien grinned, "Are things not right with your wife? You can tell me, man to man. Lucien Kazmierczak is a name synonymous with discretion from Lisbon to Lodz. 'tis a fact virtually shouted from the rooftops!"

"It doesn't matter," Ulrich shook his head; he had no intention of saying anything about Madleen to this rogue.

"My men tell me that, when they are about their

122

charitable work, the best place to find women much in need of assistance is in the back streets around *Baumwollstraße* after dark..." Lucien touched his nose and winked, "...and they'll sell you a ride for much less than old Janick did..."

*

After stabling the horses and paying the boy looking after the place for the night to rub them down and feed them properly, Ulrich went to the market square, hoping to find Madleen had returned.

She hadn't.

"Must be a very fancy bed she's found for herself," Carola said, though she sounded less certain than she had that morning.

"How is Seraphina?"

"She's been crying a lot, missing her mother..." Carola's eyes flicked between Ulrich and the girl before asking in a lower voice, "...do you think something foul has befallen her?"

The stink of blood rolling out from beneath that rotten canvas teased his nose again, "I don't know."

"I only met her a few days ago, didn't think she had the nature to abandon her little one, but... can be hard to tell."

"Has anyone gone to find her?"

Carola shook her head, "She didn't know anyone. Not been here long..." she jerked her head at the knot of men around the fire "...they think her a whore. If ill-fortune has taken her, then 'tis but her punishment for such sin."

"The sin of putting food in your child's belly?"

"'tis not what I say..."

"You fed the children?"

She bridled at that, "Yes. I did. Never had a drop of hard drink touch my tongue. I live a good life, thank you very much!" Carola glared at him, then adjusted her linen cap before adding in a softer tone, "Hasn't brought me much reward in this life, but it will in the next."

"Your husband?"

"Dead."

"I'm sorry."

"So am I. But sorry doesn't bring back the dead."

He stood awkwardly, not sure what to say or do. He thought about giving Carola more of Solace's money, but his mistress didn't possess enough to feed every refugee in Madriel. He looked at Seraphina. Two red-rimmed eyes set in a frost pale face stared back at him over the rim of the blanket he'd given her mother.

No one can save everybody...

"I will ask around," he muttered, "and see if I can find Madleen."

"Why'd you care?" Carola demanded, words dusted with ice once more.

...but everybody can save someone...

He almost spoke the thought aloud but instead conjured a hollow smile, touched his hat, and bid Carola a good night.

As his boots clipped the cobbles, he could think of only two reasons for Madleen's failure to return to Seraphina. She'd abandoned the child, or she was dead. Either way, there would be nothing he could do. He could not save

Madleen from the cruelties of this world any more than he could save himself from the consequences of Solace's desire for vengeance.

Yet he still walked towards *Baumwollstraße* rather than his mistress and her demon. Was he really trying to help Madleen and Seraphina, or just avoiding his future? Avoiding the Night's Road, as Morlaine called it. The dark path the demon followed in pursuit of Saul the Bloodless, the road Solace was determined they too should now travel.

Full night cloaked the town now. Cloud had swept in before sunset, and no moon or stars shone overhead. Oil lamps lit the market square and the main thoroughfares leading to the north and south gates; otherwise, the only light was what spilt from the lanterns, candles and rushlights burning behind shuttered windows.

Still, night came early in December, and a few people were about, mostly hurrying home, heads down, hands stuffed in pockets, eager for their fires and dinners. Those lucky enough to have them.

Others, less fortunate, huddled in doorways.

There was little to see in *Baumwollstraße*. Only the thinnest of light escaped the humble houses here. Madleen could be standing ten paces away, and he'd never know.

A dark place for dark business.

He thought of the women forced to come here and sell themselves and of Lucien's men spending their coins on them. Of couples coupling in dark, stinking alleys.

He walked further, the looming silhouettes of the houses on either side of the narrow street seemingly deformed by the weight of the night pressing down on them.

No one was about. Perhaps the men needed longer to drink, the women an even darker cloak to hide their shame.

Perhaps he should talk to Lucien's men? They came here to use the fallen women. Some must have been here last night. Someone might have seen Madleen. Some of them might have...

He thought of her next to him, sharing that blanket. They had done nothing but talk, yet, for the first time since the night Saul's foul Company came to The Wolf's Tower, he had felt something close to peace, something akin to happiness. Something-

Ulrich snorted a cloud of steaming breath. He was fooling himself. She was but a whore, a whore by desperate circumstance rather than wickedness of choice, perhaps, but only a fool fell for whores and the lies they told with their eyes and lips.

If not tonight, then tomorrow, he would be leaving Madriel, riding to his death. Why was he wasting his time loitering in these filthy back streets looking for a whore who was either dead or gone?

Something moved behind him.

His good hand dropped to the hilt of his father's sabre.

Loitering with half a bag of silver.

Well, maybe more like a third, but enough for someone to slit his throat for.

He spun around, sword hissing from its scabbard.

A figure gasped and took a step back.

A woman, slight and small.

"Looking for a lady's favour, sir?" she asked, one hand

raised to her chest but retreating no further despite his half-drawn blade.

For a heartbeat or two, he thought it was Madleen. He could barely make out her face, just a pale, round suggestion, but it did not sound like her, and this woman seemed slighter.

"Madleen?" he asked anyway, finding a strange hope in the possibility she might have spent the day selling herself here instead of looking after her daughter.

"My name's Liesl," the girl said, and he thought she *was* but a girl, though he couldn't be certain in the gloom, "though I can be anyone you want me to be if it pleases you...?"

"No, no..." he took a hasty step away. Realising he was still grasping his sabre, his fingers sprang open, letting the weapon drop back into its scabbard.

The girl stayed where she was. Slowly, the hand she had splayed across her chest stretched out, "I can be Madleen... for a coin, maybe two, whatever you can spare..."

"Are you here every night?"

The girl nodded, he thought. It was so damn dark he couldn't be sure of much.

"Do you know Madleen? I think she was here last night. Looking for... coin. Like you. She didn't come back. She has a daughter, Seraphina. She is missing her mother, she-"

"I don't know her."

"The men who come here, do they cause trouble?"

"Trouble, sir?"

"Could they have harmed her? Have you seen trouble? Women hurt? I am worried about her."

"Oh, the men who come here are always so sweet..." the girl said, then laughed shrilly.

"Do-"

"Let me be Madleen for you, please, sir..." Liesl came forward, seizing his bad hand. Even though the whole arm was half-numb to the shoulder, her fingers still felt as cold as snow-laden twigs as they tried to curl around his.

Yanking his hand free, he staggered away, heart pounding in his ears as he backed against a wall. Liesl followed him.

"I can make you happy, for a few minutes. Let me, please. We can be warm together. Wouldn't you want that?" Liesl sounded young, but something knowing and corrupt lay beneath that tender voice. It made Ulrich want to scream.

"No!" he barged past the girl, crying out as he caught her with his bad shoulder.

"I want to be warm..." she called after him.

He stumbled into the darkness, certain the girl was pursuing him, but no footsteps came.

That didn't stop him running, though.

*

"We can leave tomorrow night."

"I thought you were eager to take to the road again?"

"I am," Morlaine said, "but it will be a price worth paying if it stops your infernal pacing."

She stopped pacing.

The demon stretched out on the bed. She wasn't sure she'd spent the entire day in the room, but Morlaine didn't seem to have moved a muscle since she'd kicked off her boots and put her dark hair upon the pillow.

"He should have returned hours ago," she waved a hand at the window. She'd opened the shutters as soon as the sun set, now full dark pressed against the other side of the glass.

"These things can take time."

"You don't think something bad might have happened?"

"Something bad always happens... it is simply a matter of how long you have to wait for it."

"You make for a poor companion, Morlaine."

The ghost of a smile teased the demon's lips, then she swung her legs off the bed and started pulling on her boots.

"We're leaving?"

"Not without my horse, no."

"Do you thin-"

"Lucien is downstairs; I'll ask him where Ulrich is."

"How do you know Lucien is downstairs?"

"Just trust me, I do," Morlaine said, rising to her feet.

Solace trailed her to the door; when the demon raised an enquiring eyebrow, she said, "I'm coming with you."

"There's no need. I am not running away."

"I don't want to wear out my shoes. I haven't had them long."

Morlaine continued to stare at her.

"I'll likely pace even more on my own."

"Very well."

As Morlaine predicted, Lucien was downstairs. A flagon of ale and a half-eaten chicken sat on the table before him.

Solace wondered how much the chicken had cost but thought it better not to ask.

"Ah!" Lucien cried, licking grease from his fingers, "Divine creatures come to brighten the dark corners of my wretched and unworthy life!"

Morlaine eased herself down next to him, Solace sat opposite. She felt safer with a chicken carcass between Lucien's hands and her.

"What have you done with my cousin's husband?" Morlaine asked, swaying back to avoid Lucien's puckered lips as he swivelled to face her.

"Done? My love? I've done nothing!"

"He should be back by now," Solace cut in.

Lucien looked sideways at her, "Hark the hectoring wife! That one so young should already have become a shrew. Alas!"

"I am not a shrew!" she straightened her back.

"I would advise against it; 'tis why so many men are forced to stray from the marriage bed."

"And I thought that was solely due to their cocks," Morlaine said.

Lucien laughed and slapped the demon's knee before twisting to face Solace. Leaning over the chicken, he said, "You claim not to be a shrew, Frau Lutz, yet here you are, demanding the whereabouts of your husband after he has spent a hard day in the saddle procuring horses for your journey to Naples? If I may be so bold, you would be better served preparing the warmest of smiles and the comeliest of demeanours for his return..."

"Where is he?"

Lucien sighed, scooping up his ale, he sat back, "There's a reason I never married..."

"Lucien...?" Morlaine didn't *exactly* growl at him.

"We returned triumphantly through the town gates at dusk. The locals neglected to shower us with flower petals, but I put their oversight more down to the difficulty of obtaining flower petals at this time of year than any reticence on the part of the gentlefolk of Madriel. Young Ulrich - we are very much on first name terms now, Fraulien Lutz - immediately went to stable your splendid new horses, along with that monstrous black beast," Lucien took a gulp of ale, "I have not seen him since. Though I am sure, he will not be able to keep himself from the matrimonial embrace for a second longer than necessary!"

"So, you don't know?" Solace asked.

Lucien glanced back and forth between them, "That's what I said."

"But-"

Before she could press Lucien further, a shaven-headed man with a nose that appeared to have been broken several times and reset in a different direction on each occasion interrupted them.

"Captain,"

"Ah, Gottschall, found the bugger?"

"No."

Lucien sighed as the man set a helm upon the table and eyed the chicken, "You know, there was a time you could trust a man you were paying to soldier for you..."

"There was?" Gottschall asked.

"Most certainly! 'tis the first rule of soldiering. There must be trust between officers and men. You tell a fellow to do something; you damn well expect him to do it. Not run off... *somewhere!* Dark days, Gottschall, dark fucking days."

"I suppose," Gottschall sniffed, slate-grey eyes still fixed on the chicken. He seemed more interested in the half-eaten bird than he did his Captain's words of wisdom.

Lucien tutted, then wrenched off a leg and tossed it at Gottschall, "If he does have the temerity to come back, you've my permission to kick as many varieties of shit out of the ungrateful bastard as you see fit. Discipline, Gottschall, what's discipline?"

"First rule of soldiering, boss," Gottschall grinned, tearing off a chunk of meat with blackened teeth while scooping his helm off the table.

"Good man!" Lucien turned his attention to them, "Now, where were we?"

"Problem?" Morlaine asked.

Lucien shrugged, draining the remainder of his ale, "One of my men seems to have misplaced himself."

Morlaine hoisted an eyebrow. She did that a lot, Solace noticed.

"Deserter. Lowest kind of lowly lowlife scum known to man or God."

"How do you know he's deserted?" Solace asked.

"Why else wouldn't he come back? Went out last night and hasn't been seen since. Missed all his duties today. The only acceptable excuse is being dead. Either he's fled town or found a woman's bed. Either way, 'tis desertion."

"Perhaps he *is* dead?"

Lucien shook his head, waving his empty flagon at Anna-Lena, "No, we'd have found a body by now. My boys have been looking. And who would have killed him? We are beloved by the grateful populace we protect from the bands of bloodthirsty killers roaming the country who they haven't paid to protect them. More likely, he decided soldiering wasn't for him. Saks is a puppy; I only took him on out of the goodness of my soft heart. Some aren't cut out for it. Ladies?"

She shook her head, Morlaine did the same. Lucien gave an as-you-like shrug and lifted a single finger when Anna-Lena bestowed a filthy glare upon him.

Solace exchanged a look with Morlaine. She had a bad feeling. The demon looked like she had a bad feeling, too, though that might have had more to do with Lucien fondling her knee while he waited for his next beer.

Where *was* Renard?

Chapter Nine

Ulrich screamed.

Something had caught his ankle, tripping him. He staggered blindly into a wall, shoulder first. Sparks of pain sizzled down his bad arm. It was usually a numb, clumsy half-dead appendage he couldn't trust to pick his nose or scratch his arse but give it a hearty enough whack, and it came alive with fire and needles.

He put his back against the brickwork and sucked in a couple of breaths. The air was cold enough to make his lungs ache, which at least diverted attention from the slowly ebbing agony in his shoulder and arm.

Why had he run? The girl, Liesl, meant no harm; she was just hungry, the same as Madleen. Perhaps he'd been afraid of the temptation? Had being close to Madleen and sharing a bed with Solace woken something inside him he'd thought dead during those long months surviving in the rubble of The Wolf's Tower?

He didn't know.

Cradling his bad arm, he edged away from the wall.

The realisation came slowly that he didn't have the foggiest idea where he was. He didn't think he'd run for long, but he'd hurtled into the night without thought or care. Maybe he'd still be running if he hadn't tripped and had his wits jarred back to life by colliding with the wall.

There was little to see. A dark street, black buildings climbing towards a blacker sky. A few windows here and there fringed by faint orange light: otherwise, nothing.

It might be the same place he'd met Liesl, or he could have turned down half a dozen alleys during his panicked flight. He couldn't remember. He snorted; there were plenty of memories he wished he could dispose of so easily.

Carefully he moved on. He knew the market square and the main thoroughfares he had trudged through buying provisions with Solace, but the rest of Madriel was unknown, even in daylight. It was not a big town; he'd visited far grander cities accompanying Old Man Ulrich around Europe as his father found and lost new masters with ever-increasing haste. However, masked by the night, it could have been the greatest city in Christendom.

He was lost.

No matter. Eventually, he would find somewhere he recognised, even if only the town's crumbling wall. Still, he rested his good hand upon the hilt of his sword. The night brought out the worst in people; the Devil whispered more loudly in people's ears without the sun to distract them.

He did not want to lose the remainder of Solace's silver; he'd already been robbed once today, after all.

Several times he thought he heard someone behind him, though whenever he looked over his shoulder, there was nothing to see. It could be rats. It might have been Liesl trailing him in the hope he'd change his mind about finding some warmth. Or cutthroats with a fancy for his purse. Or refugees in need of a good coat and boots.

Most likely, it was nought but his imagination. He picked up the pace as best he could, as fearful of inflicting another blow on his damaged shoulder as he was of whatever might lurk in the darkness.

After a minute or two, the narrow street brought him to a slightly wider one, cobbles replaced mud, and a few faint glowing squares lent their meagre light to the world.

He peered one way and then the other, trying to spot something familiar amongst the dark shapes around him. He'd just about decided one unlit street looked much the same as any other when a light bloomed to his right.

As he watched, it grew brighter. A lantern. Someone to ask directions, robbers didn't tend to carry a lantern with them.

Preceded by the creak of leather and clank of metal, two men emerged. Mizzle had started to dampen the air, lending their lantern a misty halo.

"Not as pretty as some you see on street corners..." one of the men said, hoisting the lantern up to examine Ulrich. His companion laughed.

Soldiers. As the town militia consisted of old men and boys, while the watch was even more decrepit, he assumed they were Lucien's men, though their faces were too obscured by beards and helms to recognise.

Ulrich kept his chin up and held their gaze as best he could. Strange that if you spent long enough in the dark, the light made you want to shy away from it.

"I took a wrong turn. How do I get back to the *Market Inn* from here?"

"Lucky you found us," the soldier with the lantern replied.

"Could be wandering around for hours

137

otherwise," the other added. A Hessian by the sound of him, his voice a tad softer, but his eyes were as hard as his companion's, "A complete rabbit's warren, this place is."

"A nest more like. Full of vermin and filth."

Both helms bobbed up and down.

"That's as may-"

"Not safe for decent folk," the lantern man interrupted.

"All these strangers. Desperate they are. Got nothing. Cut a throat as soon as look at you."

The helms bobbed some more.

"Yes, these are desperate times, but-"

"Very desperate, oh, yes, ain't that right?"

"The worst I've seen," the Hessian nodded.

The soldier shoved the lantern towards Ulrich's face, the beard, helm and hard eyes close behind, "Best you be back to your bed. 'tis not safe out here."

"Yes," Ulrich sighed, "I'm trying to. If you can just tell me how to get back to-"

"*The Market Inn*, you said?"

"Yes?"

The lantern man's helm swivelled in the other soldier's direction, "How much's that, you reckon?"

"A taler, at least," the Hessian said.

"A taler!"

"Each," the lantern man nodded, straightening

up. When Ulrich stared at him, the soldier moved his free hand to rest upon the pommel of his sheathed sword. The Hessian followed suit.

"We don't keep these streets safe for free," Lantern said.

"Honest pay for honest work," the Hessian agreed.

"I'm not paying you for bloody directions!"

The Hessian shrugged, "Please yourself. Cost you a lot more if you get your throat cut blundering around in the dark, though."

"Thieves, robbers, cutthroats..." Lantern tutted with a sorrowful shake of the head.

"And that's just the whores," both men laughed hard enough for their sour breath to taint the damp air.

"I'll take my chances," Ulrich moved to go past the men, but the Hessian stepped in front of him.

"You sure about that?"

His good hand found the worn leather grip of his father's sabre, "Very."

The Hessian held his eye, a sneer forming behind his beard as he pushed his cloak back from his own sword.

The world went very quiet. Dying for the sake of a couple of talers wasn't sensible, but as he was going to be dead soon anyway, what did it matter? And these two would likely give him a quicker death than the one awaiting him on the road north.

A cry of alarm in the distance broke the silence. The Hessian blinked, and his companion put a hand on his arm, "Leave it, ain't worth blood..."

"Probably not," the Hessian said, though he didn't make a move to stand aside until the cry came again. This time it was much closer to a scream.

All three of them looked down the blackened street. The cry had come from the direction the soldiers had been heading, though sound sometimes carried strangely in the dark.

"More fucking trouble," the Hessian growled.

"How much do you charge to help?" the question squirmed from Ulrich's lips before he could stop himself.

The man's eyes, glinting in the lantern light, narrowed, "If cracking heads is involved, there's no charge. We do that for the fun of it."

"C'mon," Lantern said, tugging the Hessian's arm as he started down the street.

The Hessian nodded, "Be seeing you, friend," then he hurried after his companion.

Ulrich watched their swaying light retreat. The cry came again, this time a full-bloodied scream, until something abruptly cut it short. The two soldiers broke into trots, hands on the pommels of their swords.

Going the other way, he decided there was yet another thing he'd been wrong about.

Robbers did sometimes carry a lantern, after all.

*

"Most women find me utterly irresistible," Lucien gave her a black-toothed smile while he wiped beer-froth from his long moustaches.

"Really?" she looked around for Morlaine, but the demon wasn't in sight.

"The name of Lucien Kazmierczak is known from Vienna to Vaduz as an exquisite lover! Many women have told me I am the angel of their heart and the demon of their loins!"

"They... have?"

"So many, I can't recall. Simply far too many! Tell me, dear Celine..." he leaned across the table and dropped his voice to a conspiratorial whisper, "...has your cousin confessed such feelings about me yet?"

"Erm... not yet..."

Lucien slumped back and took up his latest ale, "Admittedly, some do take longer than others to fully appreciate the breath-taking skills Venus has blessed me with."

She smiled in what she hoped appeared an understanding fashion.

"Does your husband please you?"

"I beg your pardon?"

"In the matrimonial bed? I was wondering..."

"That is none of your business."

"I have a caring nature. Something else Venus bestowed on me. I am quite over-burdened with gifts, but there you are. We all get the cards we're dealt, eh?" he gulped more ale, re-frothing his moustaches in the process, "'tis just you don't strike me as being happy together. Given your youth, I would have thought-"

"Perhaps that has something to do with our loved ones being killed, our home destroyed, and our possessions stolen?"

Lucien took another slurp or two to consider this, "Well, yes, I suppose it could be. But I sense something else...?"

"Something else?"

"An air of melancholy longing hangs about the pair of you, like a stinking river fog at ebb tide."

"You're quite the poet, Captain, along with everything else."

Lucien took the comment as it wasn't intended, offered a shrug and opened his palms towards her.

"Tell me- ah, here she is! As if descending from Heaven itself!" Lucien threw his arms wide as Morlaine returned.

She stared at him as if not quite sure exactly what she was looking at, "Indeed," the demon said finally, sitting down next to Solace.

"I was just discussing melancholy longing with your cousin, but your dazzling smile chases such sanguine thoughts from my lovestruck mind. Beer?"

"I've been talking to some of your men," Morlaine offered no smile, dazzling or otherwise.

"Oh, you have? Why? I hope they have been speaking well of me. Do let me have the names of any that-"

"They tell me several people have gone missing over the last few days?"

Solace's eyes snapped in Morlaine's direction.

"Missing? A far too melodramatic explanation of events," Lucien emptied his tankard and waved it at a passing serving girl. It wasn't Anna-Lena, but Solace could guess where she'd learned to scowl, "not to mention incorrect. No one has gone missing."

"They haven't?" Morlaine did the thing with her eyebrow again. Lucien squirmed on his chair. The demon's stare was either making him uncomfortable, or it'd suddenly occurred to him his bladder was exceedingly full.

"A number of people have left town, suddenly and without telling anyone. Given the state of the world, that's hardly surprising."

Solace leaned forward, "That people would flee into the lawless, war-ravaged countryside that's blighted with brigands just as winter is breaking?"

"Most of these "missing" people were strangers. Merely passing through. No one of significance. Madriel was but a stop on the road, rumours of the war coming this way are enough to make some people run regardless of the weather."

"Like your missing soldier?" Morlaine asked.

"Like my *deserting* soldier. Precisely!" Somehow finding a reason to look pleased with himself, Lucien sat back in his chair.

"Ulrich is still not back..."

"A temporary delay, I'm sure. Nothing more."

"There are many desperate people in town... how dangerous is it out there at night?" Solace asked.

"Deadly. A snake pit. If it wasn't for my brave boys, half the town would be at the throat of the other half. As it is..." he swept a hand around the surrounding tables filled with drinking soldiers, "...I've given the town something *everybody* can hate. And fear. Making people fear you; 'tis the most important weapon you can wield. First rule of soldiering, that is..."

"So, if it's so dangerous, how do you know these missing people haven't been done to death?"

"'tis usual, when being done to death, to leave a

body behind. My boys, who have razor-sharp wits and eagle-eyed attention for detail to a man, would have noticed bodies piling up. And, even if they didn't, I'm sure the locals would have pointed them out. The buggers rarely pass up an opportunity for a good moan."

She shot Morlaine a look of exasperation. The demon's face remained as implacable as ever, but she held Solace's eye as she rose to her feet.

"I'm going to go find him."

"You can't go out there!" Lucien cried, looking aghast.

"Why not?"

"Because I was going to go to bed after this beer!" he said as the serving maid slammed another tankard in front of him, passing the table without breaking stride.

Lucien began struggling to his feet, "I will come with you. I wouldn't want you coming to any harm."

Solace jumped up as well, "As will I."

Morlaine's dark eyes bounced between them, "No, you won't."

Lucien slumped back and grabbed his drink, gallantry exhausted, "Suit yourself..."

"I-"

Morlaine took her arm and moved her out of Lucien's earshot, "I can cover more ground alone. I will check the stables and work from there. Ulrich will likely be back before me."

"But-"

"It is safer for you here."

Solace peered across the smoky Inn. She couldn't say how many men were eying them with varying degrees of gawping lechery, but it was a significant proportion.

"I am?"

"Stay with Lucien; he won't hurt you."

The mercenary captain was too busy extracting chicken remnants from his broken teeth with a blackened fingernail to catch her doubtful glance.

"I'm not certain I can make the same promise..." she muttered.

Morlaine found a rare smile and guided her back to her chair.

"Look after my cousin, Lucien; if anything happens to upset her, you'll be sleeping alone tonight," the demon said.

"With my valiant lions to protect us, no evil will befall this fair maid," Lucien boomed, sweeping a hand at the gruesome collection of killers filling the room.

"One would hope so..." with that, Morlaine swept up her cloak and headed for the door. Voices quietened, heads turned, eyes swivelled.

One burly man grabbed Morlaine's backside, the leer plastered across his scarred face dissolving instantly as she spun on her heels and slapped his face hard enough to send him crashing from his chair. Hooting laughter still echoed around the inn as the demon slammed the door after her.

"What a *woman!* What a *vision!* What an ungodly *delight!* She is more than any man could ever desire or deserve. I have eaten many oysters, but 'tis rare to find so glistening a pearl..." Lucien sighed, reaching for his beer before planting one elbow on the ale-flecked tabletop and leaning towards Solace. A twisted grin split his face as his eyebrows jigged up and down, "...now, what were you saying about your husband not pleasing you in the matrimonial bed? There's no need to be shy; you can tell me *anything...*"

Chapter Ten

He wondered if he should have been less frugal with Solace's money. The cold was seeping into his bones; the fine drizzle fell in gauzy curtains, slickening his cloak and chilling his exposed skin further.

The silver wouldn't do her much good when they died a few days or weeks hence, whereas it would have got him back to the *Market Inn* by now if he'd given Lucien's bastards what they wanted.

Now he was back to wandering these tight, black, twisting streets without knowing where he was. The two coins he'd saved didn't currently seem much of a bargain.

Again, he paused, searching for anything he recognised amongst the dark shapes surrounding him. The wind stiffened, leaving beads of moisture clinging to the bristles of his beard. He tried to make out a church tower but could see nothing beyond the buildings overhanging the street.

He'd seen no one since the two soldiers. People didn't

like to be on the streets after dark, even without the freezing rain. Between the Devil and the more earthly wrong-doers skulking in the shadows, there was little reason to wander far from hearth and bed until the sun returned.

Something moved in the darkness. A creak? A rustle? The damp squish of feet in the mud?

He peered into the rain. He stood at the mouth of another of the narrow alleys honeycombing Madriel. He hadn't even noticed how many of them there were during daylight; now, he seemed to pass one every few paces. Black chasms splitting the brooding buildings.

Maybe rats?

There weren't many cats or dogs left in Madriel to keep the vermin under control. Most people had no food to spare for animals they couldn't eat.

Or the refugees had eaten them.

He didn't know. The locals blamed the strangers for everything.

Still, whatever else befell the world, there were always rats.

He was about to move on when he heard someone sniff as if sucking up tears. That didn't sound like a rat. Still, there was plenty of misery around. He'd enough of his own.

And no one could save everybody.

"Have you seen my baby...?"

The voice seeped out of the night, as gentle as the rain falling around him.

"Who's there?"

When no answer came, he almost convinced himself

he'd imagined the voice, mistaking the patter of rain upon the world for words.

"Answer me!"

Nothing but rain. Rain on wood, rain on tile, on dirt, on stone, on leather, on felt, on skin.

He made to continue.

"Have you seen my baby...?"

The voice came again. Louder. Closer. From the alley, but there was too little light to make out anything or anyone.

"Have... have you lost your child?"

No answer.

Just some poor wretch. One of the refugees, most likely. Some of them shuffled continually around town, glassy-eyed and mumbling. Minds broken by the things there'd seen, the things they'd suffered, the things they'd lost.

The locals generally turned their faces and hurried on, ignoring them even more assiduously than they did the ones who begged or sat huddled around meagre flames in makeshift camps. But whenever Ulrich saw them, something twisted inside him, some familiarity, some kinship, for he was not so very far from them. He feared his mind, stretched by all he had seen, suffered and lost, might one day be as broken as those poor souls.

So, he did not walk on, he did not look away, he did not pretend to hear no evil or see no evil. Instead, he took a step toward the voice. He took a step into the darkness.

"Where did you last see your child? Perhaps I can help?"

Some small piece of the night shifted in front of him.

"I don't remember," the woman said, "have you seen her?"

"I don't know. What's her name?"

A figure came closer, just a fraction. He could not make out her face, only a suggestion of a white linen cap like most married women wore, but nothing else.

"I... don't remember. I know I gave her a name. Everyone has a name... don't they?"

He nodded before realising she could see as little of him as he could of her.

"Yes. Yes, they do. Are you hungry?"

"I starve!"

She spat the words out with such gut-wrenching force her pain became an almost tangible entity, enveloping him like the cold, incessant drizzle.

"I have no food... but if you come with me, I can buy you something?"

No one can save everybody...

"You have food?"

"No, I'm sorry," he patted down the pockets of his coat, once more forgetting she couldn't see any more than he could.

"You have food..." she stepped closer; the musky scent of damp old cloth came with her.

"No, really, I don't, but-"

A hand shot out, grabbing the wrist of his withered arm, fast and hard enough to make him gasp. A woman's figure followed, indistinct and all but lost to the night and the rain, but slender and a head shorter than him.

151

He tried to yank his hand away but found her grip too strong for the wasted muscles of his left arm.

"I said I don't have any food!"

He half expected other forms to emerge from the gloom, that this woman was just bait for robbers, but nothing bar the trickle of water from the surrounding roofs, chattering upon the mud and cobbles, broke the silence.

"You have food..."

He peered at the figure again, wishing for some scrap of light to make out the woman's face because her voice was starting to sound familiar.

"Madleen?"

He thought her head tilted a little, the grip on his wrist easing a fraction.

"I know that name."

"Do you know Madleen?"

"No."

"She has a child too, at-"

"Seraphina..." her voice was but a whisper; if she had not been so close, the swirling wind would have snatched it away.

"Yes! You do know her?"

The woman's other hand touched his face; cold fingers ran down his cheek and stroked the bristles of his beard.

"Have you seen my baby?"

"Is... is Seraphina, your baby?"

"I don't remember. I starve. 'tis the only thing I remember."

He put his own hand on her face; skin like winter-kissed marble, smooth and icy, trembled beneath his fingers. Was it Madleen? Had she hit her head and become addled? Wandering around town all day, not knowing who she was?

It sounded like the woman he had spoken to outside *St Lorenz's*; she was the right height and build, and the accent was the same. He had to find some light to be sure. The poor woman was so lost and confused, however, even if it wasn't Madleen, he couldn't leave her out here in this freezing rain. She didn't seem to have even a shawl to cover her head.

"Come with me. Let us get you out of the cold and get some soup for you. Would you like that?"

"I starve," she said, still stroking his beard.

He tried to move her into the street, but her feet were set hard in the sodden earth, and she refused to budge.

"Come, please? Wouldn't you like to have some soup? To get warm? To get out of the dark?

"I can't."

"Why not?"

"I can't leave the dark. He took me from the light and told me I would live in the darkness forever."

It must have been a fearsome blow to the head. Had she been attacked? Raped even? Whatever had happened, it had completely robbed her of her senses.

"Who told you?" Best to humour her, win her trust so he could get her out of this weather.

"He did."

"Who is he?"

"The man who walks above."

"Oh, Madleen..." he cupped her face and lifted her

153

chin. He had an urge to kiss her, which he thought singularly ridiculous as if this *was* Madleen she was out of her mind.

He had a sense of eyes looking up at him, glinting in whatever tiny fraction of light fell on this darkened Earth, the outlines of a face, hair, damp and slick, falling from under a linen cap.

"The man who walks above says we will all live in the dark one day."

"He does, does he?"

The face he held nodded, "He says, come the day, we will all feast upon the World's Pain..."

"The-"

"Ulrich..."

"Yes... *Madleen?*"

"I know you."

"Yes. We met last night!" For some absurd reason, his heart seemed to be pumping harder.

"I am sorry."

"You have nothing to be sorry about. You've had an accident, that's all. I will make you better."

"I am sorry..." Madleen said again, as something far colder than the rain dripped onto the fingers cupping her face, "...but I starve."

Then her face changed.

*

Lucien had moved around the table to sit next to her at some point. At some other point, a mug of wine had materialised before her. At a further point, much against

154

her better judgement, she had started to sip the wine. She'd only drunk heavily watered wine before. This wine wasn't watered at all.

He's trying to seduce me.

As no one had ever tried to seduce her before she wasn't *entirely* sure about this. Various men had come to pay her court, of course. Though they'd mostly been the fathers of the men involved or their representatives, come to discuss matters with Father. To ascertain her suitability and how large a dowry Father was prepared and able to offer. She didn't doubt other considerations were discussed, deals and favours, alliances and allegiances.

Occasionally, they had brought a son with them. A couple of times, she even exchanged a word or two with them. No marriage proposals had materialised, which made her wonder whether she was as pretty as she believed, or Father was as rich as she thought.

After many hours pondering in front of her looking-glass, she decided the problem must be money. The von Tassau's had once been very rich, they'd owned several silver mines in Silesia, but they had been mined out years before her birth.

So, she'd waited and waited while Father sought a husband, and she kept on waiting until *Graf* Bulcher decided not to take no for an answer.

But none of that business had amounted to *seduction.* It hadn't involved a man sitting rather too close to her while she drank wine that was not at all watered.

And it most certainly hadn't involved anyone putting a hand on her knee.

Lucien was showing her the blackened remnants of his teeth as his hand wandered.

"Captain, I am a married woman."

"And yet, I see no ring?" Lucien said, eyes widening a fraction, hand not budging.

It was a question she was prepared for.

"My ring was stolen as we fled. Along with most of my other possessions."

"A sorry tale..." Lucien propped his chin upon his non-wandering hand. He was still grinning.

"I do, however, still have my knife. And if you do not remove your hand from my knee..." she smiled back at him.

Lucien laughed and exchanged her knee for his beer. Then he asked a question she was not prepared for.

"Come to my bed, and I will show you what your husband is doing wrong."

Yes. She was *definitely* being seduced.

"You have already had the pleasure of my cousin, Captain. I would have thought that enough?"

"A sweet, sweet delight," Lucien sloshed more beer down his throat, "but no man should confine himself to the fruit of but one tree. 'tis not at all natural."

"And yet so many men *do* manage to confine themselves thus, do they not?"

"Yes," Lucien agreed, "the miserable-looking ones for the most part."

"Well, my husband does not look miserable."

Lucien hoisted an eyebrow at that.

On reflection, it wasn't the strongest argument she could have deployed.

"Anyway, you should know the sabre my husband carries is not for show. He knows how to use it..."

"He looks barely strong enough to lift it. And his left arm is not right; he keeps it pressed against his body and continually flexes the fingers as if trying to get them to work as they should."

"'tis an old injury."

"We all carry wounds, Frau Lutz... how long did it take you to get to Madriel? You looked like you'd been fleeing for... quite some time?"

"You ask a lot of questions when you're not about the business of seduction," she sipped wine, though harsh on the palate, it gave her something to hide behind.

"When you give someone your protection, you deserve a little truth in return."

"And we are under your protection?"

Lucien sat back and pointedly looked around the room filled with armed men.

"Yes. You are."

"And who exactly are you protecting us from?"

Lucien's gaze passed over the room again, the lips below his greying moustache twisting into a one-sided grin. As he did, the door crashed open, and two men hurried inside, shaking rain from their cloaks onto the rush-covered floor. Solace could feel the cold of the night stealing through the door from the other side of the inn.

"Some might construe that as a threat?"

That earned her a more fulsome, black-toothed grin, "Yes, some might... but I am sure you are not cursed with such a negative demeanour."

The two newcomers finally closed the door. It seemed foul out there. Where was Ulrich? What if something had happened to him? The thought made her feel terribly alone, so she instead focused on Lucien's eyes. They were a tired, dirty green, the colour of an old bottle that had spent years being weathered by sun, frost and rain.

She wondered what thoughts passed through Morlaine as those eyes looked down on her as he took his pleasures. Then she wondered, not for the first time in her life, what it would feel like for a man to take his pleasures with her.

That was something she'd expected to discover conclusively on her marriage night to a handsome young prince. Then such prospects were ripped away. There would be no marriage night for her, no prince, handsome or otherwise. The only eyes she thought of looking at her now were Saul the Bloodless', the only sounds the echo of Father's screams. The only desires left in her were for blood and vengeance.

So she told herself.

Still, she had lain awake, felt Ulrich's warmth beside her, and wondered. And when Lucien's hand squeezed her knee, that made her wonder too.

Though nowhere near enough.

Lucien wasn't saying anything else. He was just looking at her with those tired, dirty green eyes. Was this part of being seduced too? She didn't know. She sipped wine and tried to avoid the mercenary's regard.

The two newcomers were talking with Gottschall, one of Lucien's sergeants - who seemed to do most of the work organising their company while Lucien busied himself with the more important business of drinking and seducing.

One of the men was waving his arms about; the other was nodding hard enough to rattle the battered helm he still wore. Neither appeared happy. Gottschall didn't look best pleased either.

She found Lucien's eyes still on her when she looked back. Frankly, his hand on her knee was a lot less uncomfortable. She thought about telling him to put it back but decided that probably wouldn't send the right message.

"Why are you staring at me?" she asked, fidgeting with her mug.

"Because you are beautiful."

Her cheeks reddened, making her turn away, as much annoyed with herself as Lucien. Morlaine didn't blush at a compliment. She just gave people a cold blank look, maybe with a slightly raised eyebrow. Or she slapped their face. Should she slap Lucien's face? Would that make him stop looking at her?

There were times it felt natural to be setting off to hunt the demons who'd killed her father, stolen her brother, slaughtered everyone she knew and destroyed her home. That she was equipped to deal with anything this world had left to throw at her, that she was a merciless tool of God on a divine mission to right wrongs. That nothing - man, beast, demon or Satan himself - would keep her from her vengeance.

Then a man she didn't even like called her beautiful, and she blushed like the silly girl she'd once been.

If she couldn't cope with Captain Lucien Kazmierczak's wandering hands or lecherous flattery, how on Earth was she going to destroy *Graf* Bulcher, Saul the Bloodless and his Red Company?

She tossed the remainder of the wine down her throat. It didn't give her any answers, but the slight fuzziness developing behind her eyes was not at all unpleasing.

Gottschall was arguing with the two newcomers; eyes were being turned in their direction. Sadly, none of them were Lucien's.

"Tell me, Celine, how old are you?"

She was going to say seventeen before realising she no longer was. At some point, during those long, awful days in the shell of The Wolf's Tower, she'd had a birthday. She hadn't remembered it, let alone celebrated it.

So, she was going to say eighteen. But did men take a woman seriously if she was only eighteen? Nineteen seemed a far more womanly age, and she wanted to be taken seriously. She was, after all, hunting demons and seeking vengeance.

"Twenty," she said. Another year would do no harm.

"Twenty," Lucien nodded, "And no children?"

She shook her head.

"Is Herr Lutz not a fertile man? He does have that air about him."

"You're very impertinent," she met his eye and refused to look away. Until he kept on looking right back anyway.

"I, on the other hand..." Lucien showed her his, presumably, other hand, "...am *extremely* fertile. You can find the children of Lucien Kazmierczak from Minsk to Madrid, from Paris to Prague. They are more plentiful than the stars in the heavens - and twice as beautiful to behold!

If you desire children..."

His eyebrows bounced up and down again.

"Not currently," she managed to say.

Before Lucien could blurt further nonsense at her, Gottschall rolled up to their table, looking both apologetic and annoyed.

Lucien, in contrast, just looked annoyed.

"What?"

"Sorry, boss, 'tis Kott and Outman," he jerked his head at the two men he'd been talking to, who'd now taken their grievances to the bar.

"Is it money, women or beer?"

"Boss?"

"What they're pissed about," Lucien sat back, "is it money, women or beer?"

"No. 'tis Eck and Havel."

"Gambling then. Who cheated who?"

Gottschall glanced at Solace, then put his hands on the back of a vacant chair and leaned towards his captain. He dropped his voice, but she could hear him clearly enough even against the background hum of drunk voices.

"They were on the wall. Eck and Havel were due to relieve them, but they never turned up."

Lucien scanned the room, "Are the lazy cunts here?"

Gottschall shook his head, slate-grey eyes narrowing, "No, boss. I saw them leave hours ago..."

"Fuck."

She tried to raise her eyebrow the way she'd seen Morlaine do it, "More deserters, Captain...?"

Chapter Eleven

She became like ice: sharp and painful to the touch. Tiny daggers of frost speared his fingers, ready to rip the skin from his hand if he pulled it away.

But that wasn't the thing that made him cry out.

It was the way her face shifted beneath his hand, lengthening and thinning in an instant, the suggestion of her eyes, that before had held the barest glint of light, were now huge black pools darker than even the surrounding night.

"I starve!"

Frigid air slammed into his face as if he'd opened a tomb and freed something malign bottled up inside for centuries.

"Madleen!" he tried to push her away, but her hands were on his arms, not soft and gentle as he'd imagined the previous night as he'd laid next to Solace, wishing it was Madleen's breath serenading him, but like cold, hard rings of iron, binding him to her.

Teeth, long and white, flashed in the darkness. He

pulled back, staggered, boots slipping on icy mud. Something smashed into his shoulder, and pain lanced along his collar bone as Madleen snapped her jaw shut.

As he twisted away, she'd missed his neck and driven teeth into his shoulder, but the stiffened leather jerkin he wore under coat and cloak was a soldier's garb. Strong enough to turn aside some of a blade's bite, it seemed it could do the same with a demon's teeth.

Madleen was growling and yapping like a demented dog, pulling her fangs from the thick leather to try and find the soft flesh of his throat.

Unable to either break her grip or reach his weapons, he threw himself backwards to escape her wildly snapping jaws while kicking out at her legs. His boot connected with her shins and raked down them.

The footing was icy and treacherous. His standing leg slipped, and he went down, Madleen atop him. She cried out as they hit the ground together. He would have as well, but she drove the wind from him by landing on his chest.

The pressure on his arms released, the mud squelching around him, its ripe shit-seasoned stink even worse than Madleen's corpse-like breath. Thrashing his limbs, he rolled away. As soon as he was free of her weight, he tried to clamber to his feet, but a hand grabbed his ankle, yanking him back down onto one knee.

"I starve!" the demon shrieked. A hint of Madleen's voice haunted the sound, but only as a distant, bitter mockery.

The thing yanked his ankle, and he was on his back again. He kicked out with his other foot. Boot crunched bone. It screamed but did not let go.

"I must feast upon the World's Pain!"

No matter how hard he kicked, no matter how many wet, crunching sounds came back out of the darkness, the grip on his ankle didn't slacken as he was dragged back towards those teeth, back towards those jaws, back towards those lips he had wanted to kiss.

He found the hilt of his father's sabre with a flailing hand and started tugging it free of its scabbard. Hands, small but impossibly strong, were starting to climb up his body. Kicking it wasn't stopping the thing, so he planted his boot square in her face and pushed against it, levering himself back through the mud.

The demon spat and screamed, twisted its head to avoid the boot and kept on coming, kept on climbing up him, to reach the exposed flesh of his neck.

He could see little, but he felt her well enough. Those hands upon him, that body against his, her coldness, even through layers of leather, linen and wool, sucking the heat from him the way she wanted to suck away his blood and life.

He managed to wrench the sabre free, but there was no room to swing it, and no strength in his left arm to push her away. Her face was at his chest now; he could tell as much by the coldness as the pressure.

Click-click-click.

Teeth snapping together, coming closer, coming to tear and rend.

"I starve! I starve!" the thing cried, hands clinging to the lapels of his coat, climbing up him in slow savage jerks.

She was unnaturally strong, but the demon's body was still Madleen's, slight, petite and thinned by hunger.

Ulrich bucked and pushed, rolling away before she could come at him again, he sprang to his feet, swallowing gulps of burning air into heaving lungs.

Once more, a hand grabbed his ankle. Dragging his heel through the mud and almost pulling him onto his arse.

"Begone demon!" he bellowed, swinging his father's sabre. He could see nothing, but he knew the bite of steel on flesh and bone when he felt it reverberating back up his arm.

The pressure on his ankle disappeared. Something screamed, then slithered away.

"Ulrich...? Please... I starve..." a pitiful simper floated out of the night.

He stood panting, sabre outstretched before him, waiting for the thing that he tried not to think of as Madleen to come again.

Above his own heart, all he could hear was a mewling noise, like a sickly kitten.

He wanted to call out to see if some part of Madleen still existed.

Instead, he turned and ran down the street.

No one can save everybody.

He did not run for long.

How many strides he managed, he could not say, though he expected to feel a hand on his shoulder with every thundering heartbeat as his boots splashed over the rain-slicked cobbles. A hand to yank him back toward the snapping teeth of a monster.

He kept running till he barrelled into a figure that emerged from the darkness.

"Ulrich..." a woman's voice said.

"Demon!" he spat, slashing at the thing.

A hand grabbed the wrist of his sword hand, twisting it sharply till the sabre clattered to the stones below.

"Ulrich!"

He cringed away. Expecting teeth to rip his throat out.

For a moment, he was back in The Wolf's Tower, demons at every turn, snapping at his neck, breaking his honour, destroying what little he held to be true in the world.

Master...

He almost begged. Except this wasn't Saul the Bloodless. It was a woman.

He blinked. He was on his knees, the rain swirling around the figure looming over him, jewels of moisture glistening like diamonds in her night-black hair.

The first realisation was that this was Morlaine. The second, that he could see her face.

"Get up!" Morlaine hissed.

Light washed over them. Turning, he saw someone peeking around an open door, a lantern held out into the night. Other shutters, curtains and doors were ajar.

"What's all this noise?" the figure with the lantern demanded, an old man by the croaking sound of his voice.

Ulrich jumped to his feet, "Demons!"

The man held his lantern higher, a bald head craned out into the rain, "What'd you say?"

"He was attacked by robbers," Morlaine stepped across

166

him, "evil brutes, as ugly as demons!"

The old man's head bobbed up and down, "I can believe it. Those damn strangers. Weren't no thieving here before they came. Didn't have to lock my door at night before the war. This used to be a safe town. A Godly town."

He shot Morlaine a look, but she ignored him.

"Go back to your beds; we've called for the watch!"

"Fat lot of good they'll do," someone else shouted.

"Best lock yourselves inside, the rogues might still be about."

A few doors slammed shut, heeding Morlaine's advice. Other faces peered through windows, ghoulishly lit by candles held to the glass.

"I've got a crossbow," the old man said, "if those buggers come for me, I won't be afraid to use it!"

"Quite right, sir. Now, lock your door."

"Wait!" Ulrich hurried over to the man, bad arm throbbing, his shoulder afire, "Can I take your lantern?"

The man immediately shuffled back, drawing the lantern against his hollow belly.

Ulrich managed to fumble his purse and hold out a couple of coins, "For your trouble, sir. I'll return the lantern once I'm sure the... robbers have fled."

The man peered at Ulrich's outstretched hand.

"What about the oil?"

He spread a few more coins across his palm.

"And you'll bring it back?"

Ulrich nodded.

"And I can keep the money?"

He nodded again.

A bony hand reached out. Ulrich slapped the coins into it and snatched the lantern.

"Thank you, I'll-"

The door slammed in his face.

Morlaine was waiting for him in the street.

"What happened?"

A few faces still pressed against glass, but doors were closing, and curtains redrawn against the night. It was cold, and street robbery wasn't uncommon these days.

"As I said. A demon..." lantern held high, he headed back down the street after scooping up his fallen sabre, "...like you."

"A vampire? You are certain?" Morlaine caught up with him in a stride or two.

"I've seen enough of them to know," he glanced at her once he'd sheathed the sabre, "unfortunately."

It didn't take long to find the spot he'd been attacked; the alley was only a couple of dozen strides from where he'd run into Morlaine, the mud churned and broken from his struggle with the thing Madleen had become.

The lantern light did not carry far, illuminating the dancing rain for only a handful of paces. He peered into the night, but nothing disturbed the shadows. Was she still down there?

Was *it* still down there?

Madleen was no more a woman than the thing standing next to him.

"How did you escape?" Morlaine asked, eyes half-closed against the lantern's glare.

He took a few strides forward; when the demon came

to his shoulder, he nodded at the ground, "That's how."

Morlaine followed his gaze to where a hand, severed at the forearm, lay.

The demon crouched and smothered it in a large handkerchief before it disappeared within the folds of her cloak.

Ulrich stared at her when she straightened up.

"No one can see this," she explained.

"Why?"

"Because it won't rot like a mortal hand. No more talk of demons, Ulrich. Things are bad enough here."

He frowned at her, "Don't people have a right to know there are monsters about?"

"Demons mean only one thing to these people. Witchcraft. If someone starts screaming about demons, they'll be building pyres in the market square before the week is out. And whatever poor souls end up tied to those stakes, none of them will be vampires."

"We need to find her..." he said, looking away "...before she..."

"It was a woman?"

"Her name is Madleen..."

"Tell me everything."

"I will find her..." he said, moving into the alley's depths.

Morlaine grabbed his arm. The bad one. As with Madleen, the demon's fingers were cold iron too.

"Tell me what happened?"

"I don't need you... *demon!*" he hissed the last word almost under his breath.

Although he tried to yank himself away from her, Morlaine's fingers stayed wrapped around his arm.

"You do not like me, Ulrich. That is not a problem. Few people do. But you do need me. At least tonight. I need to know what happened to you, I need to find this vampire, and I need to stop her before she kills anyone else."

He frowned, "Else?"

"People have been going missing. Refugees mainly, so nobody much cared. Last night one of Lucien's men didn't come back. I had hoped it was nothing, but hope is a fool's coin. This Madleen must have taken them..." the demon tilted her head, "...how did you know her name?"

"I talked to her yesterday. She's a refugee, one of those camping outside *St Lorenz's*. I gave her food, a blanket for her daughter; I... was going to break fast with her, but she never turned up this morning..."

"You saw her *yesterday?*" Morlaine's eyes narrowed to black slits as she leaned in close, fingers digging deeper into the numb flesh of his arm.

He nodded.

"Then she has only recently been turned."

"Turned?"

"Created. Made. Sired. Yesterday she was mortal; tonight, she isn't."

"So...?"

"So, there's more than one vampire in Madriel. That was how you managed to escape from her. She is still weak, still changing."

"This other vampire..."

"Is one not much concerned with covering their

170

handiwork."

A wave of nausea crashed over him, and he slumped to his haunches.

"Ulrich?" Morlaine released his arm.

He swallowed a lungful of cold, wet air before looking up at the rain-blurred figure standing over him.

"The Red Company?"

Morlaine shrugged, "I don't know. There are others here. Some I know, some I don't. They are drawn to the Empire, to the madness and lawlessness of the war, like Suleiman. Pickings are good."

"They come to feast on the World's Pain."

Morlaine's forehead crumpled, "Solace told you that?"

He shook his head, "No, Madleen. That's what she meant; I didn't-"

Morlaine crouched down in front of him, "Are you *sure* it wasn't Solace?"

"Of course. Why?"

"She dreamt of her brother last night. He told her the undead were coming to feast upon the World's Pain."

"Solace was asleep when I left this morning. She said nothing to me, of a dream or anything else..." the cold that made him shiver then was not the one falling with the rain.

Morlaine's dark eyes stayed on him; the lantern lit her face from below, making her look far more like the strange, monstrous thing living beneath her pale skin.

"You know Solace's dreams are...?"

"Yes," Morlaine nodded, "I know."

*

Lucien was organising men to go out and search for the missing soldiers.

Or, rather, he'd sent Gottschall to haul men away from their drinks and drag them to the door under threat of curses and insults while Lucien continued to try and talk her into his bed.

It wasn't quite how she'd imagined an army operated.

Of course, this was more a gang of cutthroats hired to keep the other gangs of cutthroats out of Madriel until/if a proper army found a reason to roll up to the town walls. In which case, she suspected, it would be every man for himself.

"Ah, the burdens of command..." Lucien sighed, pouring more wine into her mug as Gottschall clubbed one inebriated intransigent around the ears and told him to get outside unless he wanted the thick end of his drink up his arse.

She didn't recall asking for more wine, or anyone bringing more wine. But a bottle had appeared on the table, nevertheless. The magic of seduction...

"Are you not going to lead your men from the front?" she asked as Gottschall herded more of them out of the door.

Lucien's dirty green eyes widened, "Good God, no! Have you seen the weather tonight? 'tis pissing down out there! No, no, there are far more important matters to attend to right here."

His hand was back on her knee. Much like the magically appearing wine, she didn't know how it kept turning up there

It was becoming a bit tiresome to keep removing it.

So, she sipped more wine instead.

Despite Lucien being more than a little appalling, she was worried about Ulrich, and every minute she lingered here amounted to another minute longer *Graf* Bulcher, Saul, and the rest of them got to keep drawing their undeserved breaths, she found the whole business of being seduced was not entirely unpleasant. She thought it possible she might even grow to quite like it if it were not for the fact vengeance would be the only lover she'd ever know.

"I should be going to my bed," she said softly.

Lucien's eyebrows, wiry and threaded with grey amongst the black, shot up, "A splendid idea!"

"Alone!"

"'tis a very cold night..."

"And my cousin will soon be warming your bed... and my husband mine!"

The thought of Ulrich made her peel Lucien's hand from her knee. In fact, it had wandered a little higher than her knee. The kind of thing a young woman really should be paying attention to.

"For all her undeniable beauty, I find your cousin a little cool... you on the other hand..."

"...am married," she pinched out a smile.

If he knew Morlaine had been drinking his blood, he'd probably think her downright cold.

The door slammed again, but it was only Gottschall pushing more men outside. Where was Renard? And Morlaine? What if they never came back?

The thought made her feel very alone.

Lucien was saying something, but the hubbub of voices and boots, metal and leather, made ignoring it easier. Renard had been by her side every day since The Wolf's Tower fell. Today he had been gone when she awoke, not just to buy horses but also to see another woman.

She'd thought herself alone ever since the two of them hobbled through the snow to escape Saul's Red Company, leaving everything she'd ever owned burning alongside the bodies of everyone she'd ever known bar her brother.

Now, in this room of bleak-faced men at arms, the realisation of what complete loneliness was, settled on her like snow in a winter blizzard.

There was little evidence God had been paying much attention to her prayers lately, but she closed her eyes and asked the Good Lord not to take Renard from her too. She could not do this alone.

After a breath or two, she steadied herself. God had kept Ulrich Renard alive for a reason. He had survived injuries and sickness few men could have, the freezing water of the lake should have killed him, but he'd lived and stayed at her side.

God hadn't done that so he could run off with some beggar woman on the street.

She opened her eyes and found Lucien turned away from her, growling at one of his soldiers, a young man with an ill-chosen fluffy blonde beard and restless eyes.

Beyond them, the remaining soldiers milled about, some finishing their drinks. A few, who had only recently returned from their duties settled themselves down, smug

174

grins splitting their faces as they offered advice on keeping the cold and damp out to their grumbling comrades heading into the night.

Her breath caught in her throat.

A figure stood against the far wall, cloaked, hooded and partially merged with the surrounding shadows eddying around him in curtains of black steam. None of the face was visible, but she felt a savage icy stare all the same.

A hand returned to her leg, and she made to slap it away before realising it was not fondling her knee through layers of skirts and petticoats, but fingers, cold and hard, dug into the skin of her thigh.

Her attention darted to Lucien. Turned away from her, arm slung over the back of his chair, he was talking to the young soldier.

And if the hand was not his...

Although there was no hand to see when she looked down, calloused skin pressed against her flesh, edging higher and higher, squirming between her leg and the skirts of her dress. There was no bulge to show anything was there, and when she dropped her hand to where she felt the touch, there was nothing... save she could not feel the press of her own hand when she pushed down on her leg.

The fingers moved around to the inside of her thigh, like some five-legged spider, working itself higher one inch at a time, insistently crawling towards her-

She snapped her legs shut.

The hand stopped moving but kept pressing against the inside of her thighs, bony and sharp, nails pushing deep as if to find greater purchase.

Breath coming in sudden brutal gasps, her eyes shot back to the figure. It was still there, still motionless. Only the shadows moved, as if the night were a sea, and its waves crashed around this thing upon its shore.

No one else appeared to have noticed it. And she was sure if someone could see it, they would. It reeked of wrongness, of something unnatural and impure.

Something of the Devil.

Out of the corner of her eye, she saw Lucien finish with the young soldier, who turned away, as oblivious as everybody else to the watching figure. The captain twisted back to face her.

His face was the colour of a cold hearth's ashes.

Her head whipped around.

He stared at her, the grin on his face entirely normal (normal for a lecherous goat like Lucien Kazmierczak, at least). Then the grin trickled away like water from a holed bucket. His eyes widened, and his pupils, large from so long in the ill-lit Inn, seemed to bleed into the rest of his eyes; black veins snuck out, dark tendrils filling the whites till only thin rings of dirty green broke the blackness.

"Do you think a child like Saul the Bloodless is someone to be scared of, my Lady of the Broken Tower?"

The voice was not Lucien's. It was not like anyone's she'd ever heard, it made her want to clamp her hands over her ears, and if that didn't block it out, she'd want to tear them from her head. A filthy, guttural noise, part hiss, part snarl, part growl, part something she had no word for. A sound that should emanate from no human throat. The noise of the pit.

Lucien's hand slapped onto the table, as grey as his face, as she watched the dirty fingernails curled, yellowed, and grew into long sharp talons.

She cried out as five sharp points cut into the soft flesh of her inner thigh.

"Wait until you meet me..."

"Who are you...? she whispered, pressing her legs together as hard as she could despite the pain. Whatever was occurring, that invisible hand was going no higher, no matter how much it hurt her.

Lucien's hand scraped down the table, fingernails gouging five grooves in the wood. Solace gasped as the fingers between her thighs did the same.

"The undead are coming, My Lady of the Broken Tower. Coming to feast upon the World's Pain..." Lucien edged forward, sharp yellow fingernails still cutting into the wood, as whatever was between her thighs cut into her flesh, "...coming to feast upon you..."

Lucien's fingernails screeched across the wood, and Solace screamed in time as what felt like five daggers slashed the inside of her thigh.

"Celine?"

She blinked.

Lucien was leaning forward, brows furrowed, skin blotchy and red rather than grey, eyes just the colour of dirty green bottles. His hand was in front of her face, fingernails reassuringly grubby and broken once more.

He clicked his fingers, and she blinked again.

"Celine?"

She painted the closest thing she could find to a smile upon her face.

"Yes?"

"You went... blank?"

"I did?"

With no further finger-clicking required, Lucien dropped his hand. It landed atop hers.

"Like you were asleep with your eyes open."

She looked at the empty mug in front of her before meeting the mercenary's eyes again. If she didn't know better, she'd have sworn something akin to concern might be swirling in there - along with the lust and lechery.

"Perhaps I took too much wine," she let out a little laugh, shrill, girlish and annoying to her ears, "I drink little!"

"Perhaps..." Lucien sat back, stared at her, then poured more wine "...though I find you can seldom have too much of any pleasure."

While he sloshed wine in the mug (and over the table) her eyes darted to the other side of the room. There was nothing to see through the pipe smoke and gloom bar the far wall, where a crude shelf holding a row of wan rushlights was the only thing of note.

"Drink," Lucien slid the wine before her. She took it and hoped he didn't notice her fingers trembling.

The tabletop bore no sign of the scratches she'd seen those wickedly sharp nails score.

She drank and stared across the room to the far wall.

What had she seen?

Her *sight* only showed itself in dreams and vague

178

feelings. An uncanny knowing of things that had or were about to happen. She'd never seen anything when she was awake. She had hazy childhood recollections of a young woman, beautiful and glowing, that nobody else could see. She'd thought her the ghost of her mother who'd died giving her life, but now, she wasn't sure if that had just been imagination and a child's yearning for a mother she'd never known. But nothing else.

If this was her *sight*, it was something new.

Her rational mind told her it was not real. No apparition had stood across the room. That awful voice had not hissed from Lucien's mouth, his eyes had not turned black, his skin had not become the colour of ashes, his nails had not grown to talons.

There was no sinister figure. There were no marks scored on the tabletop. Lucien was as he was. The world was as it had been.

That's what she told herself as she sipped the wine.

But the question she kept asking herself in reply was, if that is so, Solace, My Lady of the Broken Tower, why does it feel like blood is trickling down your leg...?

Chapter Twelve

The *obstler* eased the pain in his arm a little; the rest of him was probably beyond the help of even the strongest drink.

Morlaine watched him from across the table. She had bought a bottle, and every time he knocked the small glass back, she filled it again. Was she trying to get him drunk? Perhaps she thought he'd fall asleep, and then he'd stop insisting he was going with her to find Madleen and whatever bastard had made her a demon.

He slowly slid the glass away.

"I think I've had enough."

His hand had stopped shaking, which was the most he was likely to get from that or any other bottle.

Morlaine had found a tavern. Unlike the *Market Inn,* it was nearly empty, only a smattering of old men huddled over mugs of whatever took the chill off their bones the best. A meagre fire burned, and only a handful of rushlights restrained the darkness.

She'd steered him to a shadowy nook as far from the

scattering of drinkers as possible. Unable to stop shaking, he'd sat there glassy-eyed, mud slickened cloak still about his shoulders, the stink of the streets hanging about him until the demon returned with the bottle of *obstler*. Though she'd brought two glasses, hers remained empty.

After a couple of shots, she said, "Now tell me everything that happened? *Everything.*"

In a hesitant voice, he did. He didn't want the demon's booze, company or help but found himself too tired to refuse any of them. He was aware of the other drinkers peering at them. Those that weren't communing with their mugs alone touched heads to spit whispers in each other's ears.

"You should cover your head," he said, "They'll think you my wife rather than my whore then."

"I don't dress for the benefit of other people's traditions or prejudices," she replied, voice even, though something bright and fleeting flashed in the inky depths of her eyes before she told him to return to his account of Madleen.

"This demon," he said, his voice as low as possible, "changed her last night?"

Morlaine nodded.

He lifted his gaze to meet Morlaine's, "And there is nothing we can do for her?"

"We can kill her. That is all."

That wasn't quite what he'd hoped for.

"You... have feelings for her?" she asked, not unkindly, when he continued glowering at her.

"I liked her. I wanted to help her... I..."

"She is gone, Ulrich. Like Solace's brother is gone.

181

What remains is something else. Something that needs to be stopped."

"And she is different to you?"

Morlaine shook her head, "No, she is exactly the same. She just has no control over what has been put inside her. I do."

"But couldn't... she learn?"

She shook her head a second time.

"You did. Why can't Madleen?"

Morlaine took the empty glass to run a finger around the rim, "I do not even know how many people I killed before I learned. I still see their faces, but I cannot bear to count them. And the one who created me was a good man who tried to teach me how to control the beast. Yet still, they died, in their dozens, maybe their hundreds," her shoulders twitched, "how many deaths are you prepared to witness in order to save this woman, Ulrich? How many souls are you prepared to have chained to yours?"

He wanted to argue, but no words came. In the play of light beyond the demon, he saw Madleen as she'd been outside *St. Lorenz's*, and with each flickering sway of a dancing tongue, that fair face became something twisted and monstrous.

Instead, he poured himself another shot of the *obstler*.

"You were on the streets last night, looking for this Suleiman?"

"And the night before," Morlaine nodded as he swirled *obstler* around the glass.

"And you saw nothing, heard nothing of what was happening to Madleen?"

"If I had, I would have stopped it. I got no sense Suleiman was here, or any other vampires. I walked the streets till dawn, but sensed nothing..."

"Yet they were."

"I am fallible, Ulrich. The same as everybody else."

"If she had stayed in the church last night..." he threw back his head and let the drink burn his throat.

"She would still be alive now. But she didn't. We cannot change that; we can only shape the future, Ulrich, not the past. It is not your fault."

"As it was not my fault Saul got into The Wolf's Tower?"

"No one blames you. Solace does not."

He put the glass down and resisted the urge to fill it again.

"I helped him. I broke my oath to save my skin. All those people died-"

"Saul would have gotten in without your help. Solace told me what happened. The blame for that slaughter rests with the perpetrators, not the victims. And that is always the case."

"Now Madleen is suffering this. If I had taken her from the streets, if I had not left, if-"

"Then someone else would have. Stop wallowing, Ulrich. This is not your fault; what might have happened does not matter. What did happen does, and the important question is *why* it happened?"

His eyes moved from the empty glass back to Morlaine. "Why?"

"Vampires do not sire mortals on a whim. Even the

most debased of us accept the fewer of us that exist, the better. If we became too numerous, we will become known, and people will forget about burning witches and hunt us down instead."

"No bad thing, surely?" he spat the words out with more force than he intended.

Morlaine ignored the barb. "It isn't easy to sire someone; most do not survive the process. It is a precise business. Usually, it is done for a purpose; for gain, for companionship, for some deformed notion of love, for *something.*"

"So, you think this creature *loves* Madleen?" he snorted, filling his glass. It was rough *schnapps*, but it was growing on him.

"Whatever the reason, she was left alone after her change. That doesn't normally happen..." she tossed her head, "...of course, a vampire's normal is a very relative thing."

He chucked back another shot. If he stayed here much longer, he would keep on working the bottle till his head hit the tabletop.

He slid the glass across the table, "We're wasting time. If I can't save Madleen, I want to find the bastard who did this and kill him."

"It isn't necessarily a man."

"She said it was a man."

"She did?"

He shook his head, "Sorry, some of what happened... I forgot..."

"What did she say?"

He sucked in a breath tainted with tobacco smoke and beer fumes, "She called him... *he who walks above*... does that mean anything to you?"

"No."

"Who walks above?"

"God?"

He twisted out a dark smile, "I doubt God has come down to Madriel to make demons."

"No. But I've met plenty of vampires who have thought themselves someone of renown, from John the Baptist to Joan of Arc. None of them were. So, why not one who thinks he's God? All vampires are mad, to some degree or another..."

"And there's only one way to find where this one's madness lies."

They stared at each other, then pushed themselves to their feet in unison.

"Where do we start?" he asked once they were back outside.

The rain had abated, at least. It felt milder too, though that might have more to do with the *obstler* in his blood than the temperature.

"Where Madleen attacked you, I doubt she's gone far."

"Why?"

"A new vampire is always desperate for blood, an injured vampire is always desperate for blood, so..." Morlaine cocked an eyebrow, "...she will go as far as the first person she can find."

They walked in silence. He'd relit the lantern from one of the tavern's rushlights and held it before him, though there was little to see. No one was about.

Quite what he'd do if they found Madleen or the demon who'd changed her, he didn't know. He couldn't hold both the lantern and his sabre; the thick, numb, clumsy fingers of his bad arm weren't trustworthy enough for either task.

"The one that changed Madleen," he asked, finding the quietness of the dark town unsettling, "could it have been this Suleiman you're looking for?"

"I don't think so, he's never done anything like this before."

The alley was undisturbed; they'd walked down it once already before Morlaine took him to the tavern. There'd been no trail of blood to follow from Madleen's severed arm; the rain had seen to that.

The demon stood in the alley's mouth for a few seconds, breathing deeply. Was she trying to sniff the other vampires out?

He waited at her shoulder, hurrying after her when she set off down the alley again without warning.

He was calmer now than the first time they had checked it for signs of Madleen, but she was no more here now than she had been then.

"Are you certain she came this way?" Morlaine asked once they'd picked their way through to the far end of the alley.

"It was pitch black; I can't be certain of anything. But it *sounded* like she went this way."

Morlaine looked over her shoulder, face half shrouded by the hood of her cloak, "You should go back to Solace;

she is worried about you."

"She is?"

"Why do you sound surprised?"

He brushed past her. The alley opened onto another narrow, cobbled street, "Which way?"

"Left."

He couldn't say whether that was demonic instinct or the toss of a mental coin, but he hurried after her regardless, keeping half a pace behind her right shoulder.

"Do you not care for her?" Morlaine's question interrupted the echo of their boots.

"She is my mistress. I serve her."

"So, you do not?"

"Why the interest in our relationship?"

"Eternity can be boring."

The demon's head moved back and forth as she scanned the darkened street, right arm bent beneath the folds of her cloak. Hand no doubt resting on the hilt of the short sword she kept strapped so unfemininely to her thigh.

The street opened onto a courtyard, three-story buildings rising on each side.

Morlaine stopped. Without looking at him, she said, "If you follow me along the Night's Road, as Solace is so determined to do, you will die. Both of you."

"I know," he said, coming alongside her. An archway across the courtyard sat beyond the buildings, a black expanse beyond his lantern's kiss.

The demon tilted her head and looked at him out of the corner of her eye, "And yet you still follow her?"

"She has my oath."

"And your love?"

"I am bound to her by honour and debt. Not love."

"Love is lost to me now, Ulrich. My heart has been ice for centuries. I doubt it will ever melt again. Yours is not, and neither is Solace's. Your lives will be short. Make the most of whatever days are left to you..."

With that, the demon strode across the courtyard towards the archway.

After a shake of his head, Ulrich followed.

*

Lucien offered to see her to her room. She suspected the offer was not a chivalrous one.

When she declined, he rose with her, gave a little bow, scooped up her hand and slobbered over it.

"I will be here all night if you require me for... *anything...*"

"All night?"

"Some of my men are missing. 'tis a serious situation requiring a firm and steady hand upon the tiller to steer this honourable company through to calmer waters."

It seemed to Solace that Lucien's hand was more sweaty than steady and as likely to remain wrapped around a frothy tankard as anything else.

"I fear I will have to forgo the comforts of sleep..." he flashed a grin teetering on the salacious, "...for another night..."

After retrieving her hand, she bid him goodnight and crossed the room, discreetly wiping it on her skirts as she did so.

She kept hoping Renard and Morlaine would return right up to the moment she reached the stairs, but the Inn's door remained closed. The feeling of being watched lingered, but this time it was only the eyes of the remaining soldiers scattered about the tables that followed her. The shadows contained no suggestion of smoky malevolent apparitions.

A final glance over her shoulder caught Lucien's toothy wave as he managed the matter of the missing men by hooking his feet up onto the chair she'd just vacated as he badgered Anna-Lena for more beer.

She mounted the stairs accompanied by a sense of apprehension that grew with each squeaky step.

What would she find waiting for her in their room?

She hoped, fervently, it would be Renard but feared it would be something else.

Her *sight* told her nothing of Renard's whereabouts, and she told herself if something awful had happened, she would have an inkling of it by now. Who else did she have left in the world to worry about?

No. Renard would come back. She had no doubts. None at all...

But what of that thing she'd seen?

At the top of the stairs, several chamber lights and a single burning candle awaited her on a worn, scratched shelf. Holding one of the chamber lights to the twisting flame, the night retreated a fraction.

With the feeble light before her, she continued up to their room.

I am not afraid.

She'd survived the fall of The Wolf's Tower. She'd walked through shadows filled with real, flesh and blood monsters and lived; she was not going to start jumping at every shadow because of some spectre; her heart was not going to jump at every loose floorboard because of some ghoulish apparition.

She was a warrior. She was a fighter. She was a survivor. She was not going to go and hide under her bed until some man turned up to protect her.

Morlaine didn't need a man for that. Morlaine didn't need anyone to look after her. The demon walked the Night's Road and would do whatever it took to continue upon it, even if no end ever hove into view. And Solace von Tassau would damn well do the same!

A floorboard groaned behind her, not with the usual creak of old timber settling itself for the night but under the weight of a boot.

She whirled around, swallowing a cry and punching the chamber light before her.

There was nothing.

Cursing, she turned and walked on, the candle's light dancing upon the walls around her.

Their room was on the top floor, which meant two more flights of shadowy stairs, much narrower than the first. Each step seemingly darker than the last.

It felt like she was heading deeper and deeper into some place the sun never troubled. Before, she'd noticed nothing unsettling, only wood and plaster, dust and stains. Now every step conjured some new menace, some new horror.

Of course, before, she'd not just seen a man turn to the colours of ashes, his eyes go black while a phantom hand tried to... *deflower* her.

She wasn't sure if that was the right word, but it had been trying to do *something* unwholesome.

She hadn't been alone before either. She'd had Renard and Morlaine and-

I am a fighter! I am a survivor! God saved me for a purpose, and that purpose wasn't to hide in anyone's skirts!

She sucked in air tasting of tallow and fear.

On the corridor leading to their room, more sounds came. Scuffling feet, too distinct to be anything else. The flickering candle in the chamber light illuminated nothing moving bar the faint mist of her own breath.

She forced her feet forward, they wanted to either stay where they were or break into a run, but she let them do neither. One foot at a time. Steady as she goes.

More noise. More movement. More nothing.

Keep walking and stop that damn candle from shaking. You don't want it going out, do you?

No. She didn't.

A long mournful creak made the candle dance even more.

One of the doors ahead swung inwards, light spilled into the corridor, and a figure stepped out

A man stared at her from behind his own flickering chamber light.

Tall, gaunt, and balding, shadows filled the hollows of his face.

191

One of Lucien's men.

She wanted to lower her eyes and scurry past, but she forced herself to nod at him and offer half a smile. The man stood watching her, making no movement save with his eyes. The corridor was narrow, with barely enough of a gap to get by without brushing up against him.

His head swivelled as she approached, tracking her. As she passed, he nodded into the room. Inside was an unmade bed.

She didn't think he was asking her to make it for him.

Her eyes snapped to the front. She half expected to be yanked in and dragged to the bed, but he did nothing.

Once her back was to him, the door clicked shut, but no sound of feet followed.

She didn't glance back till she reached her own door. The man lingered outside his room; he'd twisted to watch her as she'd walked down the corridor. Above the glow of his chamber light, he appeared as inhuman as whatever Lucien had briefly become downstairs.

Her eyes turned forward again, and she hurriedly unlocked the door. Her hand shook slightly, but she did not fumble the key. Once inside, she locked the door and put her back to it.

Nailed boots clipped the uncovered boards in the corridor, growing louder, not fainter. They stopped on the other side of the door.

Her breath started coming in short, hard bursts. Bending her knees, she put her weight against the door as fear, bright and visceral, begun clawing its way up from her guts towards her throat.

Suddenly, she wasn't in a stale-smelling Inn bedchamber but hiding amongst the soot of long cold fires in a chimney place back in The Wolf's Tower, listening to the boots of soldiers looking to drag her away to the demons who'd slaughtered everyone she knew.

Heart racing, bile and sour wine filled her mouth. She wanted to gag, she wanted to scream, she wanted to run and not stop till her lungs burst.

Back in The Wolf's Tower, Renard had killed the soldier who'd found her cowering in the chimney, deciding to stand with her and not the monsters who'd promised to spare him in return for his sword and his allegiance.

But now Renard was gone, Morlaine was gone. She was alone and another monster was at her door.

She screwed her eyes shut, lips moving in silent prayer.

A sound floated under the door. A chuckle, dark and mirthless, deepening into a throaty laugh eventually accompanied by the clip of boots on wood.

Only when they faded to nothing did she open her eyes.

She crossed to the bed upon watery knees and slumped onto it, head hanging low, waiting for the gorge to splatter between her feet or subside.

It subsided.

Cold sweat slicked her skin.

I am a fighter... I am a survivor...

Slowly she hitched up the skirts of her dress, exposing her legs. She twisted her right leg, revealing the milky white flesh of her inner thigh up to the pubic hair.

Five vivid red lines cut the white.

She stared at them in the candle's restless light for a good long while.

Then she threw up.

Chapter Thirteen

Two figures huddled in the shelter of the archway.

Morlaine's unnatural eyes no doubt spotted them before the lantern's light intruded upon the shadow-choked passageway cutting beneath the buildings. As the demon had not broken her stride or reached for her blade, he assumed she did not consider them a threat.

They stood close together against the brickwork of the passageway. Both were women. At first, he thought them homeless refugees, sheltering from the only recently abated rain, until he realised neither had covered their heads. They were too old to be virgins.

"Looking for pleasures, sirs?" one asked, holding up her chin while the other pressed against her, eyes darting everywhere but on them. Both had pale cheeks, flushed bright red, from both cold and shame.

"You should not be on the streets," Morlaine told them.

The eyes of the woman who had spoken, whose dirty blonde curls the damp air had flattened around her face, widened and her face reddened further. She had mistaken

Morlaine for a man, "Begging your pardon, Frau..."

"You should not be on the streets tonight," Morlaine repeated, pulling back her hood to reveal her own uncovered head.

The women looked uncertainly at each other, then at him and then back to Morlaine. The demon appeared young enough to be unmarried, though why such a fetching lass was untaken would be a curiosity. Dressing in a man's garb, more curious still.

"We mean no harm..." the second woman, younger and sturdier than the first, blurted. Perhaps she feared Morlaine worked these streets and considered them her own.

"I have no care why you are here," Morlaine said, "it is just dangerous. Go home."

"We have no home," the first woman tugged a shawl too thin for so bitter a night tighter about bony, shivering shoulders.

Refugees then, the same as Madleen; forced to shame themselves through hunger and necessity. He wondered if they had left children somewhere to await their return too.

"There is a..." he stalled when Morlaine gave him a warning look, "...there is trouble. A woman has been... attacked. You need to be indoors."

"Our children need to eat..."

It appeared they had.

Neither woman made to budge from the covered passageway.

His hand moved halfway to the purse in his pocket before he stopped himself. Solace did not have enough money to save every refugee in Madriel, be it from demons or the consequences of war.

"Please-" was all he managed before a shriek split the stillness of the night.

Both women moved closer to each other.

Morlaine's dark eyes fixed along the passageway beyond the two women, he followed her stare, but the lantern's light only reached as far as the first cobbles of the street.

When he looked back, he found the demon pressing coins into the hands of the two women, "Get off the street. You have shelter?"

The women looked at Morlaine strangely, as well they might, "We sleep in the Lutheran Meeting House..." the first woman dropped her eyes as she added, "though they would turn our children and us onto the streets if they knew that we-"

"Go there directly," Morlaine interrupted, "Make sure you lock the doors behind you. Let no one in till morning."

"What is happening?" the second woman asked, eyes flicking up from the coin in her palm.

"Just the madness of the war..." Morlaine pulled her hood up and brushed past the women.

"Do as she says," he told them, hurrying after the demon.

The cry had sounded like a man, but nothing else had broken the night since. It might have been a husband shouting at his wife, but he didn't think so. As Morlaine had swept back her cloak to rest a hand upon the pommel of her sword, it seemed she didn't either.

She took a few long strides beyond the end of the passageway before coming to a halt in a broader street of finer buildings. They had left the poorer part of town.

As he caught up to her shoulder, Morlaine raised her head, sucking in air as if sniffing the night. The only scents he could discern were damp stone and horse shit, but her nose was undoubtedly more sensitive than his.

The two women trailed them onto the street. They both now wore linen caps upon their head, "'tis probably nothing," the older woman said, still adjusting hers, "You hear such things at night."

"You do?" he asked.

"The town is overflowing, people are worried, hungry, scared, they do desperate things," she brushed down her dress and refused to meet his eye.

He nodded. Maybe she was right; she knew Madriel better than he did.

"Where is the meeting house?"

"The other side of town."

"We wanted to be as far away as we could get... before we..." the younger woman's words faded away with her steaming breath before she could confess what they had been doing.

Morlaine started walking again; the two women scurried to his side, the younger's arm threaded inside the older one's, "Your lady is... somewhat odd, sir?"

"She is not my lady!"

"Begging your pardon, sir. No offence meant..."

He ignored them and hurried after Morlaine. Neither woman looked like Madleen, but they reminded him of her too much. The clack and scuff of down at heel shoes told him they continued to trail him.

Ahead, lights illuminated the street. Two flickering tar torches.

"Who-"

"Soldiers," Morlaine replied, "Lucien's men."

"You can tell from here?"

He could not even see how many men accompanied the torches from this distance, let alone who they were.

"They have a very distinctive smell."

He glanced at the demon. Despite travelling together for nearly three weeks, he had yet to decide if she possessed a sense of humour. He was none the wiser now.

"What do we do?"

"They are not responsible for Madleen," she said in a quiet, matter-of-fact voice, "therefore, there should be no reason to kill them."

No, still none the wiser.

"Keep walking; once they have passed and we have said goodnight to our new friends," Morlaine's hood jerked backwards at the two women behind, "we will double back. There is a vampire close."

"You are certain?"

"Very. There is blood in the air."

There seemed to be nothing in the air to him bar the fine damp mizzle that had started to fall once more, refracting the light from his lantern into hazy rainbows.

"Are we seeing these two home?"

"You can if you wish. I need to find this vampire before anyone else dies."

"Has anyone died?"

The only answer was the click of Morlaine's boots on the cobbles.

"This demon. Is it Madleen?" he demanded.

"I don't know. Her or her maker," Morlaine continued, stride unbreaking as the approaching lights grew brighter, "whichever, it is important no one knows of it. *We* must deal with it."

"People are dying..."

"And if people hear talk of demons or see corpses with their throats ripped out, as is the way of newborn vampires in the thrall of their new desires, then far more will die..." she turned in his direction, the lantern's glare making stars bloom in the darkness of her eyes, "...upon the witchfinder's pyres..."

Ahead of them, the men with torches stopped. Ulrich could see just two of them, each carrying a tar torch alight against the night. As Morlaine had said, they were both Lucien's men.

"Well, well," one of them said as they drew closer enough to make out the hard, bearded faces set under their steel helms, "'tis Lucien's whore."

"Rounding up some more for him, are you?" the second soldier laughed, nodding at the two women hanging back behind them.

When Morlaine ignored them and made to continue, the first soldier, a tall man with a flat, bulbous nose, stepped across her, "Man asked you a question, bitch."

Morlaine pulled back her hood and fixed her dark eyes on the soldier, "I am not a bitch... and he is barely a man."

The soldier snorted a plume of frosty breath into Morlaine's face, pursued by a gloved finger, "If you weren't Lucien's, I'd teach you some fucking manners."

"I am not Lucien's. So, why don't you try?" Morlaine continued to stare back boldly, with no hint of either fear or deference in her voice. It was not at all how young women were supposed to behave.

"We want no trouble, sir," he said quickly. Morlaine was keen to keep the fact there were demons at large in Madriel a secret to save people from the witchfinders, but it seemed to Ulrich, she sometimes forgot she was one of them.

The soldier's eyes flicked his way as if only just noting him, "Is that so?"

"We want to get out of the weather, nothing more."

"What you about? Where you been?"

"Just business," Ulrich smiled and kept his hand away from his father's sabre.

The soldier peered around Morlaine at the two refugees, "Saving the souls of fallen women, are we?"

His companion sniggered behind him.

"We're not fallen women!" the older of the pair snapped back, "we're good Christian folk!"

A thin smile twisted the soldier's face, "I know you... I seen you..." he spat on the cobbles. The woman dropped her eyes and shuffled closer to her friend.

"We're escorting them home," Ulrich said.

"How gallant! Eh, Piet?"

Piet sniggered again.

"Think you'd be better advised attending to your wife

202

than this sorry pair."

Ulrich shot him a questioning look.

"Getting cosy with Captain Lucien when we left," Piet explained with a wet snicker.

"Spend too long escorting *good Christian folk* home, and you'll end up with him buttering your bread for you, still..." the flat-nosed soldier looked at Morlaine and winked, "...guess that'd mean you'll be needing a new bed for the night, eh?"

Morlaine held his eye, unwavering and unflinching. After a second or two, the soldier gave a little snort and moved aside.

Ulrich ushered the two women past the soldiers whose eyes followed them above leering grins.

As Ulrich made to move off, the more talkative of the two men asked, "While you been busy escorting good Christian folk around town, you seen any of our men?"

"Some. Why?"

"Two of the boys didn't arrive on the walls to relieve the watch, plenty of whores in this town that might distract a man..." he glanced at the refugees and then Morlaine, before his attention returned to Ulrich, "...but I wouldn't have kept Hellwig Kott shivering on the walls for even the most comely of whores."

"I saw a couple earlier. I asked for directions back to the *Market Inn*, but as they wanted a taler each, I decided I'd rather freeze to death."

"Sounds like them," Piet muttered, "tight-arsed cunts."

"You get their names?"

Ulrich shook his head, "I assume they would have

charged for those too."

Flatnose glared at him, "What did they look like?"

"Tall, with beards," he told the two tall, bearded men, "think one was Hessian."

"A tall, bearded, money-grabbing, Hessian cunt," Flatnose glanced at Piet.

"Sounds like Eck," Piet agreed.

"How long ago did you see them?"

"A while."

"Which direction were they going in?"

"I don't know. I was lost. That was why I asked for directions."

"Not a lot of use, really, are you?" Flatnose sneered.

"Probably why his wife were letting Lucien have a good feel of her," Piet sniggered. He seemed partial to a snigger, did Piet.

"Anything else?"

He remembered they'd run off when they'd heard a cry. A cry that could well have been a scream. He resisted glancing at Morlaine, "No, nothing."

Flatnose gave him another long hard look, the orange light of the flaming torch dancing upon the scratched, dull metal of his helm.

"C'mon..." he finally said, striking off towards the passageway, Piet hurrying to catch up with him.

"Solace is not going to sleep with Lucien," Morlaine said quietly.

"'tis no concern of mine what she does," he spat back, surprised by the annoyance in his tone.

Morlaine gave him one of her looks, the kind that

made you think there wasn't much point in lying, then, "What didn't you tell those men?"

His eyes remained on the retreating torches, "Their friends left me to investigate a scream. I didn't think much of it at the time... screams at night aren't..."

"...always vampires," Morlaine finished for him.

"No. But do you think they could have run into Madleen? Or her maker?"

"Lucien's men aren't the most disciplined soldiers I've ever met; they could just be drinking themselves stupid somewhere..."

Flatnose and Piet reached the covered passageway; the walls glowed with fitful orange light as they walked through. Once they'd passed the shadows rushed back.

Then the screaming started.

*

Solace sat by the window, watching the square.

Occasionally, a figure or two would emerge to cross one of the isolated islands of light cast by the handful of oil lanterns hanging from poles. She eased back into the chair when each turned out not to be Renard or Morlaine.

A single tallow candle burned on the other side of the room. Despite it not being a spacious room, the light hardly made it to the window. The darkness seemed thicker somehow tonight, the light less able to penetrate the gloom. Stupid, of course. The dark was the same as it always was.

She just felt more alone in it.

Her fingers absentmindedly stroked the inside of her right thigh, tracing the five red lines cut into her skin. They smarted and tingled, though, strangely, she didn't find the sensation entirely unpleasant.

She'd rinsed her mouth and cleaned up the vomit as best she could. It only added a fraction to the room's unwholesome collection of smells, built up by countless guests over untold years, until they'd become as much part of the fabric as its scuffed floorboards and discoloured walls.

What if they don't return?

What if the night has consumed them?

What if they have run away from the insane girl and her all-consuming desire for vengeance?

"They have not run away; they are coming back..." she muttered.

The night did not reply. Nor did her *sight*.

No, her *sight* conjured ghoulish apparitions rather than anything useful.

Her eyes flicked to the window; a group of Lucien's men sauntered below, barking laughter cutting the silence along with the restless light of tar torches. No Renard. No Morlaine.

Had the apparition been her *sight* ? She was trying hard not to think too much about it.

Her hand moved to the marks on her thigh again.

She had never experienced anything like it, but the message (or threat, or warning, she was yet to quite decide which) had to have been a conjuring of her *sight*. Like the dreams and feelings it manifested itself as, a little interpretation was required.

For now, however, she had no idea what it meant.

Or how the *sight* could physically mark her.

She found her hand moving back and forth over the tingling skin of her inner thigh again. Jerking it away, she snapped her knees together. Then tugged her dress down and told herself to stop touching the wounds. It was not at all appropriate.

Her eyes drifted back to the window. The square was empty once more. The refugees were inside *St Lorenz's*, their makeshift camp deserted; everyone else was behind doors, settling down for the night.

They had intended to leave tonight, but she had made no move to change into her new travelling clothes. They would not be going now; she didn't need the *sight* to tell her that. Morlaine wanted to depart at sunset, so she had as much darkness as possible to continue their journey. But the sun had set hours ago now, so they would wait until tomorrow. Another night's rest would do them good.

She thought of sleeping beside Renard again but yanked her mind away from it as hard as she had her hand from her thigh. That wasn't appropriate either.

In truth, after weeks of trudging through the mud and rain to get here, living off berries, dried fish, and whatever Renard and Morlaine could catch, they both needed more than a couple of nights of rest and good sleep.

The girl in the looking-glass, whatever Lucien said, was hollow-eyed, thin-faced and ragged.

Not that appearance concerned her much now. She wasn't the pretty daughter waiting by the window for a handsome prince to come riding up to her castle anymore. Nothing mattered. Nothing bar vengeance.

Her hand was in her lap, rubbing the wool of her dress against her thigh. She pulled it away like an errant child playing with something dead in the street.

She really had to stop doing that!

Her eyes returned to the window.

A figure stood below. It was difficult to make much out in the shadow-filled twilight between the reach of two oil lamps. At first, she wasn't sure anyone was there as it wasn't moving. Who stayed stock still in the cold swirls of misty rain coating the market square?

She pressed her nose closer to the glass. It was cheap and subtly distorted the world on the other side of it.

Was the figure hooded? It was difficult to be certain, though it would hardly be unusual for someone to be wearing a hood, given the weather. Morlaine did, after all.

And so had the apparition downstairs.

As she watched, the figure lifted its right hand. A fist, pale as bone, emerged from the sleeve and made a knocking motion in the air.

Behind her, a fist rapped against the other side of the door.

She jumped, half turning to the door.

"Ulrich..?"

There was no answer. Of course, there wouldn't be. There was no one on the other side of it.

Outside, the figure was still motionless in the shadows, arm raised.

Light played across the cobbles, reflected and scattered by the slick stones and the little puddles caught between them. Another figure appeared; a lantern held aloft. Head lowered, shoulders hunched, hurrying through the drizzle. Another of Lucien's men heading for the *Market Inn* and its comforts.

He passed the hooded figure, neither slowing nor glancing at the motionless apparition. The lantern light glistened on the cobbles, racing in time to the soldier's rushed strides. But, as it approached the figure staring up at her window, it seemed to bounce away, as if recoiling from the darkness shrouding it and retreating towards the lantern.

If the soldier noticed anything peculiar, it didn't slow him down. His pace never faltered, and once he passed, the light seemed to hurry after him, racing away from the shadows like a dog chasing its master.

The raised fist moved again. Another knock echoed from the door.

Come...

She jumped again. And found herself on her feet.

...to me...

The fist opened, fingers splaying wide when she remained rooted to the spot. Although it was too dark and too far away, she knew those fingers ended in sharp, long yellowed nails. They moved up and down.

A scratching noise came from the other side of the door.

Come to me... My Lady of the Broken Tower...

She did no such thing. She wasn't going out there. He could scratch and knock all he damn well liked.

The hand moved once more, clawing the silken rain.

No sound came from the door. Instead, the top of her

right thigh tingled and warmed.

You carry my mark. You are mine. Come to me...

The voice was a sibilant hiss. She'd have sworn on the Holy Book that she'd heard the knocking and scratching on the door as if someone really did stand on the other side. But that voice, which sounded like a serpent on the wind, was in her head. Whispering not in her ears but in her soul.

She had pulled on her travelling coat and heavy winter cloak from their pile of provisions before she realised what she was doing.

Come to me...

For a moment, she hesitated. Actually, it was a lot longer than a moment. Then she grabbed a belt and buckled it on under her coat; a long-bladed knife hung from a sheath.

Laughter, black and amused, rolled around the room. Or maybe her head. She ignored it. Her heart gave a sick lurch as she unlocked the door. No one waited on the other side.

The corridor was as black as the laughter still echoing in her head, but she hurried as fast as she dared, all the time expecting a hand to close around her arm. She got halfway to the stairs before thinking she should have brought a chamber light. She didn't go back. She wasn't afraid of the dark. Or the things that lived in it.

Enough light dusted the stairs to make the descent easier. Floorboards creaked, distant voices, dull and muffled, sounded from the far-flung corners of the Inn.

Come to me...

She ignored them. They weren't the voices that mattered. Her thigh smarted as she walked, but she ignored that too.

Lucien still lounged at the same table, talking to one of the serving maids, who was laughing and playing with her hair. Needless to say, it wasn't Anna-Lena.

Her legs froze as he glanced in her direction, but his eyes moved over her and went back to the serving maid. The remaining soldiers ignored her too.

They can't see me...

That seemed unlikely, the bar was gloomy and thick with lingering pipe smoke, but it wasn't *that* dark. She crossed it and opened the door. No one looked up.

Outside, rain as fine as gauze chilled her face.

In the square, the hooded figure stood between the pools of lamp light, in a darkness greater than the surrounding night.

Her legs took her towards it.

She didn't want them to, but they moved of their own accord.

"My Lady of the Broken Tower," the man said, his face nought but shadow beneath the hood.

"Who are you?" she demanded, coming to a halt.

He was tall but not broad. She had to raise her chin to meet where she thought his eyes most likely to be.

"I have many names. You know none of them," his voice was deep, resonant and quite unlike the one that had hissed inside her head.

"Then give me one. I wish to know who violates my mind?"

211

"Violate... an emotive word."

"How would you describe it?" The urge to touch her thigh came so strongly she had to make a fist of her hand and press it hard against her hip to stop it.

The man chuckled.

"Call me... Flyblown."

"Flyblown?"

His shoulders moved again, "As good a name as any. Well, *Lord* Flyblown, actually. But there's no need to be formal. Is there?"

"That depends on what you want. I don't take kindly to threats."

Flyblown laughed, "You must excuse me. I have a flair for the dramatic. And I wanted to get your attention."

"You succeeded."

"Excellent!"

"Who are you? What do you want? How did you do those things earlier?"

"My, my, so many questions."

She took in a deep breath of cold, wet air, "Let us take one at a time then. Who are you?"

Flyblown reached up and slowly peeled back the hood of his cloak. She expected something ghastly underneath, like the ghoulish visage Lucien had adopted when Flyblown spoke through him.

The reality was more mundane.

A pale, sharp face with exceptionally high cheekbones, thin lips, chiselled nose, long dark hair pulled tightly back. She couldn't tell the colour of his eyes; shadows dressed the hollows of his face too deeply. He did not appear old nor particularly young. Perhaps in better light, it might be more discernible. Something about him looked unfinished, like the work of a master sculptor who still had to polish down the cruder edges of his creation.

"Your cake appears lightly sprinkled with disappointment?"

"I was expecting something more dramatic."

"A little drama seasons the expectations nicely. But melodrama should always be avoided."

"Are you a demon?"

"No. Demons are just excuses to burn people at the stake."

"I have met demons."

"You have met vampires. There's a difference."

"None of the vampires I have met can do what you do."

"I should hope not!" Flyblown said. Lifting his hand, he waved her forward. As far as she could tell, his fingernails were neither long, sharp, nor yellow, "Come, let us walk; it is a little chilly tonight."

He turned and headed across the square towards *St Lorenz's*; she hurried to his side.

"Are you real?" she asked.

He held out his hand, "Why don't you touch me and find out?"

She kept her hands where they were. Something - her *sight* or otherwise - told her she didn't want to feel this man's skin on hers.

"How did you get into my mind?" the next question blurted out as they walked across the cobbles, the church a stark silhouette against the weeping sky.

"Who said I was in your mind?"

"Lucien didn't turn grey, his eyes black, his nails long and yellow. So, it must have been in my mind. A conjuring."

"And yet you have five long scratch marks in a quite intimate location. Or are they just in your mind too?"

On the far side of the square, one of the oil lamps flickered out; darkness washed in to replace the light. She tightened her hands into a fist again but didn't answer. She could feel the wounds chaffing as she walked. They seemed real enough.

Flyblown chuckled.

"The mind, the flesh, the soul. All are malleable. As is the world itself..." his head turned a fraction, "...if you know how..."

Another lamp glowed brighter for a heartbeat before it too died.

"Are you a witch?"

"Witches, if they are anything at all, are usually cunning women who play with herbs and potions and pray to non-existent gods. They are harmless for the most part. And some of those herbs and potions even do a little good. Here and there. No, I am not a witch."

One by one the lamps were failing as they walked, the little islands of light submerging under the greater darkness.

"Are you..." she was starting to run out of possibilities, "...the Devil?"

"The Devil has no form. The Devil is the name we give our weaknesses. The Devil is greed, stupidity, lust, avarice, anger. The Devil is *vengeance*. The Devil is the darkness within us all. We are all capable of being the Devil. If anyone here is, My Lady of the Broken Tower, it is you..."

"But not you?"

"Oh, most definitely not me. I am a creature of light and joy!" Flyblown said, laughing darkly.

The last pool of light, hanging over the gate to the churchyard, blinked out, leaving only the night, the rain and the sound of their feet on the cobbles. She could still make out the bulk of the church against the fractionally brighter sky, but nothing else. Save Flyblown.

I should not be able to see his face...

But she could. His sharp, somehow unfinished features remained shadowy but defined enough to follow facial gestures. Noticing her regard, he flashed a toothy grin. His teeth appeared quite ordinary, though none seemed to be black or broken.

"Well," she said, fixing her eyes front again despite there being nothing to see, "if My Lord Flyblown will not tell me what he is. Perhaps he will do me the kindness of telling me what he wants?"

"Perhaps nothing but your delightful company?"

"What do you want?"

She sensed as much as saw the toothsome smile fade and the eyes within their black hollows harden.

"I want the same as you; I want Saul the Bloodless' head on a platter..."

Part Two

Leaving

Chapter One

She stopped. Flyblown stopped.

The rain, still fine as sighs, eddied around them. There seemed no purpose in walking, she would get equally wet standing still, and they were no closer to the church. Madriel's market square was not particularly large, and they had walked long enough to cross it several times, yet still, the tower of *St Lorenz's* remained the same distance away.

"Why?"

"Does one need a *particular* reason to stop a blood-crazed killer?"

"Yes. I think *you* do."

Flyblown puckered his lips, nostrils flaring. Despite the cold, no frosted breath steamed from them, she noticed. Just like Morlaine, just like Saul and the rest of his demons.

"Do you have dreams, hopes, ambitions, My Lady of the Broken Tower?"

"Once. The kind young women usually have, I

suppose. Then *Graf* Bulcher sent the Red Company to my home. Now my dreams, hopes and ambitions are... somewhat different."

Flyblown gave a shallow nod, "We all have them, even if they are so insignificant the world pays them not the slightest heed. Earn enough coin to afford the *good* bread, kiss the girl, buy a new blanket, repair that window, live to see your daughter married..." he shrugged, "...small curses. Some people possess bigger dreams. To better themselves, obtain patronage, wield influence, and find riches. In the great turn of the world, they are mostly as meaningless as the small curses of the little folk. Then, every so often, someone comes along... someone with bigger dreams."

"And Saul has big dreams?"

"Saul can have all the dreams he wants. Dreams are meaningless. It is the consequences of dreams that concern me. I want Saul stopped. I want the Red Company stopped. They are an affront to the world, to the natural order, and the balance of things."

"I am not sure I am any wiser."

"Creatures of the shadows," Flyblown said, "should stay in the shadows."

"And you need *my* help to take Saul's head?"

"I need tools and weapons. You are a tool. Morlaine is a weapon. Even that lad with the bad arm has his uses. I, however, cannot do the deed directly."

"Why not?"

"You do ask a lot of questions, don't you?"

"Why not?"

"Let us say it would cause me difficulties."

219

"Let us say *what* difficulties, my lord?"

"I am offering you aid and succour to fulfil your burning desire for vengeance. You do not sound entirely grateful. How puzzling."

"You are not offering me help. You are asking me to do what I intended to do anyway."

"No. What you were going to do anyway was die. With my assistance, other possibilities exist. Still, I sense a regrettable lack of trust," Flyblown lifted his head to the sky, the crumpled frown clear enough on his long face despite no light falling upon it.

"You won't tell me who you are, what you are, or why you want Saul stopped. The enemy of my enemy is my friend..." she held his eyes when they turned on her, "...but all my friends are dead."

"Perhaps a gift might earn me a little trust?"

"A gift?" she cocked an eyebrow, "What manner of gift, my lord?"

Flyblown puckered his lips, "Would *Graf* Bulcher suffice?"

"You have him?" she took a step towards Flyblown before remembering she really did not want to touch him.

He laughed, "No, of course, I don't have him! But I know how you can find him. The rest is up to you."

She turned it over in her head, "Do you know where Saul is? Where the Red Company are?"

"Actually, no. But the delightful *Graf* may well. And that was your plan, wasn't it? To ask him, not so very nicely, I presume, where the Red Company can currently be found, given his history as one of their employers?"

She nodded.

"A most excellent scheme! Although ever so slightly tarnished by the fact you have little more idea about *Graf* Bulcher's whereabouts than Saul the Bloodless'. Something I believe you neglected to mention to Morlaine when you persuaded her to let you accompany her."

"Bulcher will be a lot easier to find than Saul."

"Perhaps, but scurrying hither and tither across this war-ravaged, starving land of religious fanatics and killers, peering under the multitude of rocks available to that loathsome toad..." Flyblown cut the rain with a sweep of his hand, "...I foresee *difficulties*..."

Solace turned her bottom lip between her teeth. She did not trust this creature, but as she didn't enjoy a surfeit of allies, she had little choice.

She nodded, "Very well. Where can I find the bastard?"

Flyblown's thin lips again split to reveal his white smile, "All in good time, My Lady of the Broken Tower, all in good time..."

"Why not tell me now?"

"One problem at a time, my lady. You must leave Madriel first."

Drawing the sole of her shoe back and forth over a cobble worn smooth by countless other feet, she stared at Flyblown, "We have horses, and provisions. We are ready to depart as soon as Renard and Morlaine return..."

"Two things," Flyblown held up his right hand, two fingers raised and turned to her, "firstly, do not mention me to Morlaine. Or anybody else. But particularly Morlaine."

"Why?"

Flyblown sighed, "I knew you would ask that. Truly, my powers of perception have almost no end!"

"Why? Does she know you?"

"Morlaine knows many people. She has a *lot* of history, after all. Not as much as I do, but still, she has been around a long time."

"Does that mean yes?"

His thin lips stretched into a thinner smile," It means what it means. As everything always does."

It was her turn to sigh, "And the second thing?"

"Ah, yes..." Flyblown glanced at the fingers he still held aloft, "...and secondly, leaving Madriel might prove more difficult than you think."

"Why...?"

"Your friends have run into some difficulties..."

She stepped forward, close enough to smell something even the rain could not completely wash from the air around Flyblown, something musky, earthy and old. Something that reminded her of the family crypt beneath The Wolf's Tower.

"What has happened?"

Flyblown continued to stare at her, the corner of his mouth half turned upwards, fingers still in mid-air; she grabbed his arm and squeezed. Whatever filled the sleeve felt soft and squishy, like a half-empty waterskin.

She swallowed and ignored it.

"What has happened?"

"I told you earlier. The undead are coming to feast upon the World's Pain..." Flyblown's grin widened as he passed his fingers back and forth before her nose. The fingernails, she noticed, were once more long, sharp and yellow, "...and many of them are already here..."

*

Morlaine ran towards the screams.

He hesitated.

Behind him, the two refugee women were clutching each other, eyes and mouths wide as they stared past him into the passageway they had recently left.

I should not leave them.

I should not follow Morlaine.

The screams were not those of children, except, to his ears, everyone's screams sounded like a child's now.

"Go!" he told the women, "Go to the Meeting House, lock the door and do not open it before sunrise," he started moving away before adding, "and do not let anyone in!"

Then he ran after Morlaine, who had disappeared into the darkness beyond the reach of his lantern.

The screaming, at least, had stopped.

He wanted to pull his sabre free, but if he tried to unsheathe it with his withered left arm, it would likely just clatter to the cobbles. And he wasn't going to put the lantern down, even for a sword.

His boots echoed as he passed through the passage, the lantern light jigging upon brickwork. Emerging back into the damp night on the other side, he skidded to a halt. Holding the lantern above his head, he stood panting, the numb fingers of his left hand caressing the hilt of his sword like it were the keepsake of a long-lost lover.

"Morlaine?"

No one was in sight.

Nothing troubled the courtyard bar the mizzle. He scanned the ground for signs of blood and violence without success. Perhaps the screams had come from further away. The night could be a trickster when it came to the senses.

But he didn't think so.

He edged forward, letting the lantern's light creep ahead of him half a stride at a time.

His fingers brushed the sword again. He needed a weapon and light but could not have both.

"What happened?"

He whirled around. The two women had paid as little heed to him as everyone else did.

"What are you doing? I told you to go home!"

"'tis dark, and we have no light..." the older woman said.

"And there are murderers on the streets!" the younger woman blurted, "you said so yourself!"

"What are your names?" he demanded, returning to the mouth of the passageway where they huddled together.

"Rosi," the older woman squinted into the lantern he had thrust at their faces, "Sina," the younger one retreated a step to cower behind her friend's shoulder.

"Rosi, Sina, go home. Now!"

"But 'tis not safe. We're better to stick with you, sir," Rosi said.

"You've got a sword," Sina pointed out.

"And a light!" Rosi added.

Which was true enough, even if he couldn't use both at the same time.

"You'll be safe enough if-"

Another scream broke the silence, making the women jump. He cursed under his breath; they were going nowhere. He could tell them to piss off till he went blue in the face, but they'd likely still tag along behind.

They had the air of women much used to men yelling and swearing at them.

The scream sounded like it came from one of the smaller alleys shooting off the courtyard; he looked over his shoulder. It seemed a faint glow lit one of them. The soldiers' tar torches? Someone sticking their head out to see what the racket was?

"Very well," he said, twisting back to Rosi and Sina, "make yourself useful, take this and keep behind me," he held the lantern out to the two women. Before they started to have a chat about who should take on the vast responsibility, he pushed it into Rosi's hand. She appeared to possess marginally more in the way of wits.

"Come with me," he drew his sword with his good hand as soon as Rosi's gripped the lantern's handle.

He managed three strides across the courtyard before realising the light wasn't coming with him.

Rosi and Sina remained rooted to the cobbles.

"Come with me!"

"But... you said there's trouble?" Rosi's faltering smile tried to catch upon her lips.

"Either bring the light and come with me or leave it here and go home in the dark."

He thought their preferred option was taking the lantern and going home, but the way he growled stopped them suggesting it. After exchanging a hesitant glance, Rosi edged forward, Sina, with the air of a woman walking to her own execution, eventually followed suit.

"Stay close," he said before jerking up his sword and adding, "but not so much I'll hit you with the backswing."

They both looked blank. Or rather, blanker.

He nodded at the alley and started moving; this time the light came with him, throwing his shadow before him. If you never saw what cast it, the shadow was probably quite fearsome.

It was another narrow affair, brickwork stretching as high on either side as the lantern light reached. It smelt of damp and piss. His fearsome shadow stretched long across moss fringed cobbles; a tar torch flickered beyond it.

"Come..." he, his shadow and the lantern light moved forward.

The weight of his father's sword offered a familiar comfort. He'd tried to keep practising with it as best he could, but its blade had connected with nothing since The Wolf's Tower fell. Save Madleen's arm, of course.

If it was Madleen down here, he would have to finish her. If it was her maker...

According to Morlaine, Madleen was weak, and he'd still been lucky to escape with his life. Her maker would be far stronger, and he knew how hard it was to kill one of these wretched demons.

The women's feet scuffed the cobbles in his wake.

Walking to his own death was one thing, but leading innocent women to theirs...

He shook the thought away. Without light, he'd have

even less chance.

Water dripped somewhere; the only sound other than their footsteps. Piles of refuse stacked the walls, and he edged around each one, drawing closer to the flickering tar torch.

It appeared to be on the ground. Luckily everything was too damp to catch; half the town was built of wood and straw.

"What is it?" one of the women asked, the light swaying behind him.

He waved his bad arm to quieten her.

The tar torch smouldered, partially doused in a puddle, black smoke swirling up to meet the drizzle. More rubbish choked the alley; it seemed a place the locals deposited any and everything they didn't want. Out of sight...

Sabre half raised, he inched around the rotting remnants of an old crate no one had yet gotten around to burning for fuel.

Beyond the sputtering torch, the breeze ruffled something in one of the refuse piles, a scrap of canvas or old sheet...

He gripped the sword tighter, breath catching in his throat. Around him, gossamer rain floated earthwards on the still air.

There was no breeze.

He held his hand up. He hoped Rosi and Sina understood he wanted them to stay where they were.

He moved forward, boots splashing a filthy puddle. The light didn't come with him. He blinked moisture from his eyes, not trusting the clumsy fingers of his bad hand to do the job.

Out of the torch's reach, something moved, something that wasn't an old sheet or scrap of canvas atop a pile of rubbish.

Do you run, or do you stand?

Old Man Ulrich's voice whispered, the dampness of the night much like the spray of beer that often accompanied his father's words when he grabbed his arm to hiss wisdom in his ear.

As he reached the torch, a face separated from the shadows and turned towards him. Not from a pile of rubbish as he had supposed, but from one figure atop another. One, wearing a soldier's garb, was on his back in the filth, the second man straddled him, face dark with blood.

A face that was too long, thin and pale.

The demon hissed at him, rain washing blood from its face onto what was once a white open-necked shirt.

It wasn't Madleen. So, this must be her maker. The one that had despoiled and corrupted her. Taken her and changed her. Stolen everything she was and might ever be and debased it into something foul and unholy.

He didn't love Madleen. He barely knew her. But she'd stirred something in him, something he'd thought dead, something broken and lost. For the barest flicker of a wounded heart, something that had felt like being alive.

He surged forward, cloak flying out behind him, sabre drawn back.

An instant kill. Nothing else worked against these

things. He'd seen how fast they could heal in The Wolf's Tower.

Let's see you heal your head back onto your neck!

Old Man Ulrich's sword flashed, cutting the sodden air. Someone screamed; it might have been him.

In the shadows between the fingers of light thrown out by the sputtering tar torch, he saw Saul the Bloodless, Alms, Cleever, Jarl and the rest of the Red Company's demons. All laughing. All covered in blood. The blood of the children he now heard screaming and crying every single night. The children he'd done nothing to save.

Because he hadn't stood. He'd run, and he'd kept on running ever since.

The thing stayed where it was, one knee on either side of the soldier, large, black eyes looking up at him, unblinking, inhuman, unafraid. Rain dripped down its white cheeks like tears.

He expected it to roll away, twist and be gone. To swipe the sword from his hand, and those wickedly sharp teeth filling its slash of a mouth to be at his throat. For it to rip and rend and do to him what should have been done back in The Wolf's Tower.

To send him to Hell.

Instead, the thing choked two thick, wet words.

"Thank you..."

And then his father's sabre took its head from its shoulders.

Chapter Two

Any deal you make with the Devil is one you will live to regret...

Who had told her that? She couldn't remember for certain. It had the air of Father about it, though it might well have been Magnus. Her old tutor had a fondness for mumbling profundities almost as great as his love for cheese.

Regardless, someone had said that to her once. She wouldn't have wanted to spare the time from combing hair to think about it then. Whoever had said it, however, was undoubtedly right.

The Devil never cut you a good deal.

He always got your soul at the end of the day, and anything he gave you in return would be worth much less than that.

She thought of Saul's head on a platter.

And *Graf* Bulcher roasting over a fire.

Almost anything.

She drew her cloak more tightly around her. The shadows were deep and plentiful, but as she wasn't using her eyes, it didn't matter. She was simply following her feet.

In truth, whoever Flyblown was, he probably wasn't the Devil.

Still...

"We have a deal?" Flyblown asked.

"A deal?"

"A compact, if you prefer? An aligning of common interests. Mutual backscratching," he grinned, "How about bedfellows! Just like you and young Ulrich."

"How do you know so much about me?"

The grin stretched wider. So far, in fact, she almost expected Flyblown's pale skin to start splitting, "I have an inquisitive nature. One of my many curses."

Something about the way he said that made her want to shiver.

She added it to the list.

Then sucked in a breath, "We have a deal."

"Do you wish to shake on it?"

She remembered the way his arm had felt when she squeezed it.

Solace shook her head.

"Very well. We don't need to; you already carry my mark."

Her inner thigh smarted, seemingly in tune with his words.

"Your mark?"

"You are mine now. And I am yours. Till our business concludes."

"You've scarred me?"

His shoulders went up and down, "It's hardly

anywhere noticeable. And every honest deal does require a signature."

She lifted her chin towards his eyes. Despite the lack of light, Flyblown was visible enough, which was odd, but from whatever angle she tried, his eyes remained forever in shadow. Perhaps they really were black, like Lucien's had turned.

"Where do I cut you?"

Flyblown laughed, "You are more amusing than I expected."

Behind him, one of the dead oil lamps flared back into life.

Before she could jump out of the way, he scooped up her hand, bowed and pressed it to his lips.

Neither warmth nor wetness accompanied his kiss. It felt more like dried meat. Dried meat left by an open window one January night.

"My lady of the Broken Tower..."

When he straightened himself, several more oil lamps blinked back into existence.

"My Lord Flyblown," she nodded. She'd managed not to recoil in disgust when *Graf* Bulcher slithered his bloated pink tongue over her hand, so she could pay this monster the same courtesy.

"I suggest you find your friends. They may be experiencing... difficulties. You will find there are things requiring your attention here before you can start hunting monsters."

"Where-"

Flyblown silenced her with a raised finger, "Just follow

your feet, my lady, just follow your feet. The *sight* will always take you where you want to go. If you but let it."

With that, he turned on his heels, pulled the hood of his cloak up and walked away. The remaining oil lamps reignited in time to his heels' beat on the cobbles.

"And remember..." he called without looking back, "...no mentioning me to Morlaine..."

Then he faded into the darkness. Footsteps lingered behind him for a second or two before vanishing as well.

Only as she stood alone did she think to blurt out, "But where do I find Bulcher?!"

The only answer came from the patter of rain on stone.

And a distant scream from somewhere in the shadows of Madriel.

It was not the last one.

As she walked the dark streets, some sounded nearby, others rumbled like far-off thunder, so faint you couldn't entirely be sure you'd heard anything at all.

Every now and then, the sound of nailed boots came echoing out of the night, and she found some deep pool of shadow till they passed. Lucien's men for the most part, occasionally some of the old men of the Watch too. They all wore grim faces and frowns beneath their helms.

They looked worried. And some of them downright scared.

Was this a good idea?

Probably not.

But Flyblown had said Renard and Morlaine were in trouble. She needed to find them, and she wasn't going to spend the night sitting by her window listening to other people's screams.

Flyblown had told her something was wrong here, and her *sight* agreed. It hadn't said a lot since they'd left The Wolf's Tower, but it had peeled open an eye now. And it didn't like whatever it saw very much at all.

She didn't trust Flyblown, but the *sight* was something she'd sworn never to ignore again. If she'd paid more attention to it before, perhaps her home would not be a ruin, her father dead, and her brother... wherever and whatever he was now.

So, she would let her feet follow the *sight* and take her to Renard and Morlaine. They needed her help; they needed to be together. They were all she had.

She didn't want to be alone.

That thought thickened her throat.

Where would she be if she lost them too? She'd lost everything and everyone else in her life. It almost made her head swim, as if she stood on the battlements of a high tower, toes poking over the edge of the stonework. Darkness above, darkness below. Separated from the rest of the world, save she held the hand of a blood-sucking demon on one side and a man who had both betrayed and saved her on the other.

If those fingers should slip from hers...

More feet came hurtling out of the night behind her. She moved into a deeply recessed doorway.

Men hurried past, serenaded by clanking metal and creaking leather.

She pressed herself further back to escape the light of their torches.

Why am I hiding from them?

She'd grown up around armed men, she'd never had cause to fear Father's soldiers, but Kadelberg, Lutz and the others had been, by and large, good men, and the ones that weren't, knew better than to even so much as look the wrong way at the *Freiherr's* daughter.

But these were not good men, and Father's protection was... long gone.

Whether through *sight*, instinct or common sense, she knew running into these men at night would not be wise.

Once the light and noise passed. She sucked in a breath and tried to fathom which way to go. Following her feet to find Morlaine and Renard sounded easy, but she suspected there was far more to it than simply... following her feet.

Before she could move those feet, let alone follow them, another scream rang out. She recoiled backwards as if physically slapped, this one close, loud, and so full of terror. It sounded like those that had echoed around The Wolf's Tower the night the Red Company destroyed her life.

Were they here?

Was that what her *sight* was warning her about?

Silence returned to Madriel, but someone was dying out there. She'd heard enough people die to recognise death's song.

She stood, knees slightly bent, peering into the darkness.

Surely Flyblown would have told her if Saul and his demons were here? Wouldn't he? His fingernail marks smarted on her thigh. Why should she trust anything he said? She didn't know who he was, *what* he was or why he was helping her either. If he was helping her at-

Stop it!

Renard and Morlaine were all that mattered for now.

More screams, followed by a series of shouts, split the darkness, and she scurried back into the door itself.

Which swung slowly open behind her.

She stared at it.

Who left their door unlocked and unlatched at night?

Admittedly, she'd grown up in a castle rather than a town, but it did not seem likely in a time of war, want, lawlessness and hunger. It was a fine house too, large and built of stone, a merchant or some other monied fellow's home. Someone who owned things worth stealing and therefore even more inclined to ensure their door remained locked and barred.

Still, it was none of her business. Renard and Morlaine weren't going to be inside. And her feet certainly weren't taking-

"Help me..."

A voice rolled out of the house. A woman's. Full of misery and fear.

Part of her wanted to run. It wasn't her business. She needed to find Renard and Morlaine, saddle the horses Lucien had assured her Renard had bought with her silver and leave. *Graf* Bulcher was out there, Saul the Bloodless was out there, the Red Company were out there. And, somewhere, Torben was out there, too.

And nothing about the black rectangle before her made her think going through it would do anything but delay her finding them.

"I can't find my child…" the woman sobbed, "…I can't find my husband…"

Solace put one foot on the threshold and peered in. Candlelight seeping from a room dusted the end of an otherwise unlit corridor.

Behind her, more voices cried out. Not screams this time, but shouts of alarm. Then the crack of a pistol or musket.

The woman inside wailed at the shot, "Help me… please… someone…"

Her inner thigh started to throb. Flyblown's mark. Did that mean something, or was it just chaffed from walking?

More nailed boots came running down the street. What was happening? She stepped into the house and closed the door.

As it clicked shut, the crying stopped.

"Has some kindly soul come to help me…?"

Solace listened to the sounds of boots and voices pass by outside.

"I'm scared I'll never see my son again…" the woman sniffed. It was difficult to tell where the voice came from, though she fancied it wasn't from upstairs, "…and then Klaus won't love me anymore…"

She took a step forward.

"Where are you?" Solace asked, her voice startlingly loud in the silent house.

"Along here!" the woman said, "Have you seen my son? Bring him to me, please!"

Just a woman in distress. She could help, or ignore

her and leave. Either way, why did her hand rest on the long-bladed knife hanging from her belt? And why did Flyblown's mark tingle and smart so much? And most importantly, why did she feel a sudden and certain sense of dread.

That was the *sight*, whispering and warning. She was sure.

Yet, despite all she'd said about trusting the *sight*, the feet she was following led her down the unlit corridor towards the woman's voice.

*

Screams echoed around the alley. Once he focused on them, he decided they were more like shrieks.

Dragging his eyes from the two corpses, he checked over his shoulder. Rosi still held the lantern, though it shook enough to send their shadows jigging over the walls, free hand clamped over her mouth, eyes saucer-wide. Sina, however, was the one making the racket, bent half-forward and hopping from one foot to the other as if the Devil himself had warmed the earth beneath her feet.

"Shut up!" he snapped.

When she kept on hollering, he thought about slapping her, but as that would mean putting his sword down to free up his one good slapping hand, it was easier to live with the wailing screeches she was vomiting into the world.

He crouched next to the two bodies. The one underneath was Piet, the younger and slightly less obnoxious of the two mercenaries they'd talked to only a few minutes before.

His throat had been torn open; dark bubbles popped in the bloody wound, and a gurgling hiss escaped his lips. He still lived. Piet's eyes, wide and scared, moved towards him, though they didn't seem to focus on anything.

Ulrich rolled the headless corpse of the demon off him and found the man's hand. He squeezed it as best he could with his numb fingers. A little pressure returned through his glove.

"I am sorry, there is nothing I can do..."

Blood pooled around Piet from the gaping wound in his throat. No dressing was going to staunch the flow nor replace what he'd already lost. If Morlaine was here... he looked around. A demon's blood healed most wounds; he'd seen that in The Wolf's Tower when he'd briefly served the Red Company, but, despite Sina's shrieking, Morlaine did not return.

When he turned back, Piet's eyes had turned to glass, and the pressure on his bad hand evaporated.

"Rest in peace, brother..." he muttered.

"A devil! A devil!" Sina managed to wrestle her incoherent shrieks into words; she pointed at the corpse of the thing that had killed the mercenary.

He followed her finger to the severed head of the demon. Other than the blood smeared about its lips, nothing was demonic about the face staring back at him. It was unremarkable save for no longer being on its owner's shoulders. A round, jowly face with a reseeding hairline and a prominent wart on the cheek. The body was a little on the plump side too.

Easing himself back upright, he sheathed his sword. He didn't expect any more demons; Morlaine was no doubt pursuing Madleen, and he had dispatched her maker. Business was taken care of, but as much as he hated to admit the demon was right about anything, wild talk of devils would summon the witchfinders and get the pyres built in the square in no time at all.

"What are you babbling about, woman?!"

He put a hand on either arm when she carried on and shook her as best he could till some sense returned.

"A demon..." she said, eyes finally fixing on him, "...I've never seen such a hideous, unholy thing! 'tis witchcraft! A spawn of Satan! A-"

Now he did slap her.

"Stop talking nonsense!"

Her eyes widened and she shuffled backwards, but at least shut up. He pressed his lips together and held her eye however much he wanted to look away. He'd never hit a woman before and couldn't say he cared for it, but he needed to stop her blathering about witchcraft before it reached other ears.

She blinked, eyes already filling with tears. Which didn't make him feel any better.

"What do you think your saw, Sina?"

"A monstrosity, sir, something from the pit."

He moved aside, "What do you see now?"

Sina kept her eyes down.

"Look at him, woman! Tell me what you see?" he snatched the lantern from Rosi and stood over the corpses, "What do you see? Any demons?"

Slowly Sina raised her eyes; they moved between the two bodies, then fixed on the severed head.

"*Do you?*"

Sina shook her own head.

"It was a trick of light and shadow, nothing more. This man has attacked and killed one of the soldiers we spoke to earlier. For what reason, I do not know. But he is *not* some witch's summoning."

Sina didn't appear convinced; he considered picking up the head and shoving it in her face but decided that would be going a bit too far.

Instead, he turned to Rosi, "Did you see anything demonic?"

The older woman stared back at him for a couple of frosted breaths, "No, Nothing like that. 'tis like you said. Just a fight."

"So," he stepped back towards Sina, "no more silly talk of witchcraft or demons. Such words can cost lives. Do you understand me?"

"She understands," Rosi put an arm around the younger woman, though her eyes stayed levelled on him.

The sound of approaching feet dragged his attention away. He let his hand drop from the sword's hilt when Morlaine walked into the light. Her gaze flicked from the two women to the corpses and back again.

The demon was hard to read, but she seemed more concerned by the presence of Rosi and Sina than the dead men.

"A man attacked one of the soldiers," he said quickly, "looks like he cut his throat; I managed to kill him before

241

he pounced on us. A mad man, I'd wager."

The weight of Rosi's stare rested upon him. She didn't believe that any more than Morlaine would, but at least she had the wits not to be gabbling about demons.

"Why are they here?" Morlaine demanded, ignoring the women.

"They... followed me..." he replied, feeling the heat in her cold dark eyes.

"Get rid of them, *now!*" the demon hissed before twisting away to stand over the dead.

He spat on the ground, even though his mouth felt dry as ashes, then he jerked his chin at the courtyard, "Come..."

He headed back up the alley, after half a dozen paces looking to confirm they were picking their way through the refuse after him.

Back in the courtyard, he waited for them to catch up. The rain had abated again, though the air still carried the damp chill of its memory. Given all the screaming, he'd expected people to be out investigating the commotion, but the lantern showed no one on the cobbles.

The days they lived in. People were locking themselves indoors and praying whatever was happening outside did not cross their threshold.

Sina was still snivelling when they caught up with him; he shot her a sour look and immediately hated himself for it.

"Go back to the Meeting House this time. Directly and quickly."

Neither woman made a move to leave the circle of

lantern light.

"I think the trouble has passed; you will be safe now," he didn't know any such thing for sure. If Morlaine hadn't tracked Madleen down, another demon remained, but he had dealt with her maker, so the worst was over now.

"We will, sir?" Rosi asked him. Other things hovered on her tongue, but she didn't give them breath in front of her friend.

"You will," he said, more confidently, walking them to the passageway.

He should give them the lantern, but he had discovered what a coward he was back in The Wolf's Tower, so he held onto it and settled for seeing them through. Once out on the street on the other side, he bid them goodnight.

"Go," he said when they stood blinking at him.

If there'd gone the first time, they'd be indoors by now... they're not my problem.

"You will be safe," he insisted, though the distant crack of a pistol shot somewhere in the town rather undermined that reassurance.

"What is happening?" Rosi mouthed, one arm still slung around Sina's shoulders.

"'tis just the way the world is now..." he said, then turned on his heels and left them.

He had nothing to feel bad about, he told himself. Forcing two scared women walk home alone at night hardly compared to leaving children to be slaughtered by demons.

Was it now?

Morlaine was crouched over the corpses when he

returned to the alley.

"What are you doing?"

The demon was busy carving open Piet's savaged throat with a dagger.

"Making this look less like a vampire's work."

Once satisfied, she dropped the blade, which he assumed had been Piet's, and pulled the demon's headless corpse back on top of the soldier. After retrieving the head, she placed it on Piet's chest.

"Did you find Madleen?" he asked.

"No."

"The other soldier?"

Morlaine shook her head as she rose to her feet. She thrust a bloody hand at him, "Give me the lantern."

He did as she asked.

Carefully she unscrewed the cap and poured oil over the bodies.

"There's not a lot left," he warned.

Morlaine ignored him.

After returning the lantern she retrieved the tar torch which had all but smouldered out.

"Pity everything is so damp," she sighed, tossing it onto the bodies.

"If everything wasn't so damp, you'd likely be burning down half the town right now," he said, watching the torch splutter and fizz for a few seconds. The oil took with a whoosh, making him step sharply away. The stink of burning oil and flesh took him back to The Darkway; the screams of dying men and horses echoed around his mind.

"Ulrich?" Morlaine asked, coming alongside him.

She licked Piet's blood from her fingers, which at least drove The Darkway from his thoughts.

He shook his head.

"Those women should not have been here."

"I didn't have much choice."

"You should have left this to me."

He nodded at the burning corpses, "I killed the demon. I am not completely useless."

"I am not doubting your martial expertise, Ulrich. Did they see anything?"

"They saw its true face. It was feeding on him when I got here. I took its head, but they saw..." he shrugged, "...I convinced them they saw nothing."

"Convinced?"

"The thing's face was normal by the time it hit the ground. I told them they saw only tricks of light and shadow."

"And they believed you?" Morlaine didn't look like she did.

"I did my best."

"If they talk of witchcraft..."

"Then we had better find Madleen so no one else gets their throat ripped out," he sighed, "at least her maker is dead."

Morlaine slowly shook her head, "No, he isn't?"

"But-"

"He..." she pointed at the burning demon, "...was another new vampire, likely only made in the last night or two. A new vampire's blood is too weak to sire or heal. He did not make Madleen."

His heart sank, "How can you tell?"

"A mature vampire doesn't need to rip anyone's throat out. It leaves evidence; it leaves questions. We survive by living in the shadows, we survive by..." she waved a hand at the fire now taking the corpses, "...hiding what we are and cleaning up after ourselves."

Ulrich thought of the patches of scorched greasy earth where the Red Company had burnt the bodies from The Wolf's Tower and the village of Tassau.

"I saw plenty of people with their throats ripped out in The Wolf's Tower..." he said quietly.

"This is not the Red Company; they do not behave like most vampires..."

He looked at her. That was something. At least.

"...this is the handiwork of some other mad man..."

Chapter Three

The lighted room was a parlour and a comfortable one.

Heavy woollen curtains, good rugs, sturdy furniture, a generous number of candles burned, expensive beeswax ones too, like they used to have in the family rooms of The Wolf's Tower.

A woman sat in a high-backed chair, away from the candlelight, back rigidly straight, fingers toying with the knitting hanging from a long wooden needle in her lap. Her hair had started to grey, but only just; she was petite, a little plump in the face, but not fat. Only the very rich could afford to be fat.

Solace took all this in quickly, though it was the blood that held her attention.

The woman's gown, unfussy dark silks trimmed with lace at the sleeves and collar, was sodden. As were her face and hands.

Most of it probably came from the corpse stretched out before her. Another woman, younger, small and slight, in a simple cotton dress. She was face down on the floor in a pool of dried blood.

The sitting woman smiled at her, "I would offer refreshment, but I'm afraid Miriam..." she glanced at the body, "...isn't quite herself tonight..."

"No..." Solace swallowed, "...I can see that."

"Poor kitten," the woman dabbed her nose with a bloody handkerchief.

"What happened? Solace asked, her feet, whose trustworthiness she was starting to question, not venturing further into the room.

"Happened, dear?"

"To... your son?"

The woman dropped the handkerchief atop the knitting in her lap, "I don't know. I can't find him. Careless of me, really. I waited so long for him too..."

The rest of the house was silent and dark. Solace's stomach turned slowly. She hoped she was wrong, but she had a fair idea what might have happened to the woman's son.

"What's... what's your name?" Solace checked the corridor behind her. The woman wasn't doing anything threatening, but best to be wary of people covered in blood.

"Frau Stettin," the woman said, "I am Herr Stettin's wife. Herr Stettin is a very important man. A wool merchant and burgher of Madriel. I seem to have lost him too... have you seen Klaus anywhere, dear?"

Solace shook her head. And slowly wrapped a hand around the wired grip of the long-bladed dagger in her belt.

"It seems I am quite alone," Frau Stettin patted herself down until she found the bloody handkerchief on her lap again. She snatched it up and started wiping her eyes.

"Herr Stettin went out to find food. Tasty food, I told him. He said he was so hungry he couldn't think. He always has such an appetite that man. But that was hours ago. Simply hours..." Frau Stettin's eyes snapped in her direction and narrowed, "...he didn't send you here, did he? With food? *Tasty* food, mind?"

"No, sorry," she slipped the dagger free.

"Shame. I am getting a little hungry too..." she let the handkerchief drop back into her lap "...I don't quite know what's come over me. Ever since our unexpected guest, I've barely been able to stop myself..." her eyes brushed over Miriam's corpse, "...eating."

She should run. Find Morlaine and let her dispatch this creature. But you couldn't keep running from monsters if you wanted to destroy the Red Company. What was it Renard sometimes mumbled to himself when he thought she wasn't listening?

Do you run, or do you stand?

Yes, that was it. And Solace von Tassau wasn't running from monsters anymore. She had to learn how to deal with them.

She edged into the room.

"Your unexpected guest?"

"Yes. Nice fellow. A bit peculiar. But nice! Oh, where is my boy? Have you seen him?"

"No. I haven't. What was your unexpected guest's name?"

"Name?" Frau Stettin frowned, "My, my... I've quite forgotten! Or maybe he didn't tell me? He *was* peculiar.

From Carinthia. I remember that. They're all peculiar down there, so, no surprise, really being..." her eyes turned to the candles and narrowed "...from Carinthia. That's what he said. The Man from Carinthia!"

The Duchy of Carinthia lay in the south of the Empire, on the eastern border of the Venetian Republic. Tutor Magnus had taught her that; she remembered the maps he had lovingly unrolled across the big reading table in The Wolf Tower's library as he tried, mostly unsuccessfully, to spark some interest in geography.

As far as she recalled, he'd never mentioned anything about the peculiarity of Carinthians.

Solace took another step towards the woman, dagger held straight against her leg. It was a fencing dagger, with extended quillons to catch a sword blade. Light, long and sharp, Renard said it would be easier for her to handle than a sword. It was old, though; the blade nicked and scratched. Morlaine had lent her a whetstone and told her to sharpen it.

A blade can never be too sharp.

She'd burnt men and demons alive. She'd blown others to smithereens. She wished she'd killed more of them. She wished she'd killed them all and danced on their rotting corpses. But plunging a dagger into someone suddenly seemed a lot more personal.

Especially when that someone looked like a harmless middle-aged woman. Well, harmless if you ignored the blood covering her face and clothes anyway.

Solace tried not to look beyond the blood.

"Where is the Man from Carinthia now?"

"Oh..." Frau Stettin turned her eyes to the ceiling, "...I expect he is walking above. That's what he does. Apparently."

"And what does he do.... *above?*"

Another step. The kill had to be instant. She knew that. And as sharp as her long dagger now was, she couldn't hack off Frau Stettin's head with it.

"He spreads the word, my dear; he spreads the *word.*"

"The word of God?"

Frau Stettin laughed. Her teeth were uncommonly white behind the blood-stained lips.

"No. The word of what is to come."

"And what is to come?" Solace kept talking, kept moving, kept staring at that spot in Frau Stettin's chest where her heart resided. Had she paid more heed to Magnus' lessons on anatomy than she had geography? She hoped so.

Frau Stettin's eyes, which were almost all pupil in the wan candlelight, fell from the ceiling to fix on Solace, "The undead are coming to feast upon the World's Pain," her smile grew more fulsome. Toothy, even. "'tis the end of the world, my dear. Won't that be nice? The dead have risen, and they shall inherit the Earth..."

Her feet decided they didn't want to go any further.

"And the dead are... here?"

Frau Stettin nodded, "The Man from Carinthia brought the Word with him. He walked above and spread the Word. He gave the word to Herr Stettin and to me. We were reborn," as her gaze fell to the corpse on the floor her smile turned to a frown, "he didn't give the Word to Miriam. Not

252

worthy, you see? So... she became part of the World's Pain..."

"You feasted on her?"

"Oh yes..." Frau Stettin's tongue darted along her bloody lips "...she was tasty!"

Solace wanted to glance behind her but forced herself to keep her eyes on the demon.

"Where is Herr Stettin now?"

"I told you. He went out for food. Tasty food. We must feast upon the World's Pain before we can spread the Word too..." her mouth curled into something carnal and ill-fitting upon her soft features "...did he send you, my dear?"

"I have not seen Herr Stettin..."

"Oh... never mind... have you seen our boy?"

Solace shook her head and started moving towards the seated creature again. The wire wrapped around the dagger's grip cutting through her sweaty palm.

"We waited so long for him, then he went away. I can't remember his face now. Isn't that strange?"

"Memories can play tricks."

"Why, yes, I suppose they can. Do you remember your father's face?"

"My... father?"

Her feet stopped again.

"We all forget our father's face in the end. But never our child's. Such things should not come to pass..."

"I remember my father."

You don't possess foresight, Solace, just ignorance. Your mother was a sick and troubled woman... and clearly so are you...

She felt the sting of Father's hand on her cheek as sharply as the sting of his words in her mind. The last words he ever spoke to her, atop The Wolf Tower's barbican after she'd set the oil Torben had doused the men and demons waiting in The Darkway below with alight.

He had thought her a lunatic and a murderess, slapped her face and stormed away. She heard his boots on the icy stone, followed by the slam of the heavy oak door as he went into the castle; the same tears pricked her eyes, knowing he was going to die, knowing she was never going to see him again.

"I will never forget my father's face..." she whispered.

"That's good, dear. As it should be," Frau Stettin beamed, clasping her hands together, "and I dare say you won't forget mine either."

Her smile stretched wider.

Then Frau Stettin's soft, round face changed, and the demon she now was came flying out of the chair at her...

*

"How do we find Madleen and her maker?"

Morlaine kept her dark eyes fixed front, "We follow the bodies."

More shouts echoed from another street.

"Do you think he made more demons?"

Perhaps Lucien's men had all got roaringly drunk and were entertaining themselves with the age-old soldierly pastimes of rape and pillage, but he suspected the cries, screams and shouts that kept breaking the night's silence were even darker in origin.

"I don't know. As I said before, vampires do not make many other vampires. And when they do, they usually..."

"Usually what?"

Morlaine let out a long sigh, "Care for them."

"Care?" he lifted an eyebrow she did not see. Her eyes remained forward as they walked along the deserted street.

"The change is confusing, disorientating, terrifying. The new body and new desires can break the mind, at least temporarily. If a vampire sires someone, it is rarely on a whim. It is because they cared, or wanted, or desired, or some other reason they twisted to justify the cruelty. So, they usually stay close to..." a shrug accompanied the next sigh "...care."

"Like a mother suckling its young."

"If you like."

"Except your kind don't suckle with milk, do they?"

Morlaine didn't answer the question; instead, she said, "Madleen and the man you killed were left alone. They both sounded, from what you've told me, deranged. A vampire would normally keep their produce under lock and key so they don't run amok, so they can learn and regain their senses."

"But this one didn't?"

"It does not appear so. And it troubles me greatly."

"Troubled Piet greatly too..." he said, only half under his breath.

That did earn him a look.

He glanced away. Morlaine had a most unsettling regard.

"Why did that demon thank me before I killed him?"

A few strides worth of echoed footsteps interrupted the silence before Morlaine replied, softly and with a faraway voice, "Because he did not want to be what he had become, what he was going to become."

"Become?"

"A creature enthralled and enraptured solely by its desire for blood."

"Like you?"

Those cold dark eyes again.

"Yes, like me."

"Then why are you hunting them and not us?"

She turned her attention front again, "If all you are going to do is ask inane questions, you should go back to Solace. You are distracting me."

They arrived at a crossroads; dark houses stretched away in four directions. Nothing moved as far as the lantern reached; they'd been here at least once already. Madriel wasn't a big town. Which made getting lost in it earlier all the more galling.

Before they decided which of the turnings to take - he had no idea if Morlaine was following some arcane sense to find the other demons or they were just wandering hopefully - voices came from the street to their left, accompanied by a sudden wash of lantern and torch light.

He glanced at the demon, but when she made no move to get away from the approaching men, he did the same.

Half a dozen lights lit a group of angry-looking men; some were pointing and shouting in their direction. They started running towards them. As they grew closer, he could see they were brandishing an assortment of weapons;

cleavers, hooks, knives, cudgels, the man in front even hauled an ancient-looking broadsword.

"Should we-"

"No," she said.

"You!" a stocky man in a heavy coat yelled, pointing a chair leg at them, "Who are you?!"

There were maybe a dozen of them. A mob. Lanterns and torches danced around them.

"What business is it of yours?" Morlaine asked, pulling back her hood as she peered into the lights.

The expressions of the men changed somewhat on seeing Morlaine. They hadn't expected a woman.

The man with the broadsword shouldered his way to the front; a stringy fellow with a voluminous grey beard. He looked barely able to carry that great lump of metal, let alone swing it.

"There is witchcraft afoot, *fraulein*, so you will answer our questions!"

"Witchcraft?" he jumped in before Morlaine could say something condescending.

"Demons have been seen in town. One assaulted Herr Stockhausen's family but an hour ago!" a hatchet-faced man cried, violently waving his flaming torch enough to make the man next to him jump out of the way.

"Surely... some mistake?"

"No damn mistake. People are being attacked all over town," the old man wielding the broadsword said before raising a bony finger to jab it at him, "So, you will tell us who you are and why you are on the street after dark!"

"We are not demons, friend," he tried a smile. Given

how Morlaine glowered at the men, one of them needed to.

"Maybe not," another spat, "but *witches* must have summoned the demons. You don't get demons without witches."

"'tis the refugees, the *strangers*," the man with the chair leg shouted to a chorus of approving mutters, "they have brought devilry to our town!"

"I do not know you…" the swordsman said; he looked like he wanted to point at them with his old blade, but decided it a bit too heavy for that, "…and I know everyone in Madriel. I was born here. Lived here my whole life. I am Aumann the Apothecary. Everyone knows me, everyone trusts me. Honest and straight, pious and loyal," he half turned to the men around him, as if addressing them as much as Morlaine and he.

The mob at his back nodded as one.

"Never any trouble here before the idolatrous Catholics started the war, and the strangers came to eat our food, whore on our streets, steal our money, and frighten our children. If that was not enough, they have now brought witchcraft here too!"

More approving shouts, accompanied by assorted weapons shaken at the sky.

He didn't have Solace's *sight*. But he was starting to get a very bad feeling all the same.

"We are not refugees. We are just travelling through. On our way to Naples."

Aumann curled back his lips far enough to expose bright red gums and the blackened remnants of his teeth, "Travelling through, eh? Yet here you are, walking the streets at night while demons attack good Christian folk in their own homes."

"We should put the question to them," one man offered to further mutterings of approval.

"There are witchfinders in Lübben; we will send word tomorrow. They will help us root this evil out!" the old man announced, twisting to address the men behind him again.

"Why wait? We should put the question to them ourselves!" the man with the chair leg shouted, eyes lingering on Morlaine.

"No one is putting a question to anyone," Morlaine spat back, gaze sweeping the men, "we are not witches, we are not demons, we-"

"Be quiet, woman!" he grabbed her arm with his bad hand.

A woman standing before a mob of angry men showing not only no fear, but outright defiance was not going to persuade any of these fools they weren't worthy of questioning with hot irons.

"These are good Christian men protecting their homes and families; you will show them the respect they are due!"

Her eyes flared, but he squeezed her arm as best he could regardless.

Leave this to me.

"You must forgive my wife's cousin," he said, still gripping the demon's arm; he smiled at the men, "she is young and wilful. And will benefit greatly when she marries..."

"She seems old not to be married?" Aumann peered at Morlaine in much the way he had examined Jannick's horses that afternoon.

"Wilful," Ulrich repeated, putting his shoulder between Morlaine and the men.

"A lamentable condition," the old man said, turning hooded eyes back on Ulrich, "but-"

Another scream split the night.

Wide-eyed men raised their weapons and lights. There was nothing to see. Several muttered prayers run through the group.

"More devilry at work," the old man hissed, "more of the strangers' witchcraft."

"'tis not our doing, friend, but I am happy to lend my sword to the defence of your town against any evil," Ulrich dropped his bad hand to the hilt of his father's sabre.

"We should lock them in the gaol till the witchfinders get here," the hatchet-face man suggested.

"We have committed no-"

"There! By God, there!"

One of the men pointed down the street. A figure stood at the edge of the circle of light cast by their lanterns and torches.

Hunched and bloodied, cradling one arm against its body with the other, large black eyes stared at them from a long, corpse-white face. Tawny hair framed that awful face. Madleen wasn't wearing her linen cap anymore, but no one would mistake her for either a virgin or a whore.

Seeing her like that, hideous, terrifying, and yet pitiful, made something sickly turn inside Ulrich. He didn't know if he wanted to scream or cry.

The latest soul he had been unable to save.

For a moment, no one moved or spoke, as if everyone, Madleen included, was deciding if they should charge or flee.

Then Madleen twisted away and scuttled back into the darkness.

A man screamed, "Burn the witch!" Flaming torch in hand, he ran after Madleen. Over half the group went with him, shouting curses and brandishing their rough assortment of weapons.

Morlaine pressed her lips hard together. She wanted to get to Madleen before the mob did, but it was too late to keep word of the demons in Madriel from the locals' ears now. And Aumann the Apothecary was in no mood to let them go about their business.

The old man turned his eyes back to them, happy to leave the demon-chasing to others.

"A vile creature despoiling our fair streets! Seen with our very own eyes! No one can deny it now! Witchcraft!" Aumann's eyes narrowed, "and it appeared just as we were questioning you two...?"

The hatchet-faced man, who'd stayed at Aumann's shoulder, rushed forward and grabbed Morlaine's arm, "Come with us, witch!"

Morlaine shrugged him off and stepped back, sweeping aside her cloak to hiss her sword halfway from its sheath.

Ulrich moved across her before she could get it all the way clear.

"There's no need for-"

"A sword!" Aumann pointed, "she carries a sword! What normal maid wields a blade?"

261

"These are dark times. We have travelled far; we have to protect ourselves on the road," Ulrich protested, trying hard to keep the smile on his face.

"She is dressed like a man too," another of the mob who hadn't fancied chasing Madleen peered over Aumann's bony shoulder.

The old man nodded, "Questions must be asked about this strangeness... take their weapons and search them, lads, then to the gaol with them..."

He moved back to Morlaine's side, "You can't kill any of these fools," he hissed in her ear as Aumann's remaining men spread out around them.

"Nobody is locking me up for the witchfinders," she replied as they retreated until a wall pressed against their backs.

He dropped the lantern onto the fingers of his bad hand, the weight of it sending tremors up his left arm as he reached for his own sword.

"No one is taking my sword," he told them, dispensing with the smile, "it was my father's and nobody touches it but me."

"Hand it over, son; if you haven't done anything wrong, you've got nothing to worry about," Aumann held out a hand, twitching long, thin fingers in his direction.

Ulrich wondered how many people had heard something similar in the days before they found themselves tied to a stake surrounded by faggots of oil-soaked wood. Glancing at Morlaine, he remembered she likely still had Madleen's severed hand hidden somewhere in that long cloak of hers.

Which would take some explaining.

Damn.

He wrenched his father's sabre clear of its scabbard and faced the men surrounding them.

Chapter Four

Frau Stettin ploughed into her before she could raise the dagger.

The woman was small, but she moved fast and hit hard. Momentarily, it seemed they were flying backwards together, Frau Stettin's mouth gaping to reveal the fangs within.

Then they crashed onto the floor. The back of Solace's head smacked the floorboards, and for an instant, everything turned black. It could only have been an instant; otherwise, everything would have been black forever.

When the world came back into focus, a weight sat on her chest, while Frau Stettin tore at her clothes to find enough skin to sink fangs into.

Solace made to plunge her dagger into the demon. Save the weapon was no longer in her hand. She slapped the floor, trying to find it, but it must have skidded across the boards after she fell.

Perhaps only carrying the one weapon when fighting demons was a mistake.

When it came to such things, she had a suspicion you did not get to make many of those.

With no weapon in reach, she wriggled her hands against Frau Stettin's chest and pushed upwards. She was expecting the task to be impossible, for the creature to be too strong and heavy to shift, but she was able to push her far enough away to see those terrible long features in their entirety.

And her own face reflected in the black mirrors of the thing's eyes.

"Don't fight me, girl," Frau Stettin cried, "I'm hungry!"

The demon swatted one of Solace's arms away and lurched forward, teeth snapping, but the movement was slow and awkward as if she were not fully controlling her own body. Dry, rank breath filled her nostrils like she'd had her face stuffed in a grave.

Solace swung her free arm, knuckle cracking into the demon's skull. Frau Stettin's head jerked, but her hands were now on Solace's shoulders, pinning her down.

Although strong for a woman of any age, her strength was but a fraction of the Red Company's demons.

However, a weakling demon feasting on her blood offered Solace scant comfort.

Frau Stettin, who sat astride her, skirts and petticoats blooming around her, leaned in again, trying to get at her neck, but the movement was stiff and awkward. She could only get near enough to snap at the air before Solace's nose.

She's wearing a corset.

Of course! Her movements weren't demonic

affectations; layers of whalebone and lacquered cotton confined her.

Vanity always came at a price.

Solace bucked and writhed manically; twisting and rolling to avoid Frau Stettin's teeth and hands.

"Please stay still, dear," Frau Stettin pleaded before backhanding Solace hard enough for the ring on her finger to rip across Solace's cheek and split her lip. Blood filled her mouth. Something not lost on the demon.

"Tasty..."

Solace had grown up around soldiers, her brother forever tailing the men of The Wolf Tower's garrison with wide eyes, and she'd followed her big brother wherever he went. The men had always been wary of Torben as if he had some sickness they might catch, but they had mainly indulged the *Freiherr's* little girl.

Father had wanted her education to encompass more than the normal womanly pursuits of music, poetry, needlework and looking pretty. How much was enlightened thinking and how much necessity brought on by the possibility she would inherit the Barony of Tassau, she couldn't say. But as well as Tutor Magnus' - largely vain - attempts to engage her mind in geography, history, literature, politics and philosophy, Father had encouraged her to learn the basics of arms too.

Lutz had been a patient teacher; God rest his soul. She could load and fire a pistol. She knew the difference between a rapier and sabre and the rudiments of strategy.

She'd been too busy dreaming about handsome princes to be paying full attention. But, hanging around soldiers, you picked up certain things simply from listening to their tales, boasts and chatter; mostly in language unsuitable for a young woman looking to marry a prince.

But she'd also heard plenty of talk about how to fight.

And how it almost always paid to fight dirty.

Valour and chivalry were all well and good, but a well-placed kick in the balls at the opportune moment was far more likely to keep you alive.

So, when Frau Stettin dropped her head, Solace ignored those long, sharp, snapping teeth.

And drove her forehead into the demon.

The creature howled. So did Solace. She swung a fist. It didn't hurt as much when it connected with Frau Stettin's skull, but it proved just as satisfying.

Blood gushed from Frau Stettin's nostrils. Whatever unnatural strengths and powers these monsters possessed, their noses seemed as vulnerable to a good whack as anyone else's.

While the demon held her bloody face, Solace wriggled free. Her own face was wet too, blood from her cheek and lip trickling down her chin. Frau Stettin's blood had showered her in a cold spray, too. She wanted to wipe it away but had no time for such niceties.

After scuttling backwards, she tried to jump to her feet. Frau Stettin's hand flashed out, grabbing an ankle and yanking her back down towards those snapping teeth once more.

"Nasty! Tasty!"

She kicked the thing with her free foot. When that didn't loosen the demon's grip, she kicked again.

Something cracked and squelched. Frau Stettin rolled backwards and, with the creature still gripping her ankle, Solace went with her.

She crashed on top of the demon. Frau Stettin yelped and clawed at Solace's dress. Again, she managed to scramble free, knocking over Frau Stettin's chair in the process. Once more, the demon's hand caught her ankle. This time bringing her crashing down onto her knees.

"Nasty! Tasty!" Frau Stettin's wet snigger was in her ear as she slammed into Solace's back.

Searing pain tore through her left shoulder. Her dress was torn, revealing the pale skin beneath. Frau Stettin had pulled aside her coat and cloak far enough to sink fangs into the exposed flesh.

Solace sagged forward onto all fours; Frau Stettin came with her, teeth not letting go. Wet heat poured from her shoulder. For an instant, the pressure was gone before more pain seared the nape of her neck. The demon was working up to the soft meat where blood flowed freest. If those fangs pierced an artery, she was finished.

She didn't need Magnus' anatomy lessons or soldiers' opinion on the quickest places to cut in order to kill a man to know that.

Casting around she looked for her fallen dagger. Surely God would grant her one piece of luck. The blade, however, was neither in sight nor reach.

But one of Frau Stettin's knitting needles was.

Without thought, she grabbed the long wooden needle with her right hand and thrust it as hard as possible over her left shoulder. There was a moment's resistance before she pushed the needle in as far as she could.

A gargling hiss erupted behind her; cold wet air played across the warm, bloody skin of her neck.

Then Frau Stettin slipped off her back and crashed onto the floor, a fist's worth of knitting needle left protruding from her ruptured left eye.

Solace kicked away from the demon's corpse, right hand clamped to her neck, sliding over the floorboards till her back was hard against a wall.

She stared at Frau Stettin, once more an unremarkable, petite middle-aged woman with a slightly plump face. Just one with a knitting needle in her eye.

Heart thumping, Solace sucked in air. Eyes skirting the room for her dagger. Frau Stettin might seem dead, but everyone knew what a trickster the Devil was, and this innocuous-looking woman was one of his creatures.

She couldn't see the dagger through the jumble of upturned furniture and rugs scattered like discarded skins.

"She's dead; it does not matter..." she panted, closing her eyes.

Her head swam; her shoulder was hot and sticky with blood, her face too.

How much blood have I lost?

She opened her eyes. There was quite a lot over Frau Stettin's face, though how much was hers and how much the demon's, she couldn't say.

Solace closed her eyes again.

She felt as exhausted as she had after nights of tramping across the muddy countryside in the wake of Styx's arse.

If I go to sleep, will I ever wake up?

She forced her eyes open again. Frau Stettin was definitely dead. Definitely.

Her face and shoulder hurt abominably. The rest of her wasn't far behind. Save her inner right thigh. Flyblown's mark. That tingled. Quite pleasantly, in fact.

She had an urge to touch it again.

Instead, she focussed her attention on the dead demon. Stroking herself did not seem at all appropriate. Just the loss of blood. Silly thoughts. That's all. A little sleep, and she'd be better. Much better.

She nearly killed me.

The thought bounced around Solace's darkening mind.

Although far weaker than any of the Red Company's demons, Frau Stettin had come within a knitting needle of killing her. How was she supposed to destroy Saul the Bloodless and his merry band of monsters?

She'd been fortunate. Would she be next time?

Finding that needle had been lucky; shoving it blindly into Frau Stettin's eye had been luckier still.

Her head lolled to one side. She didn't want to think about luck or monsters. Too tired. She needed to sleep.

Only a little.

Her free hand flopped into her lap, the warmth of Flyblown's mark tingling through her skirts. She concentrated on that, ignoring everything else in the world as she slipped away from it.

Even the sounds of creaking footsteps coming from upstairs...

*

"Herr Aumann!" a voice boomed, "How it gladdens my cynical old heart to see you so concerned with the well-being of common folk, that you surround them with armed men to ensure their safety. Truly you are a beacon of hope in these dark and bitter times!"

Aumann twisted around, as did the half a dozen men who'd been egging each other on to be the first to risk the edge of their blades.

"Captain Lucien," Aumann spat, "what are you doing here?"

The mercenary bestowed a black-toothed grin on the old burgher, "My job. What, pray tell, are you doing?"

Lucien had four men at his back, none were smiling, and all had a hand on the hilt of their sheathed swords.

"These people." Aumann jabbed a finger in their direction, "are suspected of witchcraft."

"Witchcraft, eh?" Lucien's eyebrow shot up to meet the sagging brim of his hat.

"Yes, and they are refusing to come with us for questioning. A sure sign of guilt!"

"Guilt..." Lucien nodded, hitching thumbs into his weapons belt, "...or common sense. Depends from which angle you look at it, really, don't you think?"

Aumann's scowl deepened.

"These *strangers* are resisting arrest. Take them to the gaol at once, Captain Lucien!"

"It seems to the casual eye," Lucien spread his smile in all directions as he moved to put himself between them and

Aumann's men, "that this could as much be a mob of armed men accosting innocent folk about their lawful business."

"Damn it, Lucien, arrest them. That's an order!"

"I am employed by the town to ensure peace is maintained, the roads are safe to travel and the good folk of Madriel are protected from the multitudinous dangers that swirl around us due to the ongoing political situation and lamentable lawlessness befouling our fair land," Lucien adjusted the tip of one end of his drooping moustache, "in other words, I don't take orders from you."

"I am a burgher of this town!"

"You are *one* of the burghers of this town," Lucien leaned in towards the old man, "and, frankly, none of the others care for you much. So, until the town council pass an edict telling me to take orders directly from you or anybody else, I'll do as I damn well choose."

Behind the town's men the four soldiers started drawing their weapons.

"Lucien..." Aumann growled.

"Witchcraft!" Lucien laughed, addressing the ring of men exchanging glances and fingering their assorted crude weapons, "there is some misunderstanding, gentlemen. This fine fellow is Herr Lutz, a good friend of many years and his wife's cousin. You could not hope to meet more pious, godly, and upstanding people!"

He swivelled on his heels and moved to stand behind Morlaine. Slapping hands on her shoulders, he cried, "This is no witch! I can attest to this woman's impeccably devout holiness. As god-fearing a soul as you will find from

Avignon to Athens! I know for a fact that she spends an extraordinary amount of time on her knees by the bed every night, diligently giving thanks to the Lord for the *enormous* bounty his love provides!"

Ulrich glanced at Morlaine. He had not thought the demon could blush. It was difficult to tell for certain in the uncertain flickering light of lanterns and tar torches, but she suddenly seemed uncharacteristically flushed.

"That's as maybe," Aumann swept a hand towards the men around him, "but they have been seen consorting with a demon! By the eyes of all these godly men. The question must be put to them!"

Lucien turned on the nearest of Aumann's men, a pasty-faced youth with an Adam's apple almost as big as his fist, "And what did you see, my good man?"

"A demon, sir!"

"And how were my friends consorting with it, precisely?"

Lucien's hand shot up when the youth glanced at Aumann and turned his head back to face him, "I was asking you."

"Well, we were talking to them, and this hideous demon appeared!"

"Where?"

"Down there. At the end of *Nordstraße*."

"So, this demon appeared at the end of another street after you started talking to these two. Then what?"

"It... ran off."

Lucien turned to Ulrich, "And what did you see, Herr Lutz?"

"A disfigured woman, she ran off when these men's friends chased her."

"There you have it!" Lucien threw his hands up, "A disfigured woman. Madriel certainly has plenty of them; my lads know most of them very well."

Aumann glared at Lucien's men when they laughed.

"Captain, this is preposterous; people are being attacked all over town, Herr St-"

"If people are being attacked, by demons or otherwise, 'tis my job to deal with it..." he tapped Aumann's pigeon chest with a finger, "...not yours!"

"I must-"

"Go home, Herr Aumann! You must go home. All of you," Lucien cast an eye around the shuffling men, "Gentlemen. If trouble's afoot, 'tis the best place for you to be. Protecting your families, your properties, your livelihoods. Leave unpleasant business to me," he favoured them all with his broken smile, "'tis what you pay me for, after all."

Aumann's men, who'd seemed less inclined to drag them to the town gaol the moment they'd drawn their weapons and even more so when Lucien's mercenaries drew their's, started backing away.

"Do not listen to him! Aumann screeched.

In the distance, another scream broke the silence.

"Witchcraft is abroad this night; we must stamp it out!" Aumann shouted.

"Leave this to us," Lucien said, "Better to ensure your wives and children are safe than chasing... *phantoms*."

One by one the men first dropped their eyes, then their

weapons to their sides.

"We should be at home," one muttered in Aumann's direction, garnering a look that suggested the old man wished he knew enough of witchery to turn him into something unpleasant.

"You haven't heard the last of this!" Aumann spat.

He stared down *Nordstraße* before deciding he didn't much fancy pursuing Madleen alone and hurried after his companions.

"What a fine example of a civil dignitary, so hardworking, forthright and idealistic, always putting the needs of others before any petty ambitions of his own..." Lucien beamed once the old man was out of earshot, "...no wonder the Empire is run so efficiently..."

"Do you ever say anything that isn't the exact opposite of what you mean?" Morlaine asked him, sliding her blade back into its sheath.

"Of course I do," he threw his arms wide, "Oh, love of my life!"

That earnt him the kind of stare most men would find unsettling coming from a woman with cold steel strapped to her thigh.

To his credit, Lucien's smile didn't waver. Instead, he jerked his head down the street and told his men to find out what was happening.

The men nodded and hurried off into the shadows.

"Are you not going with them?" Morlaine asked.

"Oh, I find command works best with the lightest of touches," he said, "besides, as a gentleman, I find myself honour bound to see you safely back to the *Market Inn...*"

"And your bed?"

Lucien flashed another grin.

Ulrich suddenly found himself feeling even more awkward than usual.

"There's no need to trouble yourself, Captain; we can look after ourselves," he said.

"Trouble? 'tis no trouble. Besides, who knows what mischief might intervene without my steely eye, musclebound arm and highly attuned sense of danger to protect you?"

He opened his palm and waved it down the road. Ulrich assumed in the direction of the *Market Inn*. He still was not sure where he was.

He exchanged glances with Morlaine, who gave a barely perceptible twitch of the shoulders. They needed to find Madleen before Aumann's rabble, but they had no plausible excuse to get away from Lucien without raising suspicion. He didn't doubt Morlaine could keep him distracted once they got there, so he started walking the way the mercenary had indicated. If needs be, he would head out alone later.

And this time, he would do his very best to avoid getting lost.

Chapter Five

"You have made the most terrible mess of Frau Stettin..."

She opened her eyes and found she was not in the same room she'd closed them in.

It was a bedchamber. A single lantern burned low next to the bed. Although a luxurious room, the large bed, deep mattress and plump pillows brought her no comfort.

She tried sitting up. When everything swam, she immediately thought better of it and slumped back into pillows piled so high she was half sitting anyway.

A figure stood in the doorway, dressed in shadows.

At first, she thought it Lord Flyblown but this man was much stockier and the accent entirely different.

"I had hopes for her. 'tis wrong to have favourites, of course, but..."

"Who are you?"

"I am from Carinthia."

"I asked who you are, not where you come from."

"I know you did."

He made no move to enter the room; instead, remaining motionless on the threshold, hands folded in front of him.

Solace touched her neck, remembering Frau Stettin's teeth sinking into her flesh. Blood soaked her skin and ripped dress, but the wounds felt like days old scabs.

"I healed you," the man said.

Her fingers stopped moving, "You gave me your blood?"

The man adjusted his feet, head jutting forward, "You know what I am? I had a feeling you might. 'tis hard to kill a vampire, even a newborn. And all the harder if you do not know what one is. You did. So, you do. That is interesting. Tell me?"

"Am I...?" her words trailed off into a deep swallow and a sudden pounding of her heart.

"Not yet."

She shuffled up the bed. Her coat and cloak were neatly folded over a chair next to the door. The Man from Carinthia must have taken them off her. She pulled up the flap of the torn dress to cover her naked shoulder, imagining his hands on her while she was helpless, seeing the blood dripping into her mouth.

Like Renard told her the demons had done to their injured men in The Wolf's Tower to heal their wounds.

Like Saul had done to Torben...

"Why did you do that?" she managed to ask.

"Because you have the knowing of us. Few do. That will change. But, for now, 'tis unusual. I want to know how you know. I could wait till after you are reborn and ask then, but the probabilities are high that you will not survive. And then I will never know. I do not like not knowing. I walk above so that I may know everything there is to know. So, tell me?"

"You are not going to make me the same as you."

She thought he smiled, but the shadows obscuring his face were deep, "You say that as if you have a choice."

"There is always a choice."

"You are a survivor, I think. A fighter. That is useful. If you are reborn you will, in time, begat many for me, I think. The probabilities say so. I always listen to the probabilities."

"Damn the probabilities," she swung her legs off the bed. The world did not spin as much as she feared.

This time she was certain he smiled. A flash of white lit the darkness.

"What is your name?" he asked.

She wanted to run from the room, but the Man from Carinthia blocked the only door. She sucked in air. He wasn't making any immediate move toward her, so, better to talk. Buy herself time to think and straighten her mind.

"Celine," she said.

The man's head tilted, "That is a lie. Why would you lie about your name? Because your real name conceals a secret you do not wish others to know. So the probabilities tell me. You do not know me, so it is not me you wish to hide your identity from. Then who? Why? What have you done?"

Perhaps talking was not such a good idea.

She pushed herself to her feet, twisting immediately to brace her back against the wall. The Man from Carinthia stayed in the doorway, hands still before him.

"Who? Why? What have you done?" he demanded.

She almost told him. There was something compelling about his tone, or maybe it was just fear. Either way, she held her tongue. It seemed unlikely *Graf* Bulcher would hear she was alive from this demon, but she would let nothing, however unlikely, make her vengeance even more difficult than it already was.

The Man from Carinthia's head tilted the other way.

"*Graf* Bulcher..." he whispered.

"How-"

She stopped herself.

That smile came again.

"My blood is in you, so part of you is in me. Whispering like all the others who still live. It will whisper until you die or are reborn. Tell me what I have asked."

"If you can hear my mind, why do I need to?"

"Because the whispers are always the faint cries of distant lunatics, never the lucid prayers of the devout."

"Thank you for making that so much clearer..."

Her eyes darted around the room, searching for a weapon of some kind. Her dagger presumably still lay downstairs, and there wasn't even a knitting needle to hand in the bedroom. Besides, she suspected the Man from Carinthia would be a lot harder to stop than Frau Stettin.

"You cannot kill me," he sounded amused. Her eyes snapped back to him, "Tell me about *Graf* Bulcher. I have heard of him."

"What do you know of Bulcher?"

"Speaking his name sends such hatred coursing

through you, doesn't it?"

"What do you know?"

Keep talking. And stop thinking!

"He is a despicable, loathsome man who hides his weakness behind cruelty, greed and lust. He is a man of power and wealth, which sings so eloquently of why this wicked world will fall."

"It will?"

"Oh, yes. These are the End Days; everyone knows that, even those who will not admit the truth of the Word. The god of love and peace has filled the hearts of the Catholics and Lutherans with so much hatred for each other they will burn everything. Burn, burn, burn till nothing is left bar the ashes. And then we will rise and claim what remains. We will no longer be the things that hide in the shadows, no longer the unspoken thing. The Word will be said aloud, and *we* shall be the masters."

The masters...

The thought of Saul and the men who served his Red Company bubbled into her mind. They called him Master. She stamped down on it. Everything she gave the Man from Carinthia weakened her and strengthened him.

Flyblown's marks on her thigh glowed hot as if agreeing with her.

Whatever his blood had healed, the Man from Carinthia had not washed Flyblown's scratches from her skin.

"'tis just a war. It will end. They always do. The swords will be cast aside eventually," she said.

Keep talking.

How could she stop this monster? She'd killed men and demons in The Wolf's Tower. She'd killed Frau Stettin. There had to be a way!

"The swords will never be beaten into ploughshares. That is a lie. That is not the Word. They will kill and burn, burn and kill till nought remains because they believe their god of peace and love decrees it. I have seen this."

She snorted, "How have you seen this?"

There might be a way, but she needed a weapon, and she had nothing. She couldn't kill the Man from Carinthia with her bare hands, and she couldn't keep him talking forever. She had to escape him if she couldn't kill him, but the door was the only way out. There was a window, but he would cross the room long before she could open it. And they were upstairs; if she got out and survived the fall, he would catch her.

"Because I walk above."

"Above?"

"So far above. And when you go high enough, you can see everything. Everything all the way to tomorrow," he laughed. It wasn't the laugh of a sane man, but she knew that already. What did Morlaine say to her once?

All vampires are mad...

That was as maybe, but all vampires could die too.

She'd stopped Frau Stettin with a knitting needle in the eye, straight into the brain, killing her instantly. The only way you could, before their demonic healing powers saved them. But there was not even a knitting needle in the room, let alone a blade.

"What do you see?"

"A world destroyed by men, by a war that never ends, a war that destroys the cities, destroys the fields, destroys the churches, palaces and castles. That destroys all the petty monuments of mankind. The war will spread. The Holy Roman Empire will burn and fall. Europe will burn and fall. The world will burn and fall. 'tis inevitable. 'tis foretold. 'tis the World's Pain... and it will be *beautiful*."

In the Wheelhouse of The Wolf's Tower, she'd killed a demon Renard called Callinicus by blowing him to bits with gunpowder. But there certainly wasn't any gunpowder here.

"A strange kind of beauty..."

"From death comes life. We will rise and rule the world. That is the Word. I walk above. I spread the Word. I am the creator. I am the Lord. I make new life to take the place of the old. I send them out to slaughter and begat; when the glorious day comes, and the world of men falls, we will no longer be the few; we will be the many. And the world will be bequeathed to us. Because that is the Word. *Bequeathed...*"

She'd killed men in the Darkway of The Wolf's Tower too, setting light to the oil Torben had poured over the invaders. Only men had died, but she'd hurt demons too. But there wasn't any...

She forced herself not to look at the lantern next to her.

Nor think about the oil inside it.

*

"Things were different when I first came here, few listened to Aumann's bile then," Lucien said as they

284

walked, "There were people who resented the strangers, for sure, but most understood they were fleeing the war, fleeing the Catholic League, the Imperial army, the mercenaries, the brigands, fleeing hunger, persecution and death. Most were prepared to help those who arrived with nothing; to house them, give them blankets, food, mugs of milk for the children. As the war drags on and the refugees keep arriving, the town has less to give. More and more are willing to listen to Aumann and his cronies. 'tis the nature of evil to stake its claim in people's hearts by small degrees."

"And what does Aumann want?" Morlaine asked.

"To shut the gates, to turn the strangers out, to let them fend for themselves out there," Lucien jerked his head towards the town walls, "Of course, what he really wants is power for himself, to be the biggest dog in a small kennel. Adversity and want are but the means to the end, prime the fear, stoke the hatred and use it for his own ends."

"And what will you do?

"I am paid to keep the wolves from their door. The ones that are already stretched out in front of the hearth, however..." he glanced at Morlaine and shrugged, "...once he takes over, I will leave. He does not like me. Which is surprising. Lucien Kazmierczak is used to being well-liked. From Dresden to Dusseldorf, he is generally considered an exceedingly fine fellow!"

They walked on, boots clipping the cobbles. Lucien and Morlaine side by side, he trailed a pace behind. The lantern was starting to splutter, the oil running out.

"I wouldn't have thought you cared?" he said, eyes

flicking between the waning light and the mercenary's broad back.

"Cared? Who said I cared? Caring buys no beer! No, I am merely saying what I see. Aumann is whipping up hatred against the strangers for his own ends. You are strangers. Witchcraft scares people, people who are frightened by the war as it is. If he can convince the town strangers have brought it here by putting you on a pyre, he would not hesitate for a heartbeat..."

"We understand," Morlaine said, "we will be leaving soon."

"As much as it breaks my poor much-abused heart to even consider never seeing you again, I think that for the best."

"I am sure you will survive."

"Somehow," Lucien conceded before slapping Morlaine's rump.

"If you do that again," Morlaine told him without breaking stride, "I will break your arm."

Lucien laughed. Obviously, he thought the demon was joking. Personally, Ulrich was far more prepared to take her at her word.

When Lucien's chuckles subsided, he said, "So, light of my world, will you tell me what mischief you are about?"

Morlaine tilted her head, "Mischief?"

"You two have been gone for hours?"

"It is none of your business."

"Of course not, but people are going missing. Including some of my men. What do you know of this?"

"Nothing."

"Perhaps that is true. Perhaps not. But the truth is all the sourer to swallow when someone keeps secrets."

"I don't keep secrets. I just mind my own business," a colder edge than usual fringed Morlaine's voice. Lucien paid it no heed.

"Where have you been?"

Morlaine stopped, and Lucien did the same. Ulrich sloshed the lantern in the hope some more oil might somehow appear. The demon flicked her eyes towards him and then back to Lucien.

"We are lovers; where do you think we have been?"

Ulrich looked up sharply, nearly dropping the lantern onto the cobbles.

Lucien glanced in his direction. To Ulrich's way of thinking, it was a rather dismissive look.

"That seems... unlikely. Lucien Kazmierczak is a famed lover! No woman leaves his bed to jump straight into another's."

"Perhaps you hold yourself in too high a regard?"

"Don't all men? Still, frankly, witchcraft seems a more likely explanation for your absence. And I don't even believe in that nonsense."

"I am not a witch. And I am not responsible for anyone disappearing either."

Lucien swung his attention to Ulrich, "She has a birthmark under her right breast. Yes or no?"

"Yes," he blurted.

"No," Lucien and Morlaine replied just as quickly.

Ulrich opened his mouth to say something. But nothing much came out.

Lucien slapped his bad arm, "Trust me, you would have noticed!"

Absurdly, he found himself blushing.

"You did not seem overly concerned about your men earlier?" Morlaine said, thankfully moving the conversation in another direction.

"Concerned? Of course I am concerned! My boys are like children to me! They are villainous, black-hearted scum, but, still, curiously endearing," he shrugged, "besides, more are now unaccounted for. Anyone can lose one child, but when you misplace several..."

"I know nothing of what's happened to them," Morlaine lied.

"Coupled with the others in town who have apparently disappeared over the last few days. 'tis not something a diligent father can overlook. If it were not for the fact people were going missing before you arrived in town, I would be even more suspicious."

"You have nothing to be suspicious of. We are no more than we say we are," Morlaine said evenly. To be fair, she was an excellent liar.

The fact the disappearances had started before they arrived at least provided some comfort. The nagging fear that they'd led the Red Company's demons here had been swirling around the back of his mind ever since he'd discovered Madleen's fate.

"Perhaps I *should* let Aumann throw you in gaol..." Lucien said, "...the town does not employ a professional torturer, but I am sure there are several enthusiastic amateurs who would be more than happy to put the question to you..."

"That," Morlaine produced an especially cold smile before continuing down the street, "would not be wise..."

Lucien winked at him, "What a woman, eh?!"

They both hurried after her.

When they caught up, they walked in silence for a few strides before Lucien said to Morlaine, "There is something peculiar about you."

"Beyond letting you take me to your bed?"

"I was thinking more of your coldness."

"Perhaps you should do more to put some heat in me?"

"I was not referring to your demeanour. That is icy rather than cold. No, I meant to the touch. I have touched many women; 'tis Lucien Kazmierczak's curse that so many women demand his touch, so I should know."

"I've heard of worse curses," Ulrich muttered.

Lucien ignored him, "Then there is the blood..."

Morlaine's stride didn't waver. She didn't look at Lucien either.

"Just a few spots. On the sheets each morning, after I awake and find you gone. I can find no new cuts or wounds, only some almost healed scabs on my arm that I have no recollection of. Why is that do you think?"

"I have no idea."

"I have fought many battles. After all, my bravery and swordcraft are known from Dunkerque to the Dardanelles. Despite my mastery of blade and pistol, I have been wounded several times. I have had fevers and maladies, but Lucien Kazmierczak is an exceedingly difficult fellow to kill. Physicians have had much practice in honing their skills on this rugged, muscular, endlessly desirable body of mine. On many occasions, I have been bled. Bled by leeches, bled by the blade. 'tis most strange..." as they made their way down the street, Lucien's eyes were fixed upon Morlaine, "...how a night with you leaves me feeling much the same as those unspeakable charlatans did."

"Perhaps you are getting old."

Lucien snorted, "And I also find I have slept deeply for hours. Which is strange, given the need to be eternally vigilant so I may strike down my many enemies, I am usually the lightest of sleepers..."

"I thought you were well liked?"

"When you kill people for a living, even someone as loveable as Lucien Kazmierczak leaves a few regrettable grudges and misunderstandings behind them..."

Lucien continued to stare at Morlaine as they walked; Morlaine's eyes remained fixed on the street. He busied himself with the lantern.

"Then there are the dreams."

"Dreams?" Morlaine asked with a resigned sigh.

"A pale faced-creature with bloody lips and wicked fangs. Skin like snow, marbled with blue veins that pulse and throb like water running beneath ice. A face too long and thin. 'tis a terrible thing to behold, yet strangely beautiful despite its inhuman and ungodly aspect."

"Perhaps you should eat less cheese before going to bed."

"I am fond of cheese," Lucien conceded, "still..."

A crashing noise broke the awkward silence, accompanied by a woman's scream. They could see nothing ahead, but it had sounded very close.

They all stopped.

"What was that?" Ulrich raised the dying lantern higher and whirling about.

Morlaine was staring at him in the flickering light when he looked back.

Silently she mouthed a single word.

Solace...

She ran.

The lantern chose that moment to die, and the shadows closed in around them. Then the clouds broke, and the moon's cold regard fell upon Madriel.

Tossing it aside to shatter on the cobbles, he ran after her.

Chapter Six

"Tell me your name?"

His voice, soft but captivating, tugged her attention back to the door.

"Tell me yours?"

"I have no need of one. I am the Man from Carinthia. I am He Who Walks Above. I am the Bringer of the Word. I am a Bequeather. I raise the undead to feast upon the World's Pain. I am the future..." he smiled, she thought, "...and so are you."

"I will call you Fredrick then, 'tis much less of a mouthful."

He edged into the room, just a fraction, but enough for the lamplight to dust his face. Saul the Bloodless had not looked like the killer he was. However, the Man from Carinthia's true nature was writ much clearer on his features; a thin mouth, broad nose, cruel eyes, a high dome of a forehead, dark hair long and tarred back.

"What is your name? I will have it. You will tell me. I can hurt you, break you, heal you and do it again. And again. And again. I am a vampire. I have an abundance of time. Still, I would rather not. After all, time is all the more precious at the end of the world. So, tell me. Now."

She raised her gaze and held those dark eyes.

I will not show them fear.

Run or stand, I will never show them fear again.

The five red lines on her thigh tingled and warmed.

"I am the Lady of the Broken Tower. I am the Last of My Name. I am the Killer of Demons. I am Vengeance. You may be Death..." she curled out her own bitter smile, "...but not for me."

The Man from Carinthia laughed.

Which wasn't the response she'd hoped for.

So, she scooped up the oil lamp and hurled it at him.

"I bequeath you this!"

He carried on laughing.

And moved. Stepping aside, the lamp hit the wall behind him, the oil igniting as the glass shattered. Spraying him with fire.

Which put a stop to the laughter.

His tarred hair and coat burst into flame. He screamed, wildly trying to smother the fire with his hands, which took the flames as readily as the rest of him.

She'd burnt the Red Company in the Darkway, roasting men and demons alike. But Torben had poured a whole barrel of oil over them. The lamp held no more than a tankard, probably less. It wasn't going to stop him.

So she ran at the window.

There was no time to open it; the Man from Carinthia's boots thudded under the music of his screams behind her.

I am not going to die.

The marks on her leg agreed. Warming in approval. Her *sight* told her the same. God had a plan for her and Renard alike.

He wouldn't have saved them otherwise. He wouldn't have stopped the pistol she'd put under her chin after Alms slaughtered the last of her people from blowing her brains out.

He wouldn't have allowed her to clamber down the wall of The Wolf's Tower in one piece.

He wouldn't have saved Renard from the black, freezing waters of the moat and allowed her to lead him to her father's hunting lodge.

He wouldn't have saved him from his injuries. He wouldn't have brought Morlaine to them.

He wouldn't have brought them safely across the blighted war-torn land to Madriel.

He wouldn't. He wouldn't. He wouldn't.

Would he?

She closed her eyes as she hit the glass shoulder first.

Something hot brushed her ankle as the window exploded around her. Pain, sharp and searing, sliced her face, shoulder, and arm. Then coldness replaced the heat, slapping her, sucking the breath from her lungs. Tugging at her dress.

She opened her eyes and threw her arms out before her. Dark stone rushed to meet her. Her scream followed her all the way down to the cobbles.

The pain was like nothing she'd ever experienced.

Stunning, sickening, jarring. All consuming.

The world turned white, then red, then black.

The world tasted of hot copper.

The world smelt of cold stone and horse shit.

The world froze. The world burned.

She tried to speak, but nothing came save a wet gurgling sound. When she made to move, even more pain coursed through her.

I am dying.

But at least I did not show them fear.

Something moved against her inner thigh. Warm and sharp, but not unpleasant. Or she thought it did. Like the caress of a comforting hand. A comforting hand with long nails.

Something thudded next to her.

Another smell came.

Oily smoke, singed hair, burnt flesh.

She again tried to move, roll away, flail out her arms, and scream defiance. To remind God he had a plan for her and Ulrich Renard.

The pain came rolling in black waves to crash over her broken body.

"You will be mine," a voice said, "and you will feast upon the World's Pain too."

"No," she tried to say, but nothing came out, save perhaps a tooth or two.

"Praise be the Word, and the Word is *Bequeath*..."

She felt a hand on her, turning her onto her back. Stars exploded. Beneath their light, coldness rose from the stones below. Creeping at first but ever bolder, ever surer, ever quicker.

We are Death, Lady Solace... but not for you...

Other sounds came. Voices, running feet, cries.

But soon, the darkness took them too.

*

He hurtled around the corner.

Morlaine raced away from him, faster than he could ever be, even if he were still the man he'd been before The Wolf's Tower fell.

Ahead, a figure crouched over something. At first, he thought it a bundle of rags. But it wasn't.

"My lady!" he screamed. Or thought he did. He ran harder, boots skimming over the rain-slickened cobbles.

He made to draw his father's sabre, but Morlaine reached them before it came free of its scabbard.

The figure rose. Smoke, turned to silver by the moonlight, curled around it as if it had just arisen from the brimstone. It hissed something through wicked fangs.

"Get away from her!" Morlaine shouted, for once her voice carrying fire rather than ice. Her blade flashed, but the demon rolled away from it. Twisting and rising again in the instant it took Morlaine to spin back around.

"What are you doing, sister?" the thing asked.

Morlaine slashed again, impossibly fast, a strike no mortal could avoid, but the demon slid away again.

"As the world falls, we must stand together..." the demon held bone-white hands before him, dark eyes flicking toward Ulrich as he skidded to a halt over Solace, "...not with the cattle."

There was not much capable of pulling his eyes from

the sight of the smouldering demon, blackened skin and charred hair, further disfiguring its terrible face, but the bloody ruin of Solace's body did.

His sword clattered to the ground as he dropped to his knees beside her.

"My lady...?"

Her face was a mass of blood, darkening her roughly sheered fair hair, her right arm bent at an angle no arm should take, her dress was torn and bloodied, and lacerations bled from each piece of exposed skin. Shards of glass and shattered wood were scattered around her. The remains of a window. She must have jumped from one of the houses.

"In the name of God," Lucien gasped.

He did not look around. Instead, he groped for Solace's left hand and squeezed it. Her skin was cold as snow beneath the blood.

Behind him, thunder roared. The demon ducked, for an instant just a blur as dust erupted from a chunk of wall behind it. A spent pistol fell to the ground next to him as Lucien drew another from his belt.

Morlaine moved as fast, blade glinting, cutting a bloody arc across the demon's chest. It screamed and lashed out with a hooked hand, fingers missing Morlaine's face by a breath.

His eyes returned to Solace.

"My lady...?" he choked the words out upon a frosted breath.

He fumbled for a pulse. The fingers of his good hand momentarily as numb and clumsy as the withered sticks of his bad one.

"You cannot die, you cannot..." he heard himself sob.

He hated her, he loved her. He could not imagine living without her any more than he could imagine living with her. She had his oath, his honour, his debt. She led them both to their deaths at the hands of a foe they would never defeat. Her death would release him from that burden. But as he found her pulse's faint movement, he realised he did not want to be free.

Save her, and you save yourself...

That's what old Lutz had told him. And he'd been right. Without Solace there was nothing for him. No honour, no purpose, no anything. Just a broken man following a broken road. The same as his father.

"You do not die here! You know that you do not die here! God has a plan for us; you do not die here..." he moved his hand to the bloody tangles of her hair.

He wanted to scoop her up and carry her to safety, but that was impossible with his damaged, useless arm. And even if he did, it wouldn't save her. Maybe she'd live long enough to die in a bed instead of on these cold, filthy stones, but she'd die all the same.

She was slipping away, and only one thing could save her.

"Morlaine!" he cried, looking up again.

The demon had managed to close with her, one hand gripping her sword arm, the other trying to flail at her face, which was now as long and awful as his, each fang-filled slash of a mouth attempting to rip into the other's flesh.

Lucien had taken a step forward, second pistol levelled

but unable to fire for fear of hitting the wrong target. Or perhaps not even knowing which one he should shoot. In fairness to the man, his hand remained steady as a rock as his face twisted with uncertainty.

He scooped up his father's sabre and jumped to his feet.

"Take her to the Inn!" he shouted in Lucien's face.

The mercenary's eyes turned on him, though the gun stayed level on the demons.

"What-"

"Take her to the Inn as fast as you can, man. 'tis her only chance!"

When Lucien didn't budge, he forced the man's gun down, "She is a good woman! We must save her. Please!"

Morlaine and the demon crashed into a wall, and bounced off, both struggling to keep their footing on the wet cobbles. Moraine's blade span from her hand.

"Do it!"

Lucien swallowed. Looked like he wanted to argue before shoving the pistol into his belt. He bent over and lifted Solace free of the stones. Beneath, blood blackened the ground.

She moaned and twisted in his arms, then grew still.

"She can't possibly live," Lucien said, breath steady. He was strong; Ulrich prayed he was also quick.

"She does not die here," he said, pushing the man forward.

Lucien began running.

Light was starting to spill onto the street. Doors opening, voices calling. This had to finish and finish now.

The demons were spinning around, clawing, biting, kicking at each other, trying to break the other's grasp. They turned so fast. A lunatic carousel of swirling cloaks and snapping teeth.

He ran at them, sabre raised. The same dilemma confronting him as Lucien had faced with his pistol. They were so close and moving so quickly that a sword strike seemed as likely to hit Morlaine as the other demon.

But he had no choice.

She does not die today...

He pulled back his arm and swung, screaming.

Save her, and you save yourself...

The sabre slashed through the bitter night air.

Then his father's steel met a demon's flesh.

Chapter Seven

She stood atop a grey hill on a grey plain.

It was twilight. She suspected it always was here.

A breeze, surprisingly warm and pleasant, stirred the ash into transient little clouds around her feet.

"My Lord Flyblown," she nodded at the cloaked figure beside her.

"My Lady of the Broken Tower," he pulled back his hood, eyes narrowing towards the gold-tinged sky to the west.

"Am I... dead?"

"That is still to be decided," he pursed his lips, "but matters remain in the balance."

"Then our deal may prove rather short-lived."

"Life is full of disappointments. Sometimes I do wonder why we bother with it."

"What is the alternative?"

Flyblown's hand swept across the dust-blown plain and the other hills rising from it as far as the eye could see.

She sniffed, "I think I prefer life. When it is all said and done. This is a sad place. What is it?"

"The land of the dead. The land of dreams. The land of possibilities. The land of things past. The land of dust, ashes and nothingness. It can be whatever you want it to be," his eyes returned to her, "just like the real world."

"This is not real?"

He smiled, "Now we are teetering dangerously on the brink of philosophy. We should step back from that dread precipice."

Flyblown turned around and stared in the opposite direction, towards a darker horizon.

"Can you save my life?"

"Of course."

"Will you?"

"My blood cannot taint you. I am unable to intervene directly. If I could, I would end the Red Company myself. And you could do something else with your life."

"There is nothing else I want to do. My life ended when The Wolf's Tower fell. I am the last of my name, the last of my people. That must mean something."

"There is your brother."

"But he does not live anymore, does he?"

Flyblown shook his head, "Neither may you for much longer."

"And then what happens?"

"I will find another. Perhaps Ulrich. What do you think?"

"He is a troubled soul."

That made Flyblown laugh.

Figures moved against the darker horizon, shuffling

around the other grey hills. For the most part, they just circled the base of the mounds, shoulders stooped, heads lowered, dragging one foot after another through the dust. They looked impossibly tired.

When the laughter subsided, Flyblown said, "Your life depends on three things."

She cocked an eyebrow at him, much as Morlaine did.

"The sword swing of a broken man, the decision of an unworthy one and a monster breaking a promise made to herself. All three must combine. Or you will die. Or not live. I cannot see beyond that."

"You have the *sight?*"

"A... little..."

She detected a degree of probably unmerited modesty in that reply.

"Did you know the Man from Carinthia was in Madriel?"

"Of course."

"You could have told me."

"Think of it as a test."

"Did I pass?"

"That remains to be seen."

A figure stood alone on one of the distant hills, unmoving save for the cloak whipping around him.

Torben.

She found her feet taking a step forward.

Flyblown's fingers wrapped around her arm. Long, sharp, yellow nails dug into her flesh through the sleeve of her dress.

"Death awaits that way."

"He would never do me harm. Even now."

"What we want and what we do," Flyblown let his hand fall away, "do not always align."

She stared at him. His face still looked not quite finished, but his eyes... motes of light danced within the confines of their darkness, like sparks rising from a fire into a star-filled sky.

"If I go to him in this world, I die. If I go to him in... the other world...?"

"He dies."

"You know, or you want?"

"The Red Company must be stopped. It is not the way of our kind to interfere in the affairs of men. There will be consequences, dire ones, if Saul the Bloodless continues to meddle, to dabble, to live in a place beyond the darkest shadows. Your brother is part of the Red Company now."

"The Man from Carinthia said the world of men will fall. Is he right?"

"That is one possibility. But stand or fall, it should do so of its own accord. We must remain on its margin."

"Feasting on the World's Pain?"

"Things that scavenge and clean the carcass have a role in nature. That role is not to achieve dominion over the other beasts."

She pursed her lips, eyes narrowing to peer across the grey plain to the figure of her brother. He often stood motionless, body frozen as his mind wandered elsewhere. Was this the place his mind had always fled to?

"The Man from Carinthia, if I understood his rambling correctly, is creating... bequeathing vampires... to what...?

Hasten the fall? Or at least exist in sufficient numbers to subjugate mankind?"

Flyblown nodded.

"While Saul is hiring his Company out to all the petty despots tearing the Holy Roman Empire apart for their own gain?"

He nodded again.

"It would seem to me if you want to keep your kind in the shadows, the Man from Carinthia is far more of a threat than Saul and his grubby mercenaries."

"On the face of it."

"And yet you put your mark on me to destroy Saul. And failed to even mention the Man from Carinthia. Why?"

"No one listens to the Man from Carinthia. And if you couldn't deal with a mad man like him, you'd have no hope of defeating a mad man like Saul the Bloodless."

"So, this, is what? Education?"

"You could look at it like that."

"I much preferred Tutor Magnus and his infernal maps…"

Flyblown let out a hearty chuckle, once it faded into the wind, he said, "Saul is a black flame. Charismatic, ruthless, dangerous. 'tis not in the nature of my kind to work together, to co-operate, to do much at all beside despise one another. You see, we are all a mirror to each other, and what stares back at us from that shadowy glass is monstrous…"

She scratched her head, then shook it, "Do any of your kind speak plainly?"

"I shall try. The world of men will not fall because of

the Man from Carinthia and his ilk. On the other hand, Saul the Bloodless is doing something no other vampire has ever tried or achieved. He is building an army. Small, as yet, but it grows. And this endless war and the disorder it brings provide a cover for him. There is a balance in nature. We survive on the margins, in the unseen places. If the world of men falls, we will fall with it. That is the thing. We cannot exist without you. Saul dreams of bathing in the blood of the world. If he ever does, he will destroy us all. He must be stopped."

"But why me?"

Flyblown's lips twisted into an ill-fitting smile.

"It is not you."

"It... isn't?"

"No. It is Morlaine, but she is a weapon I am unable to control. You can. You have breached her; she has let you into her circle. A rare thing. A useful thing. She has walked her road of the night alone for a long time. Now she has you and your man. There will be others. To fight an army, you need an army. Gather them, use them, throw them at Saul the Bloodless and stop him any way you can. Before it is too late."

"Unless I die here, of course."

"Well," Flyblown admitted, "there is that."

She stared across the grey world at her brother. As motionless as he ever was, though now his back was straight, head high, arms at his side rather than held before him.

She took a step backwards.

"Then it is best I do not die today..."

*

Morlaine's black inhuman eyes widened even further before she spun the other demon into the path of his father's blade.

The sabre bit deep into the thing's shoulder, spraying blood into the night. The creature screamed, twisting away from Morlaine's grip to face him, mouth wide, fangs bared.

Ulrich tried a back-handed slash to take the thing's head, but it ducked away at impossible speed. A hand slashed out; fingers bent into claws. It would have taken his face off if it found flesh, but Ulrich managed to throw himself backwards. He avoided the blow but lost his footing on the wet cobbles in the process and crashed to the ground.

Pain lanced from withered arm to shattered shoulder and his sword span from his grip.

The creature loomed over him, drawing back a leg to kick him. The thing's boot would likely break his skull if it connected.

It didn't.

Instead, steel erupted from its chest.

The demon's eyes bulged, and it staggered forward. Morlaine dragged her blade from its back. In an instant it flashed and hissed again before wetly connecting with the meat.

By the time the creature's head bounced on the ground the face was human. One that carried a look of disbelief on its contorted features.

Morlaine's sword dropped to her side, her own face

that of a beautiful young woman again. Her gaze lingered upon the corpse at her feet.

"We must get rid of this," she said, not panting in the slightest.

Someone was screaming, other voices broke the night. He paid them no heed.

"There's no time!"

"He will turn to dust in hours. If people see-"

"Solace is still alive; she needs your blood, or she will die."

Her eyes moved to him.

"Lucien took her to the Inn." Ignoring the molten bolts of pain flashing up and down his ruined arm, he struggled to his feet, "We must go to her. Now!"

"But-"

"There are demons all over town, they've been seen. It's too late to keep it hidden. It isn't too late for Solace... but it soon will be..."

Morlaine remained rooted to the spot. People were edging towards them, pointing, whispering.

"Please... I beg you..."

"I warned her, if she walks the Night's Road with me-"

"No!" he faced up to the demon, shoving her with his good hand, "Save her! Do it! I don't care about anything else."

When she carried on staring at him, he shoved her again.

"People will die here," she said quietly, "they will blame witchcraft for this, and in their ignorance and fear they will send innocents to the flames."

"They can roast me on the fucking pyre if needs must but save her. Now!"

He made to push her again, but she stepped back, orange light playing across her face. People were shouting, boots hitting the cobbles. He was vaguely aware of the smell of burning wood. One of the houses was on fire. The one Solace fell from, he assumed. He didn't really care. The whole damn town could burn along with all the fools in it.

"Please..." he whispered.

Slowly the demon sheathed her sword.

Then she turned and ran.

He watched her go, before scooping up his father's sabre and fumbling it into his sheath, followed by Lucien's discarded pistol, which he tucked into his belt.

"Fire! Fire!" someone was screaming.

He looked up; tongues of flame licked the edge of a broken window in one of the houses above him. People milled about, some in nightclothes, all white-faced and wide-eyed. If there was one thing that scared folk more than witchcraft, it was a fire.

Clutching his bad arm, he turned away and hurried down the street.

"You!" someone shouted.

He ignored them. He'd take his father's sabre to them if anyone tried to stop him.

They were not far from the Market Square; Lucien should already be there, and Morlaine could no doubt run like the wind.

By the time he arrived, the demon would have given Solace her blood, and she would be saved.

Or she would be dead.

He broke into a shuffling run, bad arm screaming every time a boot hit the cobbles. He clamped the fingers of his good hand around it and gritted his teeth.

More voices called out, but no one came near him. The fire was more urgent than anything else, and people were calling for buckets. Perhaps God would hear them, and the rains would return. But he would not hold his breath; God currently seemed peculiarly indifferent to the suffering of his children.

He forced himself forward, tongue pushing in and out of the gaps left in his teeth by Bekker's boot when the Red Company's captain had kicked him in the face the night The Wolf's Tower fell.

His chest tightened, his stomach heaved.

What kind of a soldier was he now? He felt like he'd jumped out of a window rather than Solace.

And why the hell had she been there?

He shook the thought away. She could tell him when she recovered.

The street fed into the Market Square, deserted despite the hue and cry behind him. His eyes flashed to the church, dark and brooding.

Madleen was still out there.

Another thought he pushed away.

Nobody can save everyone...

He snorted at that. If he couldn't save Solace, he wouldn't even save himself.

Lights burned within the Market Inn, and he let them bring him home. One pained stride at a time. He slowed as he neared the door, sucking in the freezing air with wet, burning gasps.

Save for Herr Kehlmann and Anna-Lena, the Inn was empty; he doubted many of the mercenaries had turned in early. They both stared at him as he hurried across the room.

Anna-Lena pointed upstairs; face ghost-white.

He nodded as he went by.

"What is happening?" Kehlmann wanted to know.

Ignoring the question, he rushed up the stairs two at a time; slipping near the top, he managed to get his good hand out to stop himself from planting his face on a step. If he'd put his bad one out, his scream would have woken the dead.

At least those that weren't already awake.

He scrambled to his feet and made it the rest of the way without damaging himself further.

Outside their room, he hesitated. Light snuck under the door, but no voices.

Please...

Who was he asking? He didn't know, it had been a long time since anyone listened to his prayers.

He threw open the door.

Lucien stood beside it, almost as white-faced as Anna-Lena.

Solace was on the bed, bloody and broken. Morlaine at the end, arms folded, head lowered. She did not look around when he shut the door behind him.

"Is she...?"

When Morlaine didn't answer, Lucien did, "She is still

alive, barely," he rested a hand on Ulrich's shoulder, "'tis only a matter of time, I'm sorry, truly..."

He shook the man's hand away and crossed to Morlaine's side.

"Why haven't you given her your blood?" he hissed.

Morlaine turned dark eyes on him, "I cannot."

The two words hit him like fists in the gut.

"Why not? I know what your demon blood can do. I've damn well seen it!"

"She is too close."

"Too close to what?"

"Death," Morlaine's eyes flicked in Lucien's direction and then back to him.

"I don't understand."

"If the body is this close to death, my blood will not heal. It will change. It will make her... like me."

He moved in close enough for his nose to brush hers. She did not back away.

"I don't fucking care. Do it!"

"You've seen what the change can do. Do you want Solace to end up like Madleen?"

"That won't happen. She won't lose her mind. She is too strong."

A smile, small and terrible, turned her lips, "I thought that of someone once too. I was wrong."

He wanted to reach out and grab her by the throat. He fought down the urge, curling his hand into a tight fist instead.

"Is there no chance you could heal her without..."

Morlaine looked away and shrugged, "I cannot risk it."

"Damn well why not?"

"Because I swore I would never do it again, never pass on my curse to another, never be responsible for more death."

"Solace will not die. She will not become a demon."

"You do not know that."

"Yes, I do. We did not survive what we did for her to die here like this!"

"You speak as if there's some grand plan for us all, Ulrich? Some destiny, some purpose," she swept a few stray licks of hair from her face, "but there is none. I'm sorry."

"She is worth the risk."

"No one is worth the risk!" Anger flashed in her eyes. He'd seen her express so little emotion he'd thought her incapable of it, but the look in her eye was so intense he almost had to take a step back.

But he didn't.

Instead, he stared at Solace. Her chest rose and fell so shallowly it was barely perceptible.

"Tell me why you won't do it."

"I've told you why."

"No. You haven't. You owe me that much."

"I owe you nothing."

"Tell me, or I'll cut off your damn head and feed her your blood myself," his hand twitched towards his father's sabre. As empty threats went, it was as hollow as any he'd ever heard, but he was running out of ideas. And Solace was running out of time.

Morlaine sighed. He thought she might storm from the room, but when she spoke no anger coloured her words.

Just sadness.

"I loved a man once. A mortal man like you. When he grew old and sick, I turned him into a vampire because I could not stand the thought of living without him. He was a good man. A kind man. He did not want to become like me, though he loved me as much as I loved him. He wanted to go to God. I didn't let him. I made him kiss the vein on his death bed, and he became vampiric..."

She stared at him, long and hard, then looked away.

"That man became Saul the Bloodless. All the people he has slaughtered over centuries are because of me. All those people in The Wolf's Tower died because of me. All the children..." she swallowed, "...the ones in The Wolf's Tower were not the first. All because of me," she leaned in close enough to spit in his ear, "All because of me... it will not happen again. Do you understand me? It will *never* happen again."

"Please..."

They stood there, glaring at each other. He didn't know whether to hit her or cry. He doubted either would move the demon.

"There is another way," Lucien said, still standing by the door, back against the wall, fingers hitched in his belt.

They both turned to stare at him.

In truth, he'd forgotten the mercenary was still in the room. It was the quietest he'd been since they'd met.

"If I have been following this correctly, your blood," he first pointed at Morlaine, then Solace, "can heal her wounds?"

"He has seen what you are," Ulrich said when

315

Morlaine's only response was a glare.

Eventually, she nodded.

"Because she is so close to death," he jabbed a finger at Solace again, then bounced it back to Morlaine, "there is a danger she will become like you?"

Morlaine gave another reluctant nod.

"Whatever you are."

"It doesn't matter what I am."

Lucien pulled a face, "Not to me. No. What is important is that the magic in your blood can save this young woman's life."

"I don't like the word magic."

Lucien conceded the point with a sharp tilt of his head.

"But if you give her your blood and she becomes... whatever you are... you will know?"

Morlaine nodded.

"Then 'tis simple. Give her your blood. If she survives, everything is good, and we can busy ourselves trying to avoid being burnt as witches. If she becomes whatever you are," he held out his palms, "you kill her."

When they both continued staring at him, he added, "Assuming whatever it is you are can be killed, of course?"

Once more, Morlaine nodded.

"She deserves the chance," Ulrich insisted.

The room fell to silence, save for a few wet, gurgling gasps from Solace. Her lungs were filling with blood. She did not have long. Indecision played across the demon's face as she turned her eyes back to the stricken form upon the bed.

Somehow, he managed to keep himself from screaming in her face.

Finally, Morlaine took a deep breath, "Very well. But if she turns. I will kill her, understand me?"

It was Ulrich's turn to nod.

"And if you try to stop me," her eyes flicked to Lucien, "either of you, I will kill you too."

"Understood."

Morlaine brushed by him, sliding a dagger from her belt as she did.

"Stand by the door," she said when he made to follow her to Solace's side, "with him. Make sure no one comes in..."

He did as he was told.

"You know..." Lucien said, hooded eyes tracking him till he slumped against the door next to the mercenary, "...I am really starting to suspect you haven't been entirely truthful with me..."

He said nothing, instead watching Morlaine slice a bloody line across her palm with the dagger, open Solace's mouth with her other hand and then let her blood flow between his dying mistress' lips.

After that, there was nothing to do but pray.

And wonder if he really would let Morlaine kill her if she awoke a demon.

Chapter Eight

"How long until we know?"

"If she awakes, she is human. If she dies before she wakes, then she is not. Or she just dies. In which case..."

Ulrich went back to massaging his bad hand's stiff, numb fingers before realising the demon had not actually answered the question.

"Yes, but how long will that take?"

Morlaine, who was gazing out of the window, did not look around again, "It can vary."

He tried a more straightforward question, "Is the sun coming up yet?"

"If it were, I would not be standing here."

He stared at his ruined hand; the scar, left by Bekker's teeth as he'd slit his throat, vivid against the pale white skin. He looked away in disgust.

Solace appeared to be breathing better. He assumed it a good sign but didn't bother asking Morlaine. He'd likely get a more fulsome response from his unconscious mistress.

318

He'd washed away as much blood as he could without stripping her. Each time he checked, the lacerations cut by the glass had grown fainter. It was a miracle to behold, albeit a miracle that would see them tossed on a pyre if anyone else saw it.

He glanced at the door.

Lucien had been gone for hours.

"Do you trust him?" he asked, probably not for the first time.

"No," Morlaine said, arms crossed, back towards him, face a ghost framed in the darkened pane, "but I don't trust you either."

"You have nothing to fear from me."

"I said trust. Not fear."

"Will Lucien tell people what you are, what he saw, the other demon...?"

"I don't know."

"You know him better, I thought-"

"I've drunk his blood, which bestows a sense of his emotions and feelings, the occasional thought... but I have drunk many people's blood. It is difficult to know which thought, feeling or emotion belongs to whom. One of the disadvantages of not killing your prey."

"How... how can you stand it?"

"Who said I could?"

Her head moved as the sound of voices came from the square below.

"What's happening?"

"More madness than even floats around inside my skull."

Which was as about as helpful as most of what Morlaine said.

He sat by Solace's side; leaning across, he laid his good hand on her forehead. She was cool to the touch, not unnaturally so, but still. Was that a bad sign?

Rather than asking Morlaine, he pulled the blanket a little higher, and eased back with a wince.

"My blood could heal your arm..." she said, still not looking around.

"I know. I would rather live with the pain."

"You will not become a vampire."

"That is not what scares me."

"What does?"

He shook his head.

The sound of voices passed by and faded into the distance. Morlaine's head swivelled slowly in time, like a cat sitting in a window watching the birds outside. Tail swishing as it dreamed of ripping them to shreds.

"Will it change her?"

Morlaine looked over her shoulder. He supposed there were no more birds in view for the time being, "Change?"

"Not as in making her a demon. If she recovers, will having your blood inside her make her different?"

"If she does not turn vampiric, she will be herself. The blood restores, heals wounds, cures illnesses, and it can even reverse the ravages of time, but Solace is so young anyway. No, she will be as she was."

"Good."

"Driven half-mad with grief and a desire for vengeance that will destroy you both. My blood can heal her body; it will do nothing to her mind."

"That is... reassuring..."

The sound of approaching boots pulled his eye to the door.

"Lucien," she said before the door opened.

She did not seem unduly concerned, so he made no effort to grab the sabre propped against the wall next to him.

The mercenary knocked, and Morlaine spared him the journey to the door by crossing the room and letting Lucien in.

Rain slicked his coat, perspiration plastering thinning hair to his scalp when he pulled off his hat.

His eyes moved from Morlaine to Solace, "How is she?"

"Still alive, but not awake," Morlaine replied after peering along the corridor and closing the door after him.

"Is that good or bad?"

"That is yet to be established," Ulrich muttered, kneading his damaged hand once more.

"If your blood can heal," Lucien asked as Morlaine went back to the window, "why is his arm so wrecked?"

"That..." Morlaine went back to staring out into the slowly brightening world, "...is something you need to ask him."

"'tis a long story," Ulrich said, not meeting his eye.

He tossed his hat aside, "I would like to hear it when you have the time. Lucien Kazmierczak is famed for enjoying a grand yarn."

"Better that you don't..." was all he could bring himself to say.

Lucien moved to the end of the bed.

"What is going on out there?" Morlaine nodded down at the square.

"Chaos. But, on the bright side, it will be much worse when the rest of Madriel awakes."

"Lucien Kazmierczak is famed for looking on the bright side too?" Ulrich asked.

The mercenary found a grim smile, "An eternal optimist. 'tis one of my few weaknesses."

The smile faded, "Several of my lads are dead, town's people too. More are missing. Your demon is responsible, I take it?"

"And those he sired."

"The witchfinders will wet themselves with excitement when they get here. How many of them are there?" Lucien asked.

"I don't know. The newborn will not be able to sire others; their blood is not strong enough yet. I killed their sire, so there should be no more.,"

"I took the head of one," Ulrich said, "he'd just killed one of your men. Piet, I think his name was."

Lucien cursed under his breath and looked like he wanted to spit.

"I'm sorry."

"You should have told me."

"You would not have believed me," Morlaine said, "which is for the best."

"If I'd known, my boys could-"

"If your men had known, they would have dragged anyone they didn't like from the street for the witchfinders.

Better I dealt with it myself."

"Yes, that worked out well."

That earned Lucien a venomous glance.

"Are you going to give us to the witchfinders?" Ulrich asked.

Lucien chewed his bottom lip before replying, "They will not be here for a few days. Best you leave before they do."

"Thank you."

"I have no love for witchfinders; I've seen enough of their work. I want no part of it."

Slowly he eased himself onto the edge of Solace's bed.

"Is she a witch?"

"No," Morlaine said.

"And you? What are you?"

"'tis better to live in ignorance..." Ulrich told him, adding in little more than a whisper, "...I wish I did."

"You are asking a lot of me. If Aumann or anyone else gets an inkling of your true nature - whatever it is - I will be for the pyre too."

"We will soon be gone," Morlaine's eyes moved to Solace, "one way or the other."

Lucien nodded, "I should not be helping you, but Lucien Kazmierczak is well known as an excellent judge of character... even of people he has not taken to his bed."

Ulrich let his eyes drift away.

"Thank you." No hint of embarrassment or shame tainted Morlaine's voice. He supposed demons saw such things differently to God-fearing Christian folk.

"Aumann..." Ulrich said, "...he wanted to throw us into

gaol before... all this..."

"If anyone who saw you kill that... *creature* identifies you..." Lucien's words trailed off into a sigh, "I will protect you as best I can. Whatever the cost to my immortal soul. But I do not run this town; my influence stretches only so far."

"I understand," Morlaine said, "the man I killed, his body will turn to ash soon... that might provoke... questions."

Lucien brightened, "Well, to our immense good fortune, the fire spread to half the street. 'tis not only his body that is now ash."

"But people saw... *him*," Ulrich waved a hand before his face.

"The light was poor. I have said he was a robber and you defended yourself. That story will hold for the time being... but the more people that see these things... the more such lies will sag under the weight of the truth..."

Ulrich fixed on Morlaine, "Did you know him? The demon?"

"No. The war has attracted every lunatic vampire across Christendom. I don't know all of them."

"Vampire?" Lucien's eyebrow shot up.

"'tis what these demons are called," Ulrich explained.

"And that is what you are?" the mercenary asked Morlaine.

Nodding, she returned her gaze to the window.

"Summoned by Satan?"

She snorted a laugh.

When Lucien looked at him, he shrugged, "She is

not..." he searched for the right word; when he couldn't find it, he settled for, "...completely evil."

Morlaine cocked an eyebrow at him; he thought she might have smiled, though the light was quite poor.

"You are not Celine's cousin, are you?" Lucien asked; when Morlaine shook her head, he turned to Ulrich, "And you are not her husband?"

"No."

"I did think it unlikely."

He frowned at that, but before he could conjure a reply, the mercenary's eyes dropped to Solace, "Who is she?"

"It is better you do not know. There are people who think her dead. She wants it to stay that way."

"Other demons?"

"A more human monster, specifically," he said.

"Ah, plenty of those in the world too."

Lucien pinched his nose as he climbed to his feet, "I am going to try to sleep for an hour or two before this town starts tearing itself apart. Then you will tell more of these demons. 'tis always better to know your enemy..."

"We cannot walk in the sunlight. People will be safe until this evening. Outdoors, at least," Morlaine said.

"That is... useful." After scooping up his hat, he crossed to the door, pausing with one hand on the latch to look back and ask Morlaine, "The blood on my sheets...?"

"I did you no harm," the demon said, not meeting his eye.

He nodded, "I believe that. In fact, you did me quite some good. 'tis a long time since I felt a little happiness.

Which is strange, as Lucien Kazmierczak was once well known as a happy fellow, but lately, the way the world is..." he let himself out, his parting words fading into the shadows "...a little happiness is a rare and precious thing these days. It can buy you a lot."

*

Solace slept through the day and into the night.

His head went down a few times, and he dozed a little.

Morlaine paced, sat on the floor with her back to a wall, then paced some more. Lucien returned once with food. When Morlaine asked him what was happening in the town, he'd shaken his head, "Nothing good."

"Have any vampires been discovered?"

"Only bodies."

"There will be more."

"And not all from these creatures...."

When she raised an eyebrow, he added, "A mob stoned an old woman this morning. My men stopped it before they killed her, but they cannot be everywhere. Several strangers have been beaten. People are scared, and Aumann is stoking that fear..."

As if to reinforce his point, shouts and cries echoed from the Market Square.

"Damn..." he muttered after crossing to the window and cracking open the shutters.

"What is it?" Ulrich was too tired to get up and see for himself.

"The mobs are getting bigger..."

"What will you do?" Morlaine asked.

"Tell them to go home. Lucien Kazmierczak is famed for his powers of persuasion."

"And if that doesn't work?"

"Lucien Kazmierczak is also well known for cracking heads..." he sighed and rubbed red-ringed eyes, "...but if we have another night like the last one, then even my renowned silver tongue and feared iron fist will be insufficient to keep order."

"The vampires will soon be gone," Morlaine said, sitting in the shadiest part of the room.

"How so?" Lucien closed the shutters again.

"I will kill them."

"A noble offer, my love. But if the mob find you, they will not be able to tell the difference between you and the murderous demons as readily as Lucien Kazmierczak. Few are blessed with my sharp eye."

"They won't," was all Morlaine said in reply.

"No one will trouble you in here, for now. But out there..."

The mercenary let himself out.

*

Morlaine became more agitated as night edged closer.

Despite warning him he should keep his distance from Solace, he had stretched out beside her on the bed and slept a little. The feel and sound of her next to him was strangely comforting.

"If she awakes reborn..."

"She will not hurt me."

Morlaine gave a slow sad shake of her head and

walked away.

Later, when he awoke, it was dusk; Morlaine was at the window again, Solace remained asleep. The faint bite of smoke tainted the air.

"What's happening?" he asked, sitting up after confirming Solace still slept.

"The mobs are burning things."

"People are going to die, aren't they?"

"One way or another..." she crossed to the bed, folded her arms and stared at him, "Can I trust you to do the right thing?"

Her regard was intense. He avoided it by easing himself from the bed and onto the chair beside it, "The right thing?"

Her attention moved to Solace and back again, "The sun is down. I must go outside."

"To feed?" It was as much an accusation as a question.

Morlaine tilted her head, "To find Madleen and any others that vampire created. If Aumann and his mob finds one first..."

"Isn't it better they do? Better they burn a vampire than innocent people."

Her gaze hardened further, "The witchfinders have sent thousands to the flames based on nothing. Superstition, fear, ignorance, personal gain. If they find a vampire - a demon to you and them - how do you think they will explain the appearance of such an "unholy" creature in Madriel?"

"Witchcraft," he conceded.

"Yes. Where there are demons, there are witches.

Aumann is using fear of the strangers to take control of this town. God alone knows how many he will send to the pyre if he can prove the presence of demons here. However many it takes to get what he wants, I would wager."

"People will die regardless."

"Probably. But even more will if he can get his hands on Madleen or anyone else who has been changed."

"And how will you stop him from finding them?"

"I will kill them."

"Your own kind?"

"Not all vampires are crazed killers, but those who aren't weren't generally abandoned and left to fend for themselves like Madleen."

He swallowed and nodded, "I will come with you."

"No, you will stay here and watch Solace, and I need you to tell me you will do the right thing if she awakes changed," her eyes moved to his father's sabre still propped against the wall and back again.

"How... how will I know?"

"Trust me, you will know."

"But couldn't you... ensure she does not become a blood-crazed killer?"

Morlaine pushed back the dark curls mostly held in a loose ponytail, "No."

"So, better she dies?"

"You have not the faintest inkling how much blood stains my hands. I do not want more."

"Unless it is Solace's?"

She rounded the bed, stood over him, then bent down and clamped a hand on each of his shoulders. He tried not to wince.

"Ulrich... she will not be the person you know. She is half-mad with her lust for vengeance as it is..."

Despite wanting to protest he could not force the lie from his lips.

"I know what it is like to be fuelled by vengeance. It made me an abomination. It will do the same to her. Possibly even if she remains human, certainly if she becomes vampiric."

She stared down at him for a long time. He had to confess she had the most extraordinarily beautiful eyes. The kind a man could easily lose himself in, at least if he had no clue as to what hid behind them.

"If she is not the woman she was when she opens her eyes, kill her."

When he said nothing, she squeezed his shoulders, "Promise me. It will be the only kindness left to you. Both for her and yourself. Let her live, and every life she takes will weigh on your soul until the day you die. Trust me that is not something you want to endure."

He shut his eyes and listened to the screams of children.

"I understand," he nodded.

"Good," her hands slipped away from him. She pulled on her cloak and headed for the door.

"Morlaine," he said.

"Yes?"

"Be careful."

That earnt him half a smile, "You do not need to worry about me."

He sat staring at the door long after the demon's footsteps faded to nothing.

Then he watched Solace and waited for her to open her eyes.

His father's sabre across his lap.

Chapter Nine

Solace opened her eyes.

She was hungry. More than hungry. Starving, famished, ravenous.

Her stomach rumbled its agreement.

Sitting up, she found she was in bed, still fully clothed. Blood soiled her ripped dress.

It was night. A couple of candles burned, the fire reduced to glowing embers. The closed windows only partially muffled angry voices coming from outside,

What had happened?

Blood, pain, fear. Faces, long and awful, pale as dirty snow and marbled with blue. Fire, glass, falling, stone, cold, blackness. More pain. A man called Flyblown who wasn't really a man at all. A grey hill upon a grey plain. Dust and ashes. Torben.

To destroy an army, you need an army.

Father. Lutz. Saul the Bloodless. Karina the maid floating beneath the ice. More pain. Different. But worse.

The touch of a pistol's muzzle under her chin. Cold

metal, warm flesh. Click. Nothing.

The stink of burning oil and roasting meat. Human meat.

Her stomach rumbled again.

Do you run, or do you stand?

The sting of a hand upon her cheek.

You don't possess foresight, Solace, just ignorance. Your mother was a sick and troubled woman... and clearly so are you...

Hiding. In the dark. Sucking in air tainted with centuries of soot and ash. Sucking in tears tainted with hours of horror and loss. Listening to the sound of footsteps. Coming for me, searching for me. Taking me to the demons.

Bernard the Black, laid out in stone upon his tomb, tracing fingers through the dust so it looked like his tears had washed it away.

The Devil and The Fox.

Who was The Fox? She couldn't remember. She knew who The Devil was, though.

Saul the Bloodless.

The Devil who must die.

Vengeance. Her new master.

Five red slashes on a milky white thigh.

Pain. But only a little. Different from the other pain, though. Good pain. Tingling pain. Pain that made her want to touch herself.

A rider upon a black horse. A rider upon the Night's Road. A rider who would deliver her vengeance.

Laughter. Loud, raucous, lewd. Bulging eyes. Spittle.

Slobbering tongue on her hand. *Graf* Bulcher, leaning in close, too close. Leering. Piggy little eyes, in a big, bloated face.

The undead have come to feast upon the World's Pain.

Torben.

Why did you go with them?

Why? Why? *Why!!!!!????*

She opened her eyes. She sat up.

She thought she'd already done that once. Turned out she hadn't.

Still, it *was* night. Two candles did burn, the fire was but embers and angry voices serenaded her from below the window.

"Ulrich?" her throat was so dry his name came out in a hoarse croak that sounded nothing like herself.

Renard. Who had both betrayed her and saved her. Who loved her and hated her. Who she had entwined her naked body around to keep alive.

The last of her people.

He sat beside the bed. Eyes wide, cheeks hollow, pale as a winter morn. His sword lay across his lap; hand wrapped around its grip. So hard his knuckles were white.

"My Lady...?" he said, voice as croaky as hers.

"I'm starving!" she said, trying to smile, though she suspected it came out more of a grimace.

She felt restless and full of energy. How long had she been asleep? Why was she fully clothed? And why was her dress ripped and bloody? She frowned and shook her head to clear it.

"You are?" his grip on the sword seemed to tighten

334

further. He was shaking. The sword rattled as he slid a finger's worth from its scabbard.

She nodded, "I feel... strange."

"You do?"

She nodded again. A little more steel came into view. Was he planning to sharpen it? Yes, that must be it. Morlaine was always at hers with a whetstone. A blade could never be too sharp.

"Just sleep muddled," she rubbed her hair, finding it matted and sticking up in all manner of unnecessary directions. She remembered the girl she used to be and how horrified she would have been for any man to see her so unpresentable.

How innocent, foolish and wonderful she'd been.

Solace missed her sometimes.

She hauled back the blankets. Renard actually appeared to flinch. She had to smile at that; it wasn't as if she was naked. Save for her shoulder where her dress was torn. She tugged a flap of blood-stained fabric back into place.

"What happened?"

"You don't remember?"

She shook her head and started to swing her legs off the bed.

"The Man from Carinthia..."

"Who is he?"

She pulled a face, "I am not sure. Everything is a bit foggy."

"You jumped out of a window. You were... badly hurt."

"I was?" she froze, "Why did I jump out of a window?"

"To escape a demon."

She felt her eyebrows shoot up. Then ran a hand over her face and down her neck. Nothing hurt.

"I don't seem to be injured. That was lucky."

"You were dying," Renard said, eyes still wide, hand still gripping the sabre.

"I was?"

He nodded.

"Then... how...?"

"Morlaine. She gave you her blood. You would have died without it."

"Oh..."

A strange sense of hollowness filled her. A tear swelled in her eye. She pulled the back of her hand over it with a rough swipe. Only children cried.

She was alive. That's what mattered. Still alive to wreak vengeance. Still alive to destroy Saul the Bloodless, the Red Company and *Graf* Bulcher.

And save Torben.

The image of her brother floated somewhere behind her eyes. A distant figure on a grey hill. That seemed pretty hollow too.

But destroying the others didn't.

"My lady...?"

"I am alive; 'tis all that matters."

"Are you... yourself?"

"Myself?" she wasn't sure what that was anymore. Not the Solace von Tassau who'd been a lot more concerned about the state of her hair than most anything else, certainly. Now? All she cared about was vengeance. Nothing else mattered. Even dying.

"Yes," she said, her voice little more than a sigh, "I am myself."

Renard looked thoughtful, "Morlaine said I'd know if you weren't."

She stared at him.

He smiled back. And slid his sword home into its scabbard.

"You said you were hungry?"

She nodded as he pushed himself to his feet.

"What do you want?"

"Chicken. A whole one..." she scrunched up her nose "...possibly two..."

For some reason, her gluttony made him look relieved rather than disgusted.

*

There were no chickens to be had. Or much else.

Some coarse rye bread and barley pottage had to suffice. And the price had gone up again.

If Solace had any complaints about the food, she kept them to herself, though that might have been because the speed with which she gobbled it down precluded speech. He supplemented the meal with some salted beef and dried apples from the provisions they'd gathered.

They did not last long either.

Once done, they'd sat and talked, recounting events since he'd left to buy their horses.

"I am sorry about Madleen," she said. He thought she was going to reach over and put her hand on his, but she didn't. Which was for the best.

"I barely knew her..." he let the words trail away.

"Still..."

Her own memories were hazy, but the more they talked, the clearer they become, culminating with her throwing an oil lamp at the demon she called the Man from Carinthia. She had no recollection of jumping out of the window.

"Perhaps he threw me out?"

"It seems more likely you did it to escape."

Her fingers traced her cheek, which broken glass had sliced open the day before and now bore only the very faintest of marks. By tomorrow he was sure there would be nothing at all.

She had changed into her travelling clothes while he'd gone for food, her bloody dress now a discarded bundle in the corner. She sat cross-legged on the end of the bed. A not entirely lady-like pose.

"Why did you leave the Inn? 'tis not safe at night even without any demons."

"I thought you and Morlaine were in trouble," she held his eye, "the *sight* told me."

"My lady-"

"I am not a child in need of protection or... or *cossetting!*" she snapped, "We will face worse than this on the road ahead."

That was true enough. The road ahead was taking them to their deaths.

Her face softened, "I was worried. It was probably foolish, but I must learn how to fight these creatures."

He trusted himself only to nod.

"You saved my life again. Thank you."

"Morlaine saved your life. I just persuaded her. And Lucien."

"I thought he was only interested in getting me into his bed."

"Perhaps there's more to him than meets the eye. I think most men would have denounced us as witches or run as far away from us as possible if they saw Morlaine's true face. He chose to help."

"An unworthy man's choice..." Solace muttered.

"I'm sorry, my lady?"

She shook her head.

They sat in silence for a long while. Solace showed no obvious ill effects from her ordeal. Just a restlessness that made her follow the furrows Morlaine ploughed with her boots earlier, pacing back and forth across the room. Whether it came from the demon's blood or her own eagerness to return to the road, he could not say.

"Where do we go next?" he asked later, as much to break the silence as anything else. Wherever it was, he had no doubt he would rather be somewhere else.

The memory of Madleen sitting next to him, soft smile and pretty eyes, was one he had to shake away in order to hear his mistress' answer.

"The *sight* will tell me."

Nothing much had changed in that regard then.

"You doubt me?" she asked, seeing something in his face.

As her *sight* had led her to a lair of demons and nearly

death as opposed to their aid, he was less convinced it would help them than she was, but he shook his head all the same.

"It will show me where Bulcher is, and Bulcher will tell us how to find the Red Company."

He kept those doubts to himself too, he was happy for her *sight* to lead them a merry dance around the Empire and never come within a hundred leagues of *Graf* Bulcher and any demons, whether of his acquaintance or not.

Solace continued to pace while he laid on the bed. Although he eventually slipped into a fitful doze, his aching bad arm denied him proper sleep.

The night had stretched into the small hours when Solace suddenly stopped pacing, the town had fallen to silence, and the rhythmic creak of her boots on the floorboard had been the only sound.

"Morlaine," she said.

He could hear nothing at first; then, just when he was going to ask her what made her think the demon was returning, footsteps echoed down the corridor.

He reached for his father's sabre.

"Just in case..." he said, climbing from the bed and half drawing the sword.

Solace was already crossing the room when a knuckle wrapped on the wood.

The demon stared at his mistress when she unlocked and opened the door.

"You are recovered..."

Solace locked the door after her, and he let the sword fall back into its scabbard.

"Much. Thank you."

If Morlaine harboured any anxiety about what she might be returning to, she did not show it. Instead, she peeled off her cloak, tossed it over the back of a chair and sat down.

"I am glad."

Which was about as much emotion as the demon ever displayed about anything.

"The demons?" he eased himself back down onto the edge of the bed.

"I found three."

"And?"

"I dealt with them."

A heavy silence hung about the room.

He swallowed, "Madleen?"

"She was one of them," Morlaine said as if discussing an errant dog.

"'tis for the best..." he lowered his eyes.

"Are there more?" Solace asked.

"I don't think so."

"But... there could be?"

"The vampire who created them was of my bloodline. So, they are of my bloodline. I cannot be completely sure, but I believe I would know if there were any others close by."

"You... made the Man from Carinthia?"

Morlaine raised her dark eyes towards Solace, "The Man from Carinthia?"

"That's what he called himself. The demon who attacked me."

341

She shook her head, "No. But my blood was in him all the same. Passed on through several vampires back to me."

"Do you know who?" he asked, despite knowing himself.

"Saul... he is the only one I made who passed on the curse."

"You can be sure?"

"I only made one other. He never sired anyone. And he died a long time ago. This Man from Carinthia came from Saul the Bloodless."

"How many has Saul made?" Solace put her back against a wall and shuffled her feet as if unable to keep them still.

Morlaine stared at her own mud spluttered boots, "I do not know. But many. Enough for me to have spent centuries trying to find them. To stop them. To atone. Every life they snuff out of existence is upon my shoulders. I would say I carry that weight upon my soul. But I no longer possess a soul; only darkness, guilt and regret exist in the void where it once rested."

"You saved my life; does that not amount to some... redress?"

"I have saved many lives. I do not tally, but..." her eyes rose, dark and empty, "...no, it doesn't."

Solace's gaze flicked in his direction, but he did not meet it.

He did not know what Morlaine had done to haunt her so, what deeds so black she could never find redemption from them. He did not want to know.

Part of him thought her a demon, a creature upon

which such thoughts should not weigh.

But mostly, he thought of women and children dying, heard the echoes of their screams, heard his own voice pleading with Solace that there was nothing they could do to save them. Followed by the sound of their boots on The Wolf's Tower's stones as they left them to the demons and ran for their lives.

Were some actions so despicable they made redemption impossible?

No one can save everybody, but everybody can save someone...

He looked into Morlaine's eyes again.

It was a question he feared he knew the answer to.

Chapter Ten

"We leave at dusk..."

Beyond the closed shutters, another grey morning was dawning. The sun came late this year, which made for a long night.

A long and restless one.

Despite the time she'd slept while the demon's blood healed her, she knew she should still rest. Who knew when she would have a bed to sleep in again? The *sight* gave little away regarding such mundane matters.

"...you should stay here until then."

Morlaine stretched out on the floor, cloak folded underneath her head, eyes shut.

She'd offered her the bed, but the demon shook her head.

"Make the most of it."

"I need to replace my coat, cloak and dagger," she said.

"Send Ulrich. The last time anyone saw you, you were a bleeding, broken mess," Morlaine peeled open an eye, "best you don't provoke any more curiosity."

"I will go," Renard stood by the window, peering through a crack in the shutters. She didn't ask what he could see. It would not be anything good.

"Be careful."

He straightened his back but did not look around.

"I will, my lady."

She wished he'd stop calling her "my lady," she wasn't a *Freiherr's* daughter anymore. And every time he said it reminded her of the fact.

She forced herself to sit on the bed.

A restless energy had coursed through her ever since waking, making her skin tingle and feet itch. She assumed it was Morlaine's blood still working its magic on her. If that was the right word.

"Best I go now, my lady," Renard turned from the window.

"tis still too early, no?"

"The earlier I go, the better; most people will still be indoors. Later..." his words faded into a shrug.

"Things will get ugly?"

"I fear so."

"But if shops are not open yet...?"

"Then I will wait until they are."

She nodded and started pulling silver from her money belt.

"Enough?" she dropped coins into his palm.

"I think so..."

"Get whatever you think suitable."

His fist curled around the silver, but he made no move for the door.

"Ulrich?"

"I would like the money I am owed. My back pay..." his eyes held hers, "...if you can spare it, my lady."

Things fizzed and boiled within her. Anger and hurt chiefly. Was that all he saw her as, his employer? Or was there some other reason behind his demand?

"Are you planning to come back?" she asked, surprised at the evenness of her voice.

"You have my oath, my word, my honour. I will follow wherever you lead."

He spoke truly enough, or so it seemed. Although, of course, he had already broken his oath, word, and honour once before to save his life.

What was to stop him from doing so again?

To ride off and put as much distance between them as possible so he never had to face the Red Company and its demons again. His masters...

She swallowed. Both her fury and the words trying to force their way through her lips.

The silence stretched until she felt she had enough control to say, "I have no idea how much my father, - my dead, murdered father - paid you, Renard..." she tossed the purse of coins to him, "...take what you think is fair. Return the rest to me later..."

With that, she brushed past him and went to the window, deciding she did want to see whatever ugliness stretched out below it after all.

There wasn't much. A few souls, bundled inside heavy cloaks and coats, hurried across the cobbles. It didn't look much like any other morning on the face of it.

"Thank you, my lady. I will be as quick as I can."

She said nothing and did not turn back to the room until the door clicked shut. When she did, she found Morlaine was staring at her.

"What?"

"Do not judge him too harshly," the demon said.

"Every coin I give away is one less to fight the Red Company with. One less to bring down Bulcher, one less to give me the head of Saul the Bloodless. One less piece of silver to pay the price for vengeance. He knows that."

"The price of vengeance is not paid in silver, Solace."

"Perhaps. But I saved his life. That should be worth more than silver too!"

"And he saved yours. Twice, I believe."

"So, that it is all it is then. His due?"

"No."

She snorted and glowered, "Judas only asked for thirty pieces of silver. It appears the price of betrayal has increased since our Lord went to the cross."

"He is not going to betray you."

"How do you know that? He could take the money and run. He is terrified of the demons; he does not want to face them again."

"Then he is wise."

She wanted to kick something, but nothing was close enough other than the wall. Better she didn't; Morlaine might not be so free with her blood if she broke her foot. She sucked in air instead. It didn't calm her much.

"How do you know he isn't going to betray us?"

"Us?"

347

"Alright, *me!*"

"Because I saw the look on his face when he thought you were going to die. He would have opened his own wrist and given you every last drop of his own blood to save you. He is not going to run away. His feelings for you are too deep."

"I thought you had to share blood with someone to get an inkling of what goes on in their mind?"

"I don't need his blood for that. Rest, Solace," Morlaine closed her eyes and lowered her head back onto her folded cloak, "we leave at dusk."

*

Solace looked like he'd slapped her face when he'd asked her for the silver.

No matter, he told himself, despite the way it made a blade turn somewhere deep within him

Pastor Gehrig had a face that looked like it was continually being slapped. Bright red cheeks and wide eyes made larger still by the spectacles balanced precariously on the bridge of his long, thin nose.

"We have no room."

It wasn't the first time Pastor Gehrig had told him that since he'd badgered, bullied and barged his way into the man's office.

"Make room."

It wasn't the first time he'd said that either.

Lutheran pastors had a reputation for fire and brimstone sermons and severity. Pastor Gehrig had the demeanour of a man who jumped at his own shadow to go with his being-slapped face.

Pastor Gehrig held out a hand, fingertips mottled with black ink, "We do what we can. Which is more than we can afford. But we are unable to feed a multitude with a single loaf of bread. I pray every night for such a miracle. But, so far," he offered an apologetic smile, "none has been forthcoming."

"She has no one. She is lost and alone. Everything has been taken from her. You cannot leave her for the wolves."

"There are, to my knowledge, no wolves in Madriel."

He thought about asking if he knew Herr Aumann but managed to bite his tongue. Just.

Pastor Gehrig's too-large eyes drifted to the greyly lit window as if to reassure himself.

"Perhaps, but there are dangers here all the same."

"Indeed," Gehrig toyed with the quill in his hand, "and we do our best."

"Your best isn't good enough."

"Perhaps you would like to take over, Herr Lutz? Maybe you will enjoy more luck with that single loaf of bread, eh?"

Ulrich was leaning on the other side of the man's paper-strewn desk, trying to be as intimidating as possible. Bullying clergymen was ill-advised, but he wanted to know the measure of the man.

Was he the kind who was true to his word or the type to sneak off and spend the church's money on whores and schnapps?

He thought the former more likely but was the first to admit he was not the world's best judge of a man's

349

character.

Still, he had no real choice.

"I have more than a single loaf."

He tossed Solace's purse on the desk.

Pastor Gehrig's eyes, somehow, widened more.

"There is enough here to keep one little girl for a long time. I will be back with more at some point. I can't say when, but I expect to find her well-cared for. If she isn't, there will be no more silver... but there will be repercussions," he leaned further over the desk, ignoring the white bolts of pain fizzing up his bad arm.

Gehrig stared at the purse.

Ulrich straightened his back and presented the pastor with his palm, "Please, count it. Then tell me how long it will pay for the care of one small child. I would presume some considerable time; I doubt she eats much."

He glanced over his shoulder. Seraphina sat on a chair in the corner, feet nowhere near the floor. She smiled at him.

She looked even more like her mother when she smiled.

Gehrig jumped to his feet and scurried to the door, "Frau Balmer," he called after putting his head into the corridor.

Frau Balmer, a formidable-looking woman as grey as the weather outside, appeared before Pastor Gehrig was back behind his desk.

"Yes, Pastor?" she said, eyes flashing at him. She had tried her hardest to keep him from the Pastor and bore the look of a woman quite capable of holding a grudge.

He smiled at her. It wasn't returned.

"Frau Balmer, please take this child to the kitchen and see she is fed. She looks like skin and bone."

"But-"

"Thank you."

She nodded, and held out her hand to the little girl, "Come with me, young lady."

"Her name is Seraphina," Ulrich said.

"What a beautiful name. And you do look like an angel, don't you," Frau Balmer smiled, suddenly looking more of a kindly aunt than a fearsome harridan. It was amazing the difference a smile could make.

Seraphina's eyes moved to him, "Mama...?"

When Frau Balmer's eyes followed he gave the slightest shake of his head. Then he went to the girl and hunkered upon his haunches till he was at eye level with her.

"You must go with this nice lady. She is going to look after you for a while."

"Mama...?"

"She has... had to go away. To see your papa. These good people are going to look after you in the meantime. They'll feed you and keep you warm. They'll keep you safe."

Frau Balmer bent down next to him and held out her arms, "Come, Seraphina, aren't you hungry?"

The little girl nodded and let Frau Balmer scoop her off the chair. Holding the offered hand, she let the woman lead her from the room.

She didn't look around.

"Her mother is dead?" Pastor Gehrig asked once he'd

shut the door.

"Yes."

"How?"

"The war."

"And how did she come to be in your care, Herr Lutz?"

"'tis not relevant. I am leaving, where I am going, I cannot take her with me. I wish to see her... safe."

"You knew the mother?"

"Briefly."

"Herr Lutz," the Pastor frowned, "this is a *Christian* house, run on *Christian* values, supported by the church and the good, charitable people of Madriel. I must know-"

"Seraphina's mother was not a whore. The child was not born out of wedlock. Her father died in the war, and now her mother too. I... fought with her father, an old comrade. 'tis a debt I must pay. There is nothing... immoral here."

"I see..."

The Pastor opened the purse and poured Solace's silver onto the desk.

"You... are a most generous man, Herr Lutz."

"I am perhaps not as devout as I could be, Pastor. But I believe it is the case the All Mighty does not allow you to take your silver with you when you ascend to Heaven?"

"Indeed..."

He doubted he had long to live, and it wasn't his money anyway, but it seemed as good a reason as any. Better Seraphina be cared for than the silver fall into the hands of brigands on the road or Saul's demons. It didn't matter. However much Solace had, it was never going to be enough to destroy the Red Company.

Better to do a little good with it before he left this world.

"Your charity speaks highly of you. There is enough silver here to keep Seraphina for... several years."

"Then I will do my best to return in several years with more."

"I look forward to it."

"And to ensure she has been well cared for."

"I run a godly house, Herr Lutz. These are terrible times, but she will be fed, clothed, given a bed and a roof. She will learn the word of God and will receive an education befitting a girl of her station. That is my promise."

"I trust you are a man who keeps his promises..."

Really, he had no other choice.

Pastor Gehrig stood and offered him his hand. He accepted it with a nod.

"You are an honourable man, I think, Herr Lutz, to do such a thing as this," the Pastor swept a hand over the silver.

"I am sure many would do the same in my shoes."

"Perhaps..." the Pastor didn't look convinced.

"Everybody can save someone..." he said, turning for the door.

Even if they couldn't save themselves.

353

Chapter Eleven

It took a long time for Renard to return. Long enough for her to begin to suspect he'd just wanted to run off with her silver after all. That was her hurt and anger rather than her *sight*, but it was a fear that wouldn't stop gnawing all the same.

Morlaine swapped the floor for the bed when she'd continued to pace and fidget. Stretching out atop the blankets, hands folded over each other on her lap.

That's how a corpse is laid out...

Morlaine didn't roll onto her side, change position, or make a sound. Her chest rose and fell almost imperceptibly, which was the only movement.

Solace found it curiously unsettling, though it was hardly the most disconcerting thing about the demon.

When the squeak of boots finally floated down the corridor, she was sitting by the window. For Morlaine's benefit, the shutters remained closed, and she'd been listening to the voices in the square. Someone had been addressing a crowd; he'd talked about the Devil and his minions. He'd shouted about them even more. Other voices had shouted back, hands had clapped, and cries had gone up. She suspected quite a few fists had been shaken at the sky too.

It was raining again; its patter against the glass made for better listening. Made more sense too. She hoped it would turn into a downpour and force people off the streets.

The footsteps belonged to Renard.

Strange how she recognised the sound of his tread. He walked with no discernible difference to other men. Still, she was relieved to have him back, even if her anger still simmered too fiercely for her to show it.

"You came back?" she said after he let himself in.

In his arms, he had a bundle, "I think these will suffice, my lady." When she just stared at him, he stood awkwardly before putting his purchases on the dresser, "The blade is better than the last one; it must have-"

"You can give me back the rest of the silver now," she said, surprising herself with the coldness in her tone.

Renard straightened up.

"There is none."

"None? I know things are expensive," she glanced at the dresser and back again, "but, even after what you've bought, my father did not pay his men at arms *that* much."

He stared at her, raising his chin slightly, "I gave it to the orphanage."

"You... did *what?*"

"To take Seraphina."

"Who is Seraphina?"

"Madleen's daughter. They had no room for more children; the war has made so many orphans. I suspected that might be the case. I gave them all the coin I was owed to make them find some room. Plus the rest."

She found she was on her feet. She found she was shaking too.

"Think of it as my future pay, from now until the day I die," he said.

"Why would you do such a thing?"

He looked at Morlaine, who had opened her eyes and propped herself up on her elbows, "We killed her mother. She has no one. She should be safe now."

"I killed her mother," Morlaine corrected.

Renard conceded the point with a shrug.

"What happened to Madleen was not your fault, Ulrich," Morlaine added.

Again, he shrugged.

"I needed that silver!" Solace shouted.

"Silver will not be enough to destroy the Red Company," the demon said.

"It is all I have left, 'tis not he's..." she jabbed a finger at Ulrich, "...to give away."

"You have plenty remaining, my lady. It was only what I was due. And what I will be owed. What I do with it is my business."

"Saving one child will not bring back the ones we left to Saul," she spat, crossing the room to stand before him.

"I know."

"Then-"

"My lady, all I retain of any worth in this world is my

honour, my word, my oath..." his good hand found the hilt of his sword, "...and my father's sabre. They are all yours. Till I die. Which I suspect will not be long, so 'tis possible I have overcharged for future services. However, I will endeavour to live long enough to provide some value to you."

She glared at him. She wanted to hit him. And keep hitting him.

Instead, she settled for shouting.

"Is that how you see it? Debt and service? Nothing else binds you to me, does it? Not what we have endured together? What we have suffered? What we have lost?"

"'tis done," was all he said in reply, brushing past her to slump into the chair she had just vacated. Which wasn't the act of a servant, a retainer, a paid employee or whatever else he considered his station to be.

"Answer the damn question?!" she demanded, following him to the window.

He looked up at her with weary, red-rimmed eyes.

"Every part of me belongs to you, my lady. I will follow you to the ends of the world and the end of my days. If you want more... I have nothing else to give."

He continued staring up at her, hollow-cheeked beneath the bristles of his beard, the skin red and flaked. He appeared but a shattered remnant of the handsome young man he'd been before The Wolf's Tower fell, his shoulders sagged, his ruined arm held tight across himself, every action slowed as if he were dragging iron chains behind him.

"Solace," she had not heard the demon rise nor cross

to the window. Morlaine's hand rested lightly on her arm. Gently she pulled her away from Renard.

That was probably for the best. She'd still been trying to decide whether to hit him or hug him, and neither made for the wisest choice.

She shrugged Morlaine off but retreated all the same.

Renard's hoarse voice followed her.

"I just wanted to save a child. Just one. I could not save her mother, I..."

The sound of boots stilled his tongue, if not her fury.

"Lucien," Morlaine said, crossing to the door.

Renard hauled himself to his feet and rested his good hand atop the pommel of his father's sabre. She wanted to stand at his side but resisted the urge.

Morlaine opened the door as soon as the knock came.

It was Lucien. Clearly, she wasn't the only one in the room who could recognise a man solely by the clip of his boots.

Once in the room, he stopped and stared at her.

"Good Lord above," he whispered.

She pointed at Morlaine, "'twas more her doing."

Lucien's gaze swept the room. No black-toothed grin or wordy quip followed it.

"You must leave as soon as you can," he told them.

"We are leaving at dusk."

"Not sooner?"

"Are things so bad?"

Lucien found the room's other chair and dropped into it.

"It has started."

"What has started?" she asked.

"People are being denounced as witches. All manner of demons have been seen; one fellow swears he saw Satan himself marching down *Schmiedereihe* last night, carrying a pitchfork and sending sparks off the cobbles with his iron hooves. Bodies have been found; throats ripped out as if attacked by a wild animal. Sacrifices to the Devil..." his eyes flowed to Morlaine "...demon food."

"The fellow who claims to have seen Satan is a liar," Morlaine replied.

"They are all liars. They are all scared; the war, the food shortages, the cost of everything. The burghers who opposed Aumann are starting to fall in behind him now, terrified they'll be denounced for witchcraft themselves if they don't. The strangers will be thrown out of the town before the Lord's day. The ones that don't end up on the pyre anyway. The gaol is already filling up for the witchfinders."

"Is there nothing you can do?" Solace asked softly.

"I am trying to keep order, but, when the witchfinders get here... people will denounce the strangers to them, they will denounce their rivals, their enemies, their old lovers, they will denounce anyone they don't like. Then they will denounce their brothers, their friends, their mothers. They will denounce someone for fear if they do not, they will be denounced first. And once you are denounced..."

"But nobody can think everyone is a witch," Solace said.

"Satan walks among us. That is what they tell us every Sunday. And every day in between too. It is what people believe. And once the witchfinders start their black work on the denounced, those poor souls will eventually confess to anything, for their suffering will be so great the only mercy left open to them will be the flames of the pyre. 'tis a madness, 'tis a plague. And like the plague, it will take many lives. There is no cure for it, save waiting for it to burn itself out and praying the sickness does not visit your door before it does..." the mercenary's eyes fell to his boots, "...Lucien Kazmierczak has seen this before..."

"What will you do?" Morlaine asked.

"What can I do? If I try to stop it, I will be denounced too. Herr Aumann is a man who carries many grudges. One of them is against me. This is a time for him to settle scores."

"But your men will follow you, couldn't-"

He cut Solace off with a sharp head shake, "Several of my boys are dead. Most believe it the work of demons as much as the townsfolk. Some will look to me first, others... others will be more than willing to do as Aumann and the witchfinders bid."

His eyes settled on Morlaine, "And they are not wrong to blame these deaths on demons, are they?"

When only silence greeted him, he said again, "Leave as soon as you can. Aumann has much on his plate, but he will not forget he has already accused you of witchery. Herr Aumann is a man for keeping lists. He will not have forgotten you."

"We understand. Have any vampires been found?"

"Bodies yes, demons no. Are there any to find?"

"I killed three more last night. There could be others,

but I don't think so."

"That is something. Where are the bodies?"

"I disposed of them."

"Disposed?"

"I took them over the wall and buried them in the woods. They will be ashes in a few days."

Lucien straightened his back, "You took them *over* the wall?"

"They can do such things," Renard said, voice as hollow as his eyes.

"Ye gods. I thought I had seen all there was to see in the world, these wandering feet of mine have taken me from the high Carpathians to cold Caledonia and back again, after all. It appears I was wrong."

"I hope you never have to see my kind again."

Lucien stared at Morlaine some more, then pushed himself to his feet.

"The Watch shut the town gates at sunset; better you leave before then. There will be questions if you have to get someone to open them for you. And questions are currently best avoided."

Morlaine nodded. She did the same. Renard just stared into space.

"Thank you, Lucien," Morlaine said.

"I've done nothing."

"You know what I am, and yet you still help us."

Lucien's familiar, black-toothed grin reappeared beneath his drooping moustache, "Lucien Kazmierczak has always had a weakness for a pretty face. My one and only fault! So, how could I do anything else when..." his eyes darted between her and Morlaine "...presented with the two most beautiful women for a dozen leagues?"

Morlaine cocked her eyebrow, "Only a dozen?"

"Lucien Kazmierczak does not like to exaggerate, in fact," he added with an entirely straight face, "I doubt there is anyone between Salzburg and Seville who exaggerates less..."

With that, he nodded to each of them in turn and left the room.

*

They slipped away quietly shortly before sunset.

Thick, dull cloud had hung over Madriel like a sour mood all day, but Morlaine still wore her smoke-blackened spectacles and ensured every fragment of skin was covered, save for her face, which she hid in the shadows of her deep hood. Given the cold, that at least was not unusual.

The Market Inn boasted a back entrance, opening onto a yard reserved for pissing. A gate across the moss-flecked cobbles gave access to a narrow alley. No one was about. Which was for the best. In a town where everything and anything was now a cause for suspicion, sneaking was a practice you did not want to be caught at.

Solace remained as quiet as she had since Lucien closed the door behind him. The occasional surly glance came his way, but otherwise, she ignored him.

Morlaine said little either, but that was her way, so he read nothing into it.

His mistress would forgive him in time; she'd forgiven him betraying his oath and helping the Red Company enter

The Wolf's Tower after all. If someone could forgive that, he assumed she'd forgive trying to save a child's life.

Perhaps that was an exaggeration; maybe someone would have stepped in and taken care of the child. Charity and kind hearts had not been completely washed from the world, but they were in as scant supply as every other commodity.

He'd told Carola Madleen was dead. He didn't say how; the woman who'd added Seraphina to her brood hadn't asked either. The stories of demons, ripped out throats and missing people had swept as quickly through the stranger's camp as it had the rest of the town.

When he told her he was taking Seraphina to the orphanage, he'd expected Carola to protest. Instead, she'd turned vacant eyes on him and asked if he could take any of hers as well.

He didn't think it was a jest.

He'd mumbled something about a child always being better off with their mother.

"Not when she can't feed them, they're not," Carola shot back. Then her eyes had moved to the knot of men in the square watching them. Townsmen, several armed with cudgels. All wielded sneers and hard eyes.

Aumann's men. They were passing a bottle of schnapps back and forth. Watching the strangers, hurling the occasional insult to keep themselves warm. Never a good way to start your day.

"They're saying we're witches," Carola whispered, "blaming us for what's been happening. Reckon we'll have worse to worry about than empty bellies soon."

"You should get out of this town," he told her.

That won him a hard smile.

"'tis winter. I have six children, four pairs of shoes between them and not a coin to my name. We'd be dead before Sunday out there..."

He'd scooped up Seraphina; the girl didn't struggle. Perhaps she remembered him, or she was too cold and tired to make a fuss.

Awkwardly, with his bad hand, he peeled the blanket he'd given Madleen from the child and passed it to Carola. Then he fumbled a couple of talers out of his pocket and gave her them too.

"'tis all I can do."

Carola nodded and sniffed; her nose was red with the cold, the bags under her eyes the colour of old bruises.

When he turned to go, she'd said, "I wish she had gone to your bed... sin or not..."

So did he.

But he said nothing and took Seraphina to the orphanage.

The knot of townsmen had watched him, one demanding to know where he was going with the child. He shot him a sour look back but nothing else. Seraphina had put her arms around his neck and pressed her face against his shoulder. It was awkward carrying her with just one arm, but she weighed no more than feathers.

She'd made him think of the children of Tassau he had left to Saul, which was no surprise as most things in the remnants of his life made him think of them.

The children...

He heard Solace's voice, echoing from The Wolf's Tower as they'd made their vain attempt to reach the Library and escape, heard the screams coming from the Great Hall. She'd wanted to try and save her father, she'd wanted to save the children too.

The memory of his own voice replaced his mistress'.

...will die anyway! We cannot go in there! I've seen what the demons can do! We cannot stand against them; we cannot stop them. We can only save ourselves. You must trust me...

And she had trusted him. The man who'd betrayed her. And everyone had died except them.

He'd held Seraphina tighter and hurried past the men.

Witchery. Strangers. Whore's brat. Devils. A sacrifice for Satan. Demons. Scum.

The words, spat on steaming breaths, whirled around them, a black miasma of fear, ignorance and stupidity. He ignored them, but knew, as much as he'd known anything in his life, if one of them put a hand on him or stepped in his way, he would kill them and to hell with the consequences.

After he'd persuaded Pastor Gehrig to take Seraphina, he went back to the square to replace what Solace had lost and he'd given to Madleen, with the silver he'd kept back.

Anger still blackening his mood, he'd glared at the swelling gaggle of townsmen. Finding a home for Seraphina had made him feel no better. The weight of the silver in his pocket just made him think what else he could do with it. The money was but a fraction of what Solace's jewellery was worth. How many more could they save with that?

But Solace didn't want to save anyone, bar her brother, even though he was far beyond salvation. She wanted only to spend it on her vengeance. Madness gripped Madriel, but madness held sway over his mistress' soul too. And he would follow her, because she held his oath, his word, his honour as firmly as the madness held her.

Run or stand?

That was always the choice. And they always ran. Saving only themselves.

He didn't even know his feet would take them to the townsmen till they did.

"Go home," he snarled at them, "leave these people alone."

"They've bought witchcraft to our town," one of the men snarled straight back. He was middle-aged with a big gut and a pock-marked face. Ulrich recognised him as one of the men who'd been with Aumann the night before last. "We're keeping them from mischief till the witchfinders arrive."

"Go home," he'd said again, planting his feet on the cobbles before them.

"Or what?" another laughed.

He half drew his father's sabre, "Or I'll cut you all down!"

It sounded like an absurd boast, but it stopped the laughter. Several of the men backed away from him, others exchanged nervous glances. A couple, however, seemed less inclined to let a one-armed swordsmen tell them what to do.

"Piss off," one of them barked in his face, stepping

366

forward where his companions had stepped back.

There was always one.

Booze soured the man's breath, suspicion narrowed his eyes, "Why so keen to stand up for these people?" he demanded, "There are witches amongst them, you one, eh?"

"Saw him on the street the night the demons came. Shifty and suspicious he was, we were talking to him when that hellspawn appeared," the pock-faced man who'd been with Aumann said.

A mutter ran through the group.

"Go home," he repeated, "there's no damn witchcraft here, just hungry people who've lost everything!" He showed them another finger or two of steel.

If his sword cleared the scabbard, he would have to use it.

But most of these men didn't want to fight; even with such odds on their side, they knew a blade could maim or kill a couple of them, and they were in no mood to see who won that prize. And there must have been something in his eye that told them he was not bluffing.

He'd spent every second he'd lived since the fall of The Wolf's Tower being afraid, but now he only felt a calmness. He'd fought demons. Maybe he'd dishonoured himself, betrayed his oath, left children to die and run away, but he had fought them. They had terrified him, and they were worthy of his terror, for they were abominations.

A few ignorant fools, on the other hand, were something else entirely.

The sour-breathed man glared at him, lips curling back to show the stumps of his teeth. Then one of the others put a hand on his shoulder and pulled him back.

"Leave him, Karl..."

As his friends edged backwards from whatever they saw in Ulrich's eyes, Karl jabbed a finger at him and then tapped his temple, "I've got your face friend; when the witchfinders get here, they'll be hearing about you..."

With that, he spun away, and the group moved across the square, muttering and repeatedly glancing back at him.

He slid his blade home.

It was only when he turned around, he saw the soldiers behind him.

"'tis fortunate you didn't draw that blade, son," Gottshall, Lucien's sergeant, said.

Perhaps he had not looked as fearsome as he thought he had.

"Not looking to cause trouble."

Gottshall's eyebrow shot up, "No? Well, I'd hope not. We've got enough to be dealing with as it is."

Gottshall had three men with him; none of them smiling.

"Best avoid the likes of them," Gottshall nodded in the direction of the retreating townsmen, "we won't always be around."

"They were-"

"Standing around talking shit. I know."

"They were watching the refugees, accus-"

"And I was watching them. As for accusations. There's going to be a lot of them flying around in the next few weeks. The clever fellow ensures he does nothing to get on the end of one."

"Thanks for the advice," he'd brushed past Gottschall, strangely disappointed he hadn't been able to draw his father's sabre all the way out of its scabbard and headed off to spend the remainder of Solace's silver.

Chapter Twelve

Renard insisted on leading the way.

Morlaine needed no such chivalry, while Solace was still too angry to appreciate the gesture.

They had slipped out of the *Market Tavern* and were now cutting across town to the stables burdened with their provisions. Of course, Renard had considerably lightened her load regarding the silver she had to carry. However, the weight of his charity inconvenienced her far more heavily than the missing silver would ever have.

In truth, it was but a fraction of what she had. But that was *all* she had. He had no damn right to-

She stopped herself.

It was done. Not for greed, self-gain or spite, but to aid a motherless child. He had no right to do it, and it would do little more good than spitting in the wind given the state of the world, but if she could not forgive him for it, she might as well cut him free of his oath and let him go.

Still, the thought of never seeing him again filled her with an unfamiliar unease.

I need him, that is all.

She needed every hand she could find to help her destroy The Red Company; the fact Renard only had one that worked properly was neither here nor there.

She fixed her eyes on his back as they walked through the gloomy byways of Madriel, but that just made her think of following him through the even gloomier corridors of The Wolf's Tower.

Morlaine trailed a pace behind her, most of their provisions on her back despite needing none of them herself. The weight was less of a hindrance to her than the remaining dregs of daylight.

They emerged onto a wider street. Renard paused, glancing at her as she came alongside, "The stables are nearby," he said, eyes sweeping both ways, good hand not far from his sword.

People were still about, but fewer than usual, she suspected. The night was the time for the Devil's work, and the Devil had come to town.

They didn't know Morlaine had dealt with the demons for them already.

As they started down the street, a heavily laden wagon came trundling towards them; two men sat atop. Both stared at them as they went by. Neither smiled.

Morlaine stopped as the wagon clattered by, her hooded head swivelling to watch it pass.

"What is it?" Solace asked.

Renard answered, "The wagon is loaded with faggots of wood."

She watched it continue down the street in the

direction of the market square.

"Herr Aumann is most efficient," Morlaine's voice floated out from under the deep recess of her hood, "I will give him that."

"The wood is..." her voice trailed off.

"...for the pyres," Renard finished the sentence for her.

"Already?" she whispered.

"No one likes to look slack if there are witches to burn. Sloth might be easily confused with complicity..." Morlaine said, "...everyone is competing to look more eager to find and burn witches than their fellows for when the witchfinders come."

"Is there nothing we can do?"

"I can save people from monsters, I can save people from sickness, I can save people from injury..." Morlaine said, her voice almost lost in the gentle breeze flitting down the street, "...but I can never save them from themselves..."

"No one can save everybody..." Renard said, continuing along the cobbles.

Shutters banged shut as they passed, and a few suspicious eyes peered out at them from shadowy interiors. Whenever she stared back, they quickly retreated.

The windows of one house they passed had been put out, the shattered door hanging off its hinges.

Two boys huddled together on a doorstep, "What happened here?" Renard asked.

"Witches lived there," one of the boys, eyes wide and cheeks red, told him.

"Get inside!" a woman screeched, an ashen face pressed against the window, "What did I tell you about talking to strangers?"

The boys scurried through the door, and the woman stared at them like they were cloven-hooved devils themselves.

They walked faster to the stables.

A group of men waited on a corner ahead. She heard Renard curse under his breath, but as they drew closer, she saw they were Lucien's men. They didn't exactly offer heartfelt smiles and cheery waves, but they said nothing and, more importantly, did nothing.

Shouts echoed from a nearby street. The mercenaries exchanged resigned looks and hurried off towards the commotion.

"Are you sure you found all the demons?" Solace asked out of the corner of her mouth.

"No. I think so, but it is impossible to be certain; I doubt the Man from Carinthia successfully sired more than five newborn in such short a time," Morlaine said, "but we cannot stay longer to find out."

She nodded. Lucien had been right. A plague had broken out, and it was spreading fast. Neither reason nor prayer was going to stop it now. All they could do was get out before they became engulfed by it.

"How do you know he was only here a short time?"

"If he'd been here longer, the town would have been knee-deep in corpses by the time we arrived..."

The stables were still open. Horses were valuable, and the stable owner had told them he employed boys to watch them all night when Morlaine had stabled Styx.

"You want to take them now?" a tousled haired

adolescent asked when they found him pouring grain into a bucket.

"We have to leave in a hurry," Renard said.

"You done something wrong?" the boy straightened up quickly.

"No. But I might stick the toe of my boot up your arse if you don't open the stables for us pronto."

Renard fished out a copper coin when the boy did nothing and flicked it at him. The lad moved quick enough then.

She waited in the stable yard while Renard went with the boy to ready the horses, shuffling feet to keep warm. Morlaine remained as still as any statue.

No sensible person would be leaving the town after dark. No sensible person would commence a long journey in winter either. The cold and dark were no inconvenience to Morlaine, but they could kill Renard and her. She pulled her cloak around her. It was a good one, thick and lined with wool. It would keep the chill out well enough tonight. But if heavy snow came in the weeks before Christmas, they might freeze in the saddle. After Christmas, the likelihood of snow increased greatly, but she saw little point in thinking so far ahead.

Even if Morlaine would countenance waiting out the winter, Solace wouldn't. She'd given the Red Company enough of a start. She wouldn't give the bastards anymore, no matter how cold it got.

The stable lad returned with each horse in turn. Styx made a grand sight, and the boy looked half terrified as he led the beast out. The two mounts Renard had bought were less impressive. Particularly given how much he'd paid for them.

"They were the best I could get," he said, as if reading her mind.

She shook her head. Neither seemed about to imminently die or go lame. So long as they weren't ridden too hard, they would get them where they were going.

As soon as she worked out where they were going.

She'd been waiting for Flyblown to tell her where she could find Bulcher, but they'd been nothing, either in the real world or the one of dust and ashes.

For now, simply out of the town gates would suffice.

She left Renard and Morlaine to check the harnesses, buckles and straps of the riding tackle. When the boy asked about money, Renard jerked his head, first at Morlaine and then her.

He gave Styx a baleful glance and came over to her.

"You're paid up for another two days," he said, "but Herr Dekker deals with the money and 'tis all locked up for the night. If you come back in the morning..."

"We'll be back in a day or two; we'll collect the money we're owed then," Morlaine didn't look up from adjusting one of Styx's stirrups, "Dekker can be trusted not to spend it in the meantime?"

"Herr Dekker is an honest man," the lad said, without much in the way of conviction.

"Good, we'll see you when we get back."

The lad looked at Renard for confirmation; he appeared uncomfortable discussing money with women.

Renard gave him a curt nod and bid him goodnight.

The boy lingered for a moment, then scurried off.

"Why did you say we'll be back for the money?" she asked.

"It's a lot less suspicious than saying we won't be."

More silver gone. Morlaine had paid for Styx's stabling; she'd paid for theirs. Or rather Renard had. With her coins.

'tis no time to become a miser...

Once the horses were ready and their provisions stowed in saddlebags, Morlaine vaulted effortlessly onto Styx's back. When Renard offered to help her up onto one of the horses, she snapped at him, "I know how to ride."

She also knew the better horse and hitched herself up on the bay mare. She wasn't as graceful as the demon but climbed into the saddle well enough.

It was more of a struggle for Renard with his one good arm, but once he managed it, they rode to the North Gate.

It was shut and barred when they got there.

*

"Open the fucking gate!"

"There's no need for profanity, sir..." the man, who looked old, tired and not best pleased to be sworn at, rested on his pike.

"We have urgent business; we need to leave now," Ulrich told them.

The second Watchman shook his head and the huge beard it hid behind, "No one's allowed to come or go between sunset and dawn."

"Since when?"

"Since Burgher Aumann told us this afternoon."

"This is ridiculous!"

The bearded Watchman rolled broad shoulders and shifted his weight from one foot to the other; his potbelly shifted with him, "What business is it you and these two ladies have out of town on such a bitterly cold night, may I ask?"

"'tis none of your concern."

"Sorry, sir, but we can't. Witches are communing with devils out in the woods at night," the first Watchman leaned forward and lowered his voice.

"Dancing naked, making sacrifices, summoning all manner of evil on the town," the bearded Watchman added.

His friend edged further forward, his voice dropping another notch, "Fornicating too... with *demons*. Would you believe such a thing?" he shook his head, "Filthy buggers!"

Ulrich sat back in his saddle and tried to fight down his frustration. Beyond the two watchmen, the heavy wooden gates stood within there stone arch. Barred and shut.

There were only these two old watchmen preventing the whole town from running off into the woods to fuck with demons, but he couldn't see a way to open the gates other than by cracking their heads together.

Well, he could think of one.

"How much?" he demanded wearily.

"How... much?"

"Yes. How much for the pair of you to go and take a piss for five minutes?"

"What... *together?*" the bearded Watchman looked appalled.

"Whatever your *business* is," the first Watchman glanced at the two women behind him, "it will have to wait until morning,"

He looked over his shoulder; perhaps feminine charm might work where simple bribery didn't. It was a typical example of his luck that the town of Madriel employed the only two honest watchmen in the Holy Roman Empire.

The sound of approaching hooves diverted his attention. A horseman emerged from the thickening gloom, bundled inside a heavy winter cloak.

"Ah," Lucien beamed, "here you are!"

Ulrich scanned the shadowy street for more of the mercenary's men, but none followed.

"Captain..." he said as Lucien reined in his horse between Morlaine and Solace. Ulrich hoped, for the sake of Lucien's mount, that the stable had keep Morlaine's stallion as well fed as they'd promised. Styx gave the newcomer an interested look and pawed the cobbles with an iron hoof.

Lucien shared his black-toothed grin with all and sundry before fixing it on the two watchmen.

"Jeremias..." he nodded first at the bearded man, then his companion, "...Matteo. What a bitter night to be on the gate! Who did you upset, eh?"

"Just doing our bit," Jeremias nodded back, though a scowl accompanied the gesture rather than a smile.

"As are we all!" Lucien boomed, "'tis the least we can do in these dark days."

Both men scowled.

The horses shuffled, mainly to put some room between themselves and Styx's teeth. He seemed even more inclined to sink them into flesh than his mistress.

Lucien beamed at everybody. Morlaine stared blankly back at him; Solace raised an eyebrow. Had she used to do that so much before she met Morlaine? He couldn't remember.

"Now, why don't you fellows open the gate, eh? Will help to keep you warm, I wager."

Jeremias shook his head, "Burgher Aumann said no one is to enter or leave between sunset and dawn. Told these people that. They don't seem to believe me."

"Well, Burgher Aumann is a wise and sensible man. We're all aware of the unbounded limits of his wisdom. Aren't we, boys?"

"We're just following orders."

"Of course. But now you have new orders."

"We do?"

"Yes. Open the gates."

"Whose order?"

"Mine."

The two watchmen exchanged a glance, "Burgher Au-"

"Is not charged with the security of this town! I am. A considerable amount of your taxes go into my pockct to prove it. Whatever edict Burgher Aumann has made, it does not apply to these people..." his grin stretched wider and grew colder, "...or me."

"But-"

Lucien held up a gloved hand, "The truth, and this is for your ears only - if you blab, I'll have your hides to decorate my hearth - is that these people possess vital intelligence for the witchfinders and must not be delayed.

The very fact they are leaving at night demonstrates the urgency of their information."

Matteo pulled himself up to his full height, which, in truth wasn't particularly impressive. He was a short and thin old man; if the wind picked up any, only his boots and helmet would keep him at his post, "Burgher Aumann was quite clear, no one-"

Lucien leaned so far out of his saddle he appeared in danger of diving onto the shit-stained cobbles.

"Of course he did! Who do you think this intelligence is about?"

Matteo's eyes widened, "But.... but..." he flapped.

"Bugher Aumann is no more a witch than I am," Jeremias spluttered.

"Is it not often the case that the fellow who blusters the loudest and points the finger most vehemently has the best reason to direct attention elsewhere?" Lucien gave each of the men a significant look, "And once the witchfinders have this intelligence, Jeremias, that last statement of yours is one you will have great cause not to repeat."

"Burgher Aumann..." Matteo mouthed "...I never would have thought..."

"Thinking is not required. Just open the gate and keep your mouths shut. If Aumann gets wind of what we know... the Devil himself might come knocking at your window."

The watchmen looked at each other before putting their pikes aside in unison, They hurried under the archway together to unbar the gates.

Lucien straightened in his saddle.

Then winked at him.

Chapter Thirteen

Upon the Road, The Electorate of Saxony, The Holy Roman Empire - 1630

"What do you think you are doing?" Morlaine demanded once they were clear of the gates.

"Helping, my love," Lucien replied.

"Do not call me my love,"

"Why not?"

"I don't care for it."

"Very well, my darling."

The demon glowered at him. Styx gave the mercenary a baleful glance too. Solace wasn't at all sure which was the more unsettling. Not that Lucien appeared unduly perturbed by either.

He started whistling.

Once the town's walls were just a black line in the distance behind them and she was confident no one was trailing them, Solace reined her horse to a halt and asked the same question.

Lucien turned to Renard, "Do these women always express their heartfelt gratitude so freely?" When he didn't reply, the mercenary's smile faded as his eyes returned to her, "I thought you might need some help getting through the gates."

"And we are grateful, truly," her eyes dropped to the saddlebags behind the mercenary. They looked exceedingly well packed, while Lucien was dressed in heavy travelling clothes.

"Lucien Kazmierczak is a man no longer wanted in Madriel. While Lucien Kazmierczak no longer wishes to be in Madriel. An alignment of interests that has persuaded me it is time to return to my wandering ways. Lucien Kazmierczak is a very well-travelled man. He has seen a great number of things during his many daring adventures, where he crossed all of the seven seas to each corner of the Earth. For many a long year he was of the opinion he'd seen everything," he turned his head towards Morlaine, "but he has recently concluded that is not the case after all."

"You cannot travel with us," Morlaine said.

"But the roads are so dangerous! And you are so fair, my sweetheart. Another sword to protect you is highly recommended in these uncertain times."

"I need no protection."

"Perhaps..." he looked back along the shadow-washed road. A faint smear of light still haunted the clouds to the west, but it was rapidly fading before the night, "...but the witchfinders will be here soon. I have no care for such work, but if I do not help them, I will join their list of people to question. 'tis a lengthy list already. Aumann has collected a great number of grudges over the years. I do not wish to lengthen it further. Lucien Kazmierczak knows little of the future, but he is not destined for the pyre."

She did not know what to make of Lucien. At first, she'd thought him a lecherous boor only one (very small) step up from the brigands who plagued the war-ravaged lands of the Empire. But he'd helped save her life and had carried on helping even after he knew Morlaine's true nature.

Perhaps they should not turn his offer aside so quickly.

"Where we are going, what we are doing," she said carefully, ignoring the warning looks coming her way from both Morlaine and Renard, "is likely to lead to all our deaths. You should follow a different road away from Madriel."

"I have no idea what you are about, but it sounds dangerous and ill-advised," he grinned, "therefore, I accept your invitation!"

"There was no invitation," Morlaine said.

"There's no better man to find at your side than Lucien Kazmierczak when faced with hopeless odds and a fearsome foe!"

"I'm sure your beer-stained wit provides a most welcome distraction when facing certain death," Renard almost spat.

"It has been told thus several times," Lucien looked around, "So, we are decided. I will ride with you!"

"No," Morlaine said.

Solace held up her hand.

"To fight an army, you need an army..." she said.

The five red lines on her thigh warmed as if a lighted candle passed back and forth over them. It felt approving.

"My lady, we do not have an army, and he..." Renard jerked his head at Lucien, "...does not constitute one."

"No, I don't have an army. But now I have a Captain."

Renard looked mortified.

"I'm not taking orders from him!"

"No," she smiled. Thinly, "You take orders from me."

*

He didn't trust Lucien.

Old Janick had warned him the mercenary was a snake and he thought it good advice, even if it came from a man who had fleeced him over the price of two very mediocre horses.

The moon broke intermittently through clouds racing on a bitter wind. Lucien continued to grin inanely, despite Morlaine and his insistence it was a mistake to let him join them.

Solace, however, had made up her mind.

"I do not need you two; I *certainly* do not need him," Morlaine said, looking down on them from her high perch upon Styx's back.

"You do need us. All of us," Solace kept her eyes on the silver-washed horizon ahead.

"I travel the Night's Road alone."

"And how close have you ever come to finding Saul the

Bloodless?" Solace asked.

Morlaine did not reply, though he fancied a scowl crossed her usually expressionless face.

"You need me to find him. But finding him is only half the problem, isn't it?"

Again, Morlaine said nothing.

"Who is Saul the Bloodless?" Lucien asked him.

He ignored the question.

"The other half of the problem," Solace answered her own question, "is how to deal with him when we find him."

"I know how to deal with him," Morlaine shot back.

"If he travelled alone, perhaps you would. But he doesn't..." now Solace turned her head to stare at the demon, "...does he?"

Morlaine lapsed back into silence.

"Who does he travel with?" Again no one answered Lucien.

"When we find him, we need the means to destroy him *and* The Red Company. Yes?" When Morlaine refused to answer, she asked him, "How many demons are there in the Red Company, Renard?"

Saul, Alms, Cleever, Jarl, Wendel. Others I never caught the name of..." he hesitated before adding, "...and now Torben."

Solace's horse whinnied, and she patted its neck.

"More than you can defeat alone," she told the demon after a laden pause.

"One must know one's enemy," Lucien offered, as much to himself as anyone, "first rule of soldiering, that is."

"So. You need me to find them, and we'll need help

defeating them. You can't defeat them alone; we can't defeat them between the three of us. Therefore, we need him," she nodded in Lucien's direction, "and we'll need more. We need an army to defeat an army."

"Well," Lucien piped up when no one else did, "you have made an excellent start; Lucien Kazmierczak's sword is worth a hundred!"

"Your proposition overlooks one small fact," Morlaine said, ignoring Lucien's boasting, "you don't actually know where Saul is. And you've still not come up with any insight into where we can find him, have you?"

"I told you, *Graf* Bulcher will tell us."

"And where pray tell, is this Bulcher? We are heading down this road," she indicated the rutted, muddy excuse before them with a jerk of the head, "but you have no idea where it is taking us."

"I have every idea where it is taking us."

"Really?"

Solace raised her eyes towards the half-crescent of the moon.

"Magdeburg. The way to find Bulcher is in Magdeburg..."

Ulrich's eyes darted to his mistress. It was probably just a trick of the wind flitting spitefully around their ears, but that hadn't sounded like Solace. Not just in inflection and intonation. It had sounded like someone else entirely.

He glanced at Morlaine. If she'd heard anything, it wasn't showing on her face. Though few things ever did.

"How do you know that?" Morlaine asked.

"I... just... do..." Solace said, hesitance accompanied

by a curious expression. She shuffled in her saddle to scratch the top of her leg.

"'tis a hard ride to Magdeburg," Lucien said, "and things are bad there. The city rose up against the Emperor after the Swedish king entered the war. 'tis said an Imperial army has gone there to put the rebels down."

"Things are bad everywhere," Solace said, "'tis the World's Pain..."

He looked at Morlaine, who was, in turn, staring hard at Solace. He wanted her to say it was nonsense. That she wasn't going to go to Magdeburg, that she didn't need their company, didn't need their help, that they'd caused her enough trouble already.

He wanted her to tell them she travelled The Night's Road alone.

He wanted her to tell them they had to find their own path. One that didn't lead to Saul the Bloodless and his cursed Red Company.

As with so many things in his life, he was disappointed.

Morlaine nodded and turned her eyes to the road.

"Magdeburg..."

They rode on in silence for a little while before Lucien said, "Perhaps this is an opportune time to take me into your confidence and enlighten me as to your motives and plans. As it stands, I feel I am lacking a little... *detail*..."

"There is no hurry, Captain; we have an abundance of time," Solace said, her eyes, like Morlaine's, only for the darkness before them.

"There's a very long road ahead of us..."

A Dark Journey Continues...

The Night's Road – Book Three

Empire of Dirt

Follow Solace, Ulrich, Morlaine and Lucien's journey as they pursue *Graf* Bulcher and Saul the Bloodless in *Empire of Dirt*, the next instalment of *The Night's Road*, due for publication in December 2022....

In the Company of Shadows

If you'd like to read more dark tales from the world of *In the Company of Shadows*, there are currently two free novellas (available as eBooks only) – *The Burning* & *A House of the Dead* – available. Both are set shortly before the events of *Red Company*. To get your free copies just visit andymonkbooks.com.

The Burning

The madness of the 17th Century witch burning frenzy has come to the sleepy village of Reperndorf.

Adolphus Holtz, Inquisitor to the Prince-Bishop of Würzburg, is keen to root out evil wherever he deems it to be. His eye has fallen on young Frieda and he fancies she'll scream so prettily for him when the time comes.

Frieda has already witnessed one burning and knows from the way her friends and neighbours are looking at her that she will be next. She seems doomed to burn on the pyre until a mysterious cloaked stranger appears out of the depths of the forest...

The first novella of *In the Company of Shadows* expands the dark historical world of *In the Absence of Light* and the shadowy relationships between humans and vampires.

A House of the Dead

All vampires are mad...

The weight of memories, loss, the hunger for blood, the voices of your prey whispering in your mind, loneliness, the obsessions you filled the emptiness inside yourself with, the sheer unrelenting bloody boredom of immortality could all chip away at your sanity.

And love, of course, one should never forget what that could do to you...

Mecurio has hidden from the world for twenty years in the secret catacombs beneath the city of Würzburg known as the House of the Dead, a place of refuge for vampires away from the eyes of men.

He tells himself it is so he can complete his Great Work without the distractions of the mortal world. But it isn't true. Time is slowly stealing the woman he adores from him and he has hidden their love away in the shadows of the House of the Dead to await the inevitable.

When a vampire whose bed he fled from a hundred and twenty-seven years before, arrives in search of information, he sees the opportunity to do a deal to save the woman he now loves for a few more bittersweet years. But all vampires are mad, one way or another, and when you strike a deal with one you may not end up with what you bargained for...

Books by Andy Monk

In the Absence of Light
The King of the Winter
A Bad Man's Song
Ghosts in the Blood
The Love of Monsters

In the Company of Shadows
The Burning (Novella)
A House of the Dead (Novella)
Red Company (The Night's Road Book One)
The Kindly Man (Rumville Part One)
Execution Dock (Rumville Part Two)
The Convenient (Rumville Part Three)
Mister Grim (Rumville Part Four)
The Future is Promises (Rumville Part Five)
The World's Pain (The Night's Road Book Two)
Empire of Dirt (The Night's Road Book Three)

For further information about Andy Monk's writing and future releases, please visit the following sites.

www.andymonkbooks.com

www.facebook.com/andymonkbooks

Printed in Great Britain
by Amazon